The breathtaking promise of the English countryside can lift even the heaviest spirits . . .

Willow Armstrong, the once-famous "Queen of Weight Loss" and president of Pound Busters, succumbed to stress eating after her divorce. Now the scandal of getting caught on camera binging on pizza, and the internet-wide mocking of her new curves, may destroy her career. Add in a business advisor who drained her finances, and Willow is out of options—until she learns she's inherited a house in England's most picturesque locale, The Cotswolds.

Willow's trip across the pond to sell the property and salvage her company soon becomes its own adventure: the house, once owned by grandparents she never met, needs major work. Plus, single dad Owen Hughes, the estate's resident groundskeeper and owner of a local tour outfit, isn't thrilled about the idea of leaving . . .

Yet as Willow proceeds with her plans, she's sidetracked by surprising discoveries about her family's history—and with Owen's help, the area's distinctive attractions. Soon, she's even retracing her roots—and testing her endurance—amid the region's natural beauty. And the more she delves into the past, the more clearly she sees herself, her future, and the way home . . .

Visit us at www.kensingtonbooks.com

Books by Sharon Struth

Blue Moon Lake Series
Share the Moon
Twelve Nights
Harvest Moon
Bella Luna

The Sweet Life
The Sweet Life
Willow's Way

Published by Kensington Publishing Corporation

Willow's Way

The Sweet Life

Sharon Struth

LYRICAL PRESS
Kensington Publishing Corp.
www.kensingtonbooks.com

First Electronic Edition: April 2018
eISBN-13: 978-1-5161-0356-0
eISBN-10: 1-5161-0356-4

First Print Edition: April 2018
ISBN-13: 978-1-5161-0359-1
ISBN-10: 1-5161-0359-9

Printed in the United States of America

This is dedicated to my daughter Katherine, whose semester in England gave me a reason to visit and explore the stunning Cotswold countryside.
And...
To my friend across the pond, Rachel Brimble, for all your advice about being British and helping critique this book.

Acknowledgments

I'd like to thank the readers of my books, who often tell me they get lost in the worlds I create and wish they'd never end. Knowing others join me on this journey is the icing on the cake of each book I write.

Thanks also to Paige Christian, editor extraordinaire, my agent Dawn Dowdle, and the staff at Kensington Publishing, a place that feels like family.

To my husband and daughters—you guys are everything.

Inspiration comes from many places, so I'd like to pass along a special thanks to my neighbor Jillian A. Her love for my dog Milo—a quirky, lovable, and always happy PBGV—helped inspire both Henry and Jilly in this book.

Special thanks to all my writer friends, because without you who would I talk to about writing? And especially Terri, who wastes no time when I message her with a grammar question and is always there to support me in a crisis.

To my wonderfully supportive mother, thank you for giving out so many of my business cards.

A special nod to Beverly, because you rock!! I'm so glad we're friends.

Last, to my friends, your support is immeasurable. I love you guys!

Chapter 1

Willow Armstrong could hardly breathe as she stared at the video playing on her laptop. Stupid. She'd been so stupid. Once again, she'd let urges rule her choices, and this time, she'd been exposed.

Willow squinted at the blurred image. Maybe that wasn't even her. Heck, she'd seen clearer pictures of Sasquatch. "Are you sure that's me, Becky? I mean, lots of people in Manhattan could own a black Lexus."

Her assistant remained silent on the other end of the phone for a little too long then said, "Give it a sec. Keep your eyes on the rearview mirror."

The camera zoomed on the inside of the car and the front mirror came into focus. Willow paused the tape and leaned on the marble kitchen counter to get a closer look. A shiny object hung off the car's rearview mirror. Was that…?

Nooooo!

Dread wormed through her, twisting and turning like a knife in her gut. The silver folded-fork symbol associated with Willow's weight-loss empire, Pound Busters, dangled off the mirror.

She groaned. "I can't believe this."

"I'm sorry. I figured you'd want to know."

"You made the right call."

"Now I'm not sure. Why don't you shut it off?" Becky couldn't hide her worried tone.

Willow's heart warmed for her concerned assistant, who had given Willow ten dedicated years of service. Loyal right to the end. And this could be the end.

On the screen, the arrow hovered over the play button. Terrified to see what the rest of the world would, she froze, her hand stilled on the computer mouse.

Thirty minutes and four thousand "likes" ago, Celebrity Secrets had posted the video to their Facebook page. Dear God! Over seven hundred comments she didn't dare read, and some three hundred shares, all over a slip into Tony's Slice of Heaven. The mouthwatering goodness of the slice barreled toward her with a vengeance. Just a few moments of cheesy bliss. Was it too much to ask for?

"You there, Willow?"

"Yes." She drew in a breath that somehow boosted her courage. "I really should watch this."

She hit the play button. The camera moved and refocused, closing in on the shadowy figure in the driver's seat until the picture became perfectly clear.

A blond woman, whose hoodie barely hid her face, ate—no, more like shoved—a hot slice of Tony's extra-cheese thin crust into her mouth. Willow could still taste their trademark sweet sauce laced with fresh basil, the stretchy, melted mozzarella, the crust toasted to perfection in a brick oven. She salivated. So damn tasty.

The show paused right at a second messy bite and the camera panned back to their main studio, leaving the screen view of Willow pinned, mid-bite, in the upper corner. Show host Lindsay Star stood on the set, her body turned to the video of Willow. Her thigh-high, sleeveless, sequined dress seemed more suitable for clubbing. Suddenly, the pretty brunette swung to face the camera, her sly smile suggesting she'd just heard the century's juiciest piece of gossip.

Willow turned up the volume, prepared to face the jury of one.

"Once again we find Pound Busters founder and CEO Willow Armstrong in the spotlight. Just over two years ago, her then-husband, Lieutenant Governor of New York Richard Carter, announced he planned to leave Ms. Armstrong for his campaign manager.

"Viewers might remember Pound Busters made news earlier this week when Ms. Armstrong's long-trusted business advisor, Tom Comstock, embezzled both her company and personal funds, leaving the country without a trace. Word on the street is the Pound Busters' board isn't too happy with their founder, as it was at her urging that they kept Mr. Comstock rather than firing him six months ago. And Ms. Armstrong's significant weight gain since her divorce has caused Pound Busters shareholders to blame her for lower profits and dropping stock prices.

"It makes this reporter wonder if this is the end of the line for the woman known as the queen of weight loss. Earlier today, I interviewed Nikki Winslow, President of Pound Busters' Board of Directors. After seeing our clip of the firm's CEO during her visit to Tony's Slice of Heaven, here's what Ms. Winslow had to say..."

The video of Willow vanished, replaced by a taped interview of Nikki with the brunette reporter. Outside her Upper East Side co-op building, Nikki stared at the camera, her thin face always angry and holding the dire expression of a woman who wished she'd eaten more for lunch. Wrapped in a beige Burberry trench coat, the Manhattan sophisticate clutched a Gucci shoulder bag while the doorman held an umbrella over her head. She pursed her thin lips, causing the cosmetic-tight-skin around them to twist unnaturally.

Willow's heart raced. The board had exhibited tolerance with her assurances that she'd been trying to lose the weight gained after Richard's public humiliation. After all, how many marriages ended that way? Hell would have to ice over before she'd forgive him for not telling her privately first. She'd owned her role in the gain, even though by many people's standards Willow's weight would be considered average. She ran a hand along the dip in her waist, full in an area where no curve had existed for decades. In the world of selling weight-loss services, going from a size six to a size ten—sometimes a twelve—was sacrilege.

"I'm dismayed to see this tape." Nikki shook her head. "Ms. Armstrong has lost sight of the company's vision. Pound Busters has seen a steady decline in her commitment to our goals. Because of her belief in Tom Comstock, we kept him on. A huge mistake. And now this latest episode proves she's been lying to us about a desire to return to her previous weight. We will be having a meeting soon about the direction and management of the company. A direction that may or may not include Ms. Armstrong."

Bile clogged Willow's throat. Fired. Tossed out on her butt from the company she'd started some twenty years ago. Her blood, sweat, and vision had gotten this firm off the ground when others merely laughed at her idea. If she knew one thing, it was how it felt to be fat and get skinny. Then get fat again, and lose it. Rinse, lather, and repeat. The sad story of her life.

Only after college had she figured out how to lose the weight and keep it off. A strict food regime and military workout routine. One often balked at by the experts.

But both celebrities and the public loved it.

One Pound Busters location led to ten, then to a hundred. The firm grew in leaps and bounds, finally so enormous she'd taken the company public. A move that seemed smart at the time, but now a board of nine people controlled Willow's destiny.

Becky quietly asked, "You okay, Willow?"

No. She wasn't. "I'll be fine. Thanks for the heads-up. I need to think about what I'm going to do. See you tomorrow."

She hung up and headed to the refrigerator, automatically reaching for the handle. She jerked her hand back as if she'd touched a hot metal rod.

Come on, Willow! Fix, don't feast. Commandment Four of Pound Busters' Five Commandments of Weight Loss.

She plunked down on a stool at the kitchen island, reaching for an apple from the basket then tossing it back in without taking a bite. Drawing in a deep breath, she closed her eyes. The depth of her current problems coiled around her like a cobra, getting tighter, tighter, tighter, until it sapped her energy.

Weight gain sat at the center of her work problems. Much as she wanted to stand up and scream at those who criticized her gain, how could she?

Every day of her forty years, she'd been aware of her weight. A chubby early childhood. Those plump adolescent days, turning into plus-sized teenage and college years. Every single moment living in the shadow of a mother who'd once modeled, worsened by a stepfather who'd pounded in her head that she'd better be smart, because with her weight, only her brain would get her places.

Getting thin at the end of college had given her the acceptance she always wanted. Deep inside of her, though, lurked the same person. The one who let dark demons in the pantry lure her to comfort. But who was she, without food in the equation? She'd asked that question too many times lately, making it hard to fight off the people who now fat-shamed her.

She stood and walked to her apartment window, searching the twinkling lights of the cityscape for answers. In the past, if she gained a few pounds, she'd sneak off to the spa upstate nestled in the Catskills. Maybe it made her a fake, but she couldn't afford to fail. This time, she faced a bigger loss obstacle. Five pounds had turned to ten. Ten to twenty. Twenty to thirty.

Her problems beat her silly, pummeling away at the idea she could salvage this. What had she done to herself? She rubbed her throbbing temples.

Stupid. Stupid me! All because of stupid Richard and his affair.

She dug into the Pound Busters Commandments, reviving number two: Believe, don't blame.

Inside her head she repeated, *I believe I can lose this weight* three times until her frustration slowly lifted.

If she could just get to Golden Bridge Spa, she could fix this. A month in secret seclusion, eating only what their dieticians provided while this video blew over. When she came out, she could reappear closer to her old self, even laugh at her lapse of judgment. Except she needed money for that secret seclusion. As Nikki so rightly pointed out, Tom had run off with both Willow's and the firm's money, leaving her without a dime. She could borrow it from her stepfather? No. No borrowing, from anyone.

There had to be money she could use. Somewhere.

Then it hit her.

She raced to the bedroom closet. Tossing shoe boxes and boots out of the way, she dug deep into the back for the cardboard box she'd shoved away a while ago and ignored since. Heart thumping, she set it onto her bed but hesitated to open it. Swallowing the lump in her throat, she opened the flaps and pushed past the personal items, a mishmosh of things she had no other place to store. A large manila envelope made her pause. Her mother's things.

Her stepfather's maid had delivered the envelope a week after the horrible car accident that ended her mother's life. Maria had handed it over, simply saying, "These were in your mother's closet. Your stepdad said you should have them."

That night, Willow opened it, surprised to find it filled with photographs. She'd removed a handful of the aged photos, tried to figure out who these strangers were to her mother. But with her gone, Willow would never be able to ask, or get answers to her questions. In her sadness, she'd shoved the photos back inside and figured one day she'd try to learn more. But life took over and she'd forgotten they were here.

Willow exhaled and returned to her task, looking past the large envelope as she rummaged for the bank passbook, of course, finding it at the bottom.

After opening the small booklet, a relic of banking's past, she blew out a relieved sigh at the eight-thousand-dollar balance. Plus interest. At least she had money. She'd call the bank in the morning. Placing the passbook on the nightstand, she thanked her lucky stars she hadn't closed out the account when she got married or shared this account with her former business advisor.

As she folded the box top to put it away, her mother's envelope beckoned. She removed it and tipped it, allowing the photographs to spill out. An envelope and a small black velvet jewelry case fell out, too.

She picked up the jewelry case. Mom's twenty-third birthday. The cook had made a breakfast tray and Willow ran ahead of her stepfather into the bedroom with this case, wrapped in shiny paper. Her stepfather had personally helped her purchase the gift at a swanky jeweler on Fifth Avenue, a big moment for five-year-old Willow, who'd lived rather modestly with her mother until she'd married Charlie. Willow could still remember Mom's beautiful smile as she'd removed the rosebud necklace and put it on. The fond memory faded. Willow lifted the hinged lid. She ran a finger over the silver granulated pendant, across the bumps of the tiny rosebud surrounded by three leaves. The dark oxidized finish highlighted the flower's grooves, a gift Willow had been certain her mother would love. Rose was Willow's middle name.

With years of sadness starting to unravel, Willow slipped the silver chain over her neck. A thickness filled her throat. Avoiding these special things had allowed her to cope with the loss.

She gathered photos left scattered on the mattress. On top was one of her mother as a young woman holding hands with a man around the same age. Willow gave him a closer look, noting a familiarity in the man's face. Mom only shared the occasional story about her life in England before moving to the States. Could these people have been from that life? Were they relatives Willow never knew about?

She put down the photos and took the long, thick envelope. The postmark date was a year before her mother died, the contents from a lawyer in Bath, England.

The flap had been opened already. Willow removed the multipaged correspondence.

On top was a letter, dated October 15, 2006, indicating that due to the recent passing of her mother's parents, the attached will was being executed. 2006? Mom had always said her parents died before she'd left England. The postmark and date made no sense. She flipped to the will, read the details, *Bitton Property willed to Chloe Armstrong Van Dassel by Derrick and Sarah Armstrong.* They'd left her mother their house? Why hadn't she claimed it?

A voice inside her head shouted, "You had grandparents," but she couldn't quite grasp the reality.

Her mother had lied?

Was there other family Mom had hidden? Willow would have given anything to learn there was family out there besides her mother. She'd even asked her mother a few times over the years, but was told there wasn't.

She continued reading and, almost at the end of the will, Willow blinked at a single line, not sure she'd read it correctly. She read it again.

In the event of Chloe Armstrong's death, Willow Armstrong will be bequeathed the property.

Willow put down the will and went to the other envelopes. Each contained a follow-up letter, asking her mother to confirm receipt of the will. The final letter, dated almost a year after the first, said the property would be held in trust if she didn't respond soon. Based on the postmark, her mother had passed away one month later. So a month before she died, she hadn't claimed the house...

Which meant Willow owned property in Bitton, South Gloucestershire?

Excitement she hadn't felt in ages bubbled inside her. A house in England must be worth something. The passbook might be small potatoes compared to the money she could get from selling a house.

She gathered the passbook, will, and photos, then scurried down the hallway to the kitchen, flying on the wings of hope. A search on the internet for this address should provide more details on the location.

The passbook money could get her to England, where she could see about selling the house. With any luck, while there, she could start to piece together the empty spaces of her life.

Chapter 2

"Unreserved seats found in cars one and two only!" The Paddington Station conductor waved his arms toward the opposite end of the track from where Willow stood to board a car.

Passengers standing in the same line as Willow groaned and half of them abandoned their spots to rush to the other end of the track.

Willow didn't have a seat number or car number that she could see so she went up to the conductor. "Excuse me. Am I in the right line?" She showed him the ticket.

He leaned over to look, squinting as he scanned it. "No. Car one. Best you hurry, Miss. Those unreserved seats fill fast on a bank holiday. Next time it's worth a little more money to pay to ensure you get a seat."

"Thank you." That explained why she'd gotten such a bargain when she'd booked online.

She ran toward the others who'd left her line, a yawn slipping out as she dragged luggage that got heavier with each step. Sleep was all she wanted after the overnight flight to Heathrow, where she'd been too wound up to get a second of shuteye.

Since her arrival in England at eight a.m., she'd taken the express train into London to a branch of the law firm handling her grandparent's estate. There, they'd given her a key to the house, located near Bath. Now she navigated Paddington Station. Stunning with its high, curved ceiling, modern in style, and open-air tracks, it was also jam-packed with people.

At the first car, she squeezed into the thick of the crowd, gripping her luggage and inching toward the door. She'd always heard that forming a queue was as British as scones and tea, but perhaps it wasn't true on a bank holiday.

By the time she hauled her luggage up the steep steps and swung the bag onto the top of a luggage rack near the entrance, sweat beaded her forehead. She ambled down the aisle glancing both ways for a free seat, squeezing past passengers who stood talking to other passengers. Two-thirds of the way back, she blew out a sigh of relief when she spotted a few empty seats.

She plunked into one, shimmied off her light jacket, and took a moment to pat some of the sweat off her forehead. Tipping her head back on the headrest and closing her eyes, she clasped the rose charm on her mother's necklace.

Since slipping it on three days ago, she hadn't taken it off and now wore it as a symbolic way to have her mother with her on this trip. She couldn't imagine why her mother had lied about what she'd left behind in England, but there must've been a good reason.

Someone took the seat beside her. She dropped her hand, opened her eyes, and glanced over. A tall, slender man sat down and stretched his long legs out in front of him, giving her a nod as he did. She did the same and turned to the platform as last-minute passengers ran for the train.

The necklace pressed a spot just beneath her collarbone. *Mom, we're here. We're really here.* A bittersweet mix of joy diluted with sadness washed over her as she wished they'd taken this journey together.

The man to her side shifted in his seat and Willow heard a few beeps. Looking through her purse, she glanced at him out the corner of her eye. He held a cell phone to his ear. Great. A talker.

She double-checked her wallet pocket, where she'd stored the house key from the estate solicitor. According to Mr. King, her grandmother had died in 1998, leaving her grandfather in the house alone for eight years. A neighbor found him dead when she'd noticed he wasn't picking up his mail.

"Hi, baby. I'm on my way back from London."

Willow stared out the window, trying not to listen.

The man laughed softly. "Okay. What are you wearing?" He paused. "Perfect. Exactly what we talked about."

Pain squeezed her chest and jerked her back to the moment she'd found Richard on his cell phone in their bedroom whispering, "Will you wear the teddy I bought you?" At least that's what she swore she heard, a fact he denied when confronted. The truth came out two weeks later at a press conference, when he told the world he planned on leaving Willow. Had he hated her so much he couldn't do it in private? Or had public disgrace been the only way to get her attention?

"See you soon." Her seatmate undid the tray in front him and dropped the phone there.

The train doors shut. Finally. A muffled announcement came over the speakers about their arrival time in Bath, and the train smoothly pulled from the station.

Willow watched out the window, trying to ignore the pressing ache in her chest over Richard. After two years, his leaving shouldn't bother her, yet it niggled at the insecurity owning her since childhood.

She wasn't good enough. Wasn't skinny enough.

As they flew past the outskirts of London, she removed a bag of crackers and a book from her purse. Eating the snack, she watched fields and the occasional house passing outside the train window.

"Tickets, please."

She handed it over to the conductor, and could feel the stare of the man to her side. Like a good New Yorker, she ignored him.

The portly conductor clicked the ticket and gave her a quick smile. "Enjoy your day."

"Thanks." She inhaled and sat back, anxious to see the house.

The day after the will discovery, she'd called Abe, thinking legal advice would be prudent before she got too excited about what she'd found on the internet. Right now, her lawyer was about the only one she trusted.

One website had described Bitton as located in a well-traveled area of England, where tourism dollars might yield a big price for the right house. Abe had worked his magic and by noon he'd talked to someone in the UK and told her they estimated the property to be worth a million pounds—a greater sum in US dollars.

She tipped her head against the window and closed her eyes, the rose necklace shifting on her throat, like a gentle tap from her mother. How many times had her mother ridden a train like this from London to Bath, where once at the station a family member would give her a lift home to Bitton? An unexpected tear slid down her cheek, knowing she'd go there too, but to an empty house.

"You okay there, Rosebud?"

She opened her eyes and glanced to her side to the man seated there, surprised to find him staring at her. "Are you talking to me?"

He nodded and lowered his folded newspaper while watching her over reading glasses that slid halfway down his nose.

"My name isn't Rosebud."

He offered a closed lip smile. "Your necklace. It's a rosebud."

"Oh, yes it is." She reached up and touched it. "Thanks. I'm fine." She shifted to face out the window again, but stopped when he kept talking.

"You're American, are you?" He placed the paper on his lap. His British accent sounded crisp and friendly, so much classier than American men.

"Did my accent give it away?" She grinned.

He smiled. "First trip here?"

"It is."

"Right then." He shifted in his seat, facing her and appearing ready to settle in for a long conversation. "Are you staying in Bath or headed somewhere nearby?"

"Bath." The stranger didn't need to know everything about her.

"You'll love it. The place was founded by the Romans as a thermal spa." He reached into his pocket and pulled out a candy bar. A Cadbury Double Decker. *Chocolate.* A word that transcended continents. He tore away the paper. "Bath became an important center of the wool industry in the Middle Ages. A lot of history there. Want some?" He tipped the chocolate bar her way.

She pulled her gaze from it. "No. I'm sorry for staring. Just a bit jet-lagged."

He took a bite, chewed and swallowed. "Bath also has wonderful architecture. Georgian-style designs built with Bath stone."

"What's that?"

"It's local limestone found in most of the buildings around town. You'll also find neoclassical design at the Roman baths. An amazing site. The Romans..."

He talked. And talked. Willow studied his long face, the slope of his nose, the rugged crags of his profile and dark eyes, the same color as his unkempt black hair and thick brows. He wore a light leather jacket over a white dress shirt and black jeans. Though tall and even a bit lanky, he seemed confident in his skin. He also liked to talk. Pleasant compared to most American men she knew, who weren't very chatty. The soothing quality of his accent relaxed her.

"...and they remain intact to this day. Any special thing you might try to see?"

"I saw Stonehenge was nearby and would love to get there if I have time. But everything you mentioned sounds very interesting."

A man hurrying down the aisle slowed at their row. "Hey there, mate!" He stuck out his hand right in front the man seated next to her. "It's been a long time."

He glanced away from her and a grin spread. "Well, Roger Barton. How the hell are you?"

"Never been better. What are you doing back in England? Last I heard you were all over Europe."

The ready grin left her neighbor's face, replaced by a shadow of sadness. "I came back a year ago. Time to come home." His solemn tone shifted, more upbeat. "Where are you these days?"

Willow gave them privacy and watched out the window, shocked by what she'd been missing. Farms. Sheep. Fields that stretched for miles. Excitement vibrated inside her chest. *This* was how she pictured England.

Fitting some travel into her life over the years should've been easy. Richard used to remind her they had no money issues or children and could go anywhere in the world. Her answer? Always no.

Work. Work. Work.

Success meant everything. Couldn't he see that work also made her forget the two miscarriages? Forget the doctor's news she could never have a child?

Her seatmate's deep voice rumbled beside her. "That's one of my mates from growing up. A real blinkered fella, but he seems to have changed."

Blinkered? She turned to him, about to ask what it meant, but he held out a bag of almonds. "Have a few."

"Sure." She reached in and motioned to the small bag of crackers near her book. "Want some?"

He shook his head. "It's salt and chocolate for me today." He reached into the pocket of his jacket and removed a card. "Listen, I run a tour company if you're in the market for one. Can I interest you in a card?"

"Sure. I don't know what I'll be doing each day, but a tour sounds fun." And she meant it, but only after she got the house on the market.

Rolling up the top of the almond bag, he stretched his long legs into the aisle and tossed the snack on the tray. "Great. Well, cheers then." He smiled and shut his eyes. "Enjoy the rest of the ride."

"You, too."

She smiled. Men could sleep anywhere.

When she'd first landed in England, she'd been exhausted. But the excitement of getting closer to the house worked like a jolt of caffeine. With any luck, this journey would not only bring her much-needed cash, but a family history she sorely desired.

Chapter 3

A muffled voice over the train's loudspeaker announced, "Next stop, Bath Spa."

Willow closed her book. The man still slept to her side. She debated on whether to say something, but he yawned and his eyes slowly opened.

She gathered her jacket and backpack from the floor beneath her seat. When the train stopped, a more sizable crowd than at the previous stops stood to leave. Her seatmate rose, then stepped aside and waved his hand to the aisle. "After you."

"Thanks." She smiled and squeezed out, following the crowd down the aisle.

At the luggage rack, she stopped. Two bulky suitcases sat on top of hers. She tugged her handle to slide it out, but nearly knocked the other two down. People exiting bumped her as they moved quickly to the doors. Her adrenaline pumped. What if the doors shut and the train pulled away?

A hand suddenly shot over her head and took the handle of her bag.

"I'll get it." Her seatmate stood close, towering over her. "Go ahead out to the platform."

She hesitated. A bona fide New Yorker knew better than to leave her personal belongings in the hands of a stranger. People again banged into her trying to enter the train. Putting her faith in the stranger, she stepped outside the doors, staying close in case he planned to run off with her belongings. On one level, a ridiculous notion, but tourists were easy victims.

That very second he turned around and stepped out, her luggage in hand. "Here you go."

"Oh. Thank you so much." She grabbed the handle and felt like an idiot for the few seconds of distrust. Nobody in this country had been anything but kind.

"Well, then." He glanced around. "You know where you're headed?"

"Yes. I'm getting a cab."

"Okay, then. Take the lift over there with your bag up to the main level. There are always cabs outside." He glanced toward the building. "I'm parked in the station lot. I can give you a ride somewhere, if you like."

"That's very nice of you, but I'll stick with my plans."

"Okay, then. I'm off." He passed her a grin that probably got him far in life. "Enjoy your stay in England."

"Thanks."

As he walked away, he blended into the crowd of passengers. For a minute, she felt utterly alone. Hell, she was alone.

After a stop in the ladies' room, she took the elevator to the street level, where she struggled to get through the train station turnstile with her large luggage until a nice employee politely let her out a regular door, all while smiling and welcoming her to town.

She stepped outside and inhaled the crisp fall air while searching the parking lot. A nice new van approached, the words *Wanderlust Excursion Cotswold Tours* emblazoned in red letters against the white vehicle's side, with a street address in Bath. In the driver's seat sat the man who'd been next to her on the train.

He stopped and rolled down his window and the new car smell drifted out. "You sure I can't offer you a ride?"

Sure, the guy possessed charm. So had Ted Bundy. Beyond his van, she spotted a cab with the driver standing outside his car door. "No. I think I found myself one. Enjoy your day."

She hurried off, waving to the older gentleman with a scruffy white beard, who waved back.

In a thick British accent, he asked, "Hello there, miss. Need a ride?"

"I do." She walked closer to him. "To Bitton."

As the driver placed her luggage in the trunk, she watched the tour guide's van pull aside in the parking lot.

"What address?" The driver opened the back passenger door and she climbed inside.

She read him the address and he took off.

The cab pulled out into traffic and careened around a corner. Willow braced herself for impact with an oncoming car. She'd never get used to driving on the opposite side of the road. Crossing the street in London, she'd nearly been run over.

According to the driver, the ride on A431, a road running from Bath to Bristol, would get them there in about ten minutes. The Bath cityscape disappeared and they drove along the Avon river, where the terrain became flat and less busy.

Minutes passed before the driver said, "We are entering Bitton, miss."

She straightened in her seat, aware of every detail outside the window. At first, they drove past fields stretching as far as she could see, but when they crossed an intersection, a few houses appeared, the volume increasing as they entered town. Sights her mother must have seen. The swell of regret made her heart ache. If only she'd pressed her mother harder about the past. A trip here together could've opened up a world of conversations they never shared.

The cab slowed as they entered a busier area. Light beige-and-white brick buildings, with flat fronts and small windows, lined the street, a restaurant, corner market, and a few pedestrians on the sidewalks.

"Are we close to the house?"

"Just down the road."

They drove straight, rounding a couple of traffic circles that made crossing Fifth Avenue at rush hour seem like a stroll in the park. The car slowed and turned into a private driveway, stopping at a fork on the property.

The driver studied his GPS. "I think we want to go left." He motioned to a dirt road. "What do you think?"

She shrugged. "I've never been here before. Your guess is as good as mine."

He started down the isolated road, with trees lining both sides. Sleeping alone in this place could be a little creepy. Living in a big city, Willow never felt unsafe. Neighbors were close by.

A clearing appeared up ahead. The dirt road ended, and a paved brick driveway began.

"Ah, there it is!" the driver exclaimed.

Willow ducked her head to see out the front window. Straight ahead stood a sizeable house, bigger than she'd expected. The cab pulled in front of it and stopped.

A paper from the London attorney called the place a Victorian, but the structure looked nothing like those of the same name in the States. The multistoried home exterior, made of rough-finished stones, welcomed with a pretty front porch. Creamy beige wood trim outlined the porch and second-level dormered windows.

Willow fished the key from her purse. "Can you wait while I make sure I can unlock the place?"

"Yes, ma'am." The driver reached over and released the trunk, getting out as she did.

Willow approached the wide steps leading onto the porch. Weeds popped up from the driveway stones, pointing to years of neglect. The lawyer had said a caretaker kept an eye on the property in case of emergencies and made sure to pay the taxes, but nothing else.

Her heart raced. Family of *hers* once lived here. Willow squeezed the old key in her palm and approached the solid, dark-wood door. Holding her breath, she worked the key into the lock and it clicked open.

"Miss? Here's your bag."

She turned to find the driver at the base of the porch. She squared away the fare. As the cab drove away, the loneliness washing over her at the train station returned.

Drawing in a breath, she imagined her mother at her side. *Here we are, Willow. The home where I was raised.*

Willow swallowed the lump in her throat, took the luggage handle, and hoisted it up the steps. A low howl of a dog, followed by rustling from the nearby woods, made her pause.

She turned to the sound, laughing as a short-legged, shaggy dog approached, its long tail raised high in the air, wagging like a flag of surrender. The cute canine bellowed another generous howl and came toward Willow; she swore it wore a smile—if a dog could.

Willow stepped off the porch. "Hello there, little fella." She crouched down and extended her hand. "Come here."

Woooowoooowoooo. This time he offered a softer, less frantic cooing that warmed and welcomed. He swarmed her calves while she ran a hand along his thick, wiry fur, trying to figure out the breed. A body like a basset hound, with the same white, black, and tan coloring, yet his thick, wiry hair was very un-bassett-like.

She touched his long, silky ears. "You're a cute little guy."

With that he rested his short, thick legs on her knees, giving her the once-over, too.

Long snout. Pronounced black nose. Smiling dark brown eyes peeked out beneath a mop of hair atop his crown-shaped head. A real cutie. He licked her cheek.

"Are you lost or just part of the welcome wagon?" He licked her again. "Then part of the welcome wagon it is."

She checked his collar for ID. A metal tag read *Henry* and listed a phone number.

"Well, Henry, why don't I call your—"

"Henry!" A child yelled. "Henry!"

The voice came from the direction of the same thick trees where the dog had exited.

"He's over here," Willow hollered back and a moment later a young girl of maybe five or six dressed in jeans and a long-sleeved T-shirt emerged. She marched over. "Oh, Henry." She shook her head and her fawn-colored pigtails danced. "You are not always a good listener."

The dog abandoned Willow. As he rushed to meet the girl, his back end swayed to one side, as if it couldn't keep up with his front half. He ran right into the young girl, but she braced herself from falling and leaned over to give him an affectionate pat on the back.

"Henry! You can be such a bad boy."

Henry licked her cheek, making the girl giggle. Willow couldn't wipe the smile from her face if she tried. Besides the young girl's contagious laugh, her accented voice and reprimand sounded so grown compared to American children.

Willow walked toward them. "What kind of dog is he?"

"Oh, he's a petite."

"I've never heard of those." Willow squatted down and ran her hand along his low, long body. "Just a petite?"

"No. A Petite Basset Griffon Vendéen." She pronounced the words with a beginner's French accent.

"That's a mouthful. Well, I've definitely never heard of that either."

"That's why we call him a petite, or sometimes a PBGV." She cupped the dog's snout in her hands and kissed the top of his head. "My mum used to breed them." She frowned. "Now we only have Henry."

"Oh, so she doesn't breed them anymore?"

She quieted and stroked the dog's long ears. "My mum passed away. But my daddy let me keep Henry."

Sadness tore at Willow's chest. To hear that such a young child had suffered the loss of a parent didn't seem right. "I'm sorry about your mother. I lost mine, too. It's hard."

The little girl played with the dog for a bit then glanced up at Willow. "You're American?"

"Yes. I just arrived in the country. Do you live near here?"

"Through those trees. Are you the lady who owns this house?"

She nodded. "I'm Willow. What's your name?"

"Jillian. But everyone calls me Jilly." She scrunched her nose, the bridge of it dotted with freckles. "Willow is a funny name."

"It's definitely unusual." Kids were always so straightforward, a quality she possessed herself that was not always admired by other adults. "My mother told me Willow meant slender and graceful."

In her chubby childhood years and adolescence, Willow had wished she could change her name to anything else. Not once in her life had she *felt* slender and graceful.

"Really?" Jilly's eyes went wide.

"Oh yes." Willow lifted her arms over her head, joining her fingertips together then sticking out her leg with the toe pointed. "Graceful like a ballerina. See?"

Her reward came when Jilly's chestnut-brown eyes brightened and she nodded. "Oh yes, you look just like one."

"Why, thank you so much." Willow took a bow, accepting a compliment far from the truth.

"My daddy helps take care of your house." Jilly picked up a stick and threw it. The dog bolted off in pursuit. "It used to be my mum."

The lawyer had given Willow the name O. Hughes with a phone number. "And where do you live again?"

Jilly pointed to the trees as the dog returned and dropped the stick near her navy-blue sneakers. "In the cottage over there. Me and my father."

When she'd picked up the key, the lawyer had briefly mentioned a cottage on her land, saying it hadn't been included in the home's original estimate. An unexpected cha-ching on her cash register.

A woman in the distance yelled, "Jilly! Come home now."

The child picked up the stick. "I have to go now. Come, Henry!"

She waved the stick and took off for the trees, with Henry galloping at her heels and baying his cry of reveille.

Willow soaked in the joy of watching them, the feeling swiftly replaced by unexpected regret. When she and Richard hadn't been able to have children, he'd refused to adopt. She'd never know if that might have helped root their marriage.

As the dog and child disappeared through the trees, Willow turned to the house. A tremor of excitement rumbled in her chest as she made her way to the front door.

* * * *

"What do you mean Billy called in sick? Again?" Owen Hughes stood in the reception area and stared at Margo.

"Billy has a bug." Owen's feisty office administrator glared back at him and spoke with a stern tone, which he accepted because, as his mum's friend, Margo had known Owen since he wore diapers. "Can't have him getting the customers sick, can we?"

"No. Of course not." He'd taken his anxiousness out on the wrong person. "It's the last thing I needed today. I'm tired. Left the house at sunrise to get into London for a nine o'clock meeting."

"How'd it go?"

He sat on a metal office chair near Margo's desk and crossed his ankle on his knee. "We have a new hotel client who'll send tours our way."

"Fantastic." Margo threw up her hands, more glee than Owen could muster at the moment. "Wanderlust Excursions Cotswolds Tours is starting to come into its own."

"It is." So why didn't he feel great? "Appears as if I'm the only one left to take over Billy's tour today. I hope Bea can keep Jilly longer. This single parenthood thing isn't easy some days."

Margo leaned forward and crossed her arms over her ample chest. "I already called Bea. She said of course. I told her you'd be heading home from the tour after five."

"You're the best, Margo. Sorry if I'm a bit ruffled. I got an email while at my appointment. Seems I may get kicked out of the cottage soon."

"Kicked out? Why?"

"The owner showed up. Can you believe it? After all these years. The lawyer says they want to sell the place fast as possible."

"Suddenly it's an emergency." Margo's thin eyebrows arched. "When the owner died and Tracey moved into the cottage... Well, it must be over ten years ago."

The mere mention of his ex-wife stirred up sadness. They had married because Tracey got pregnant with Jilly—the marriage lasting a mere six months—but he'd always cared about her. Her unexpected death last year had shocked the whole town. Only those close to Tracey understood the depth of her depression.

"Why the rush to sell?" Margo asked.

"I don't know, but they did say the owner is American. I'm worried about telling Jilly the news."

Jilly's tears in the months following Tracey's death had nearly ripped Owen apart, most notably when he'd told her they might have to move. *But Daddy, how will Mommy know where to find me?* she'd asked over and over. How did he talk to a child about suicide? About death? God knows he tried. The child psychologist didn't seem to help. But a great gift from a guardian angel had come when the lawyer for the house asked if Owen would assume Tracey's role as caretaker. He'd grabbed the chance to give his baby girl one less thing to worry about.

"Perhaps the new owner will let you stay if you explain your situation." Margo's optimism never failed her, a trait he normally found uplifting.

He shook his head. "They have every right to sell."

"Come on, Owen. You could try."

"And say what? Please don't sell your property. I used all my savings to buy into a Wanderlust Excursion franchise here in Southern England and need a cheap place to live. Oh, and my daughter will be upset if we move because she's worried her dead mother won't know where she's gone." Tightness tugged at his chest. "Good grief, Margo, they'd laugh in my face. Even if they offered to sell me the cottage, I don't have a dime to buy a place right now."

Money. It controlled everything. Owen could almost hear his father crow over Owen's choice to invest in the tour business when he learned the latest news. Owen barely had one foot back in Bitton to care for Jilly when Dad had pushed him about joining the family roof-thatching business. How many times did he have to say no?

"Yoohoo. Earth to Owen."

He looked up at Margo. "I'm sorry. What?"

"I said you don't know what the owner will do unless you give asking a try."

"I can't. It sounds like a soap opera and nobody's problem but mine."

The bigger obstacle would be finding a cheap rental that allowed for a dog. Not all places accepted animals and Henry—with all his quirks—was Jilly's guardian angel.

He smiled to ease the worried expression on Margo's face. "So tell me the details on Billy's tour."

"A group of librarians, here for the Jane Austen Festival. They want the half-day tour."

He glanced at his watch. "Just enough time for me to grab lunch then head over to the meeting point."

He made a quick call to Bea, wolfed down a burger at a place down the street from his Bath office, and then picked up his customers.

As he drove the group of eighteen to their first stop, he methodically pointed out landmarks and tried to sound enthusiastic. Never a struggle when he'd worked as a tour director for Wanderlust's other European destinations, far from Bitton. In those places, he didn't have to deal with his father.

He slowed the van as they neared the car park on Bratton Road.

"We're going to stop so you can see the Westbury White Horse." He motioned to a distant hillside. "When you exit the van, take a look that way and you'll see the symbol for the town of Westbury. A salt engraving of a horse that stands at one hundred eighty by one hundred seventy feet."

As the passengers exited, he heard the usual ooo's and aah's. When had his passion for the sights of the Cotswolds fizzled out? All he knew was he hated being back home, the sacrifice made only for his daughter's well-being.

While he stood with the tour group talking about the salt horse, a thatcher service truck flew by on the road. An idea tumbled toward him, although it stung a bit, like salt on an open wound. What if he worked part-time for his dad? He'd sworn he never would. But the extra money could help his finances, at least until the tour franchise made better profits. Yeah, it could work, but at what cost to his happiness?

Chapter 4

Willow pushed and the front door opened with a foreboding creak, like every horror movie she'd ever seen. She laughed off the omen and entered, inhaling a dank, musty scent. The scent of neglect and passing time.

In her imagination, arriving at her grandparents' house conjured images of a greeting filled with the sweet scent of cookies baking and a toasty fire in the fireplace. The stale air and dimly lit foyer weren't even close. She released her luggage handle, aware of a gentle throb in her hand from her tight grip.

She owned this house now. She'd make it homey, so prospective buyers didn't run out the door screaming.

Light would help. Tipping her head back, she studied a brass fixture hanging from the ceiling with scarlet shades shaped like tulips. On the cracked plaster wall to her right, she found a switch, but when she flipped up nothing happened.

Stepping in further, she peeked through a doorway opening to her left. The living room. Dim, just like the entryway, due to tightly drawn shades on a tall bay window. Sheets covered several objects. Judging from the size, she guessed furniture.

A creak came from above. Or was it below? She stilled.

"Hello?" Her voice reverberated against the walls. Nobody answered.

A quiver traveled her spine. Forget imaginary monsters or ghosts. All kinds of critters could be roaming in a vacant house, especially one in the country. Why hadn't she thought about that before?

According to the lawyer, the caretaker's limited responsibilities included watching the property and hiring seasonal maintenance for outside of the house, not upholding the interior.

She drew in a deep breath. Old houses made noises. *Get over it, Willow.*

Turning into the dark living room, she navigated piles of newspaper and boxes to reach the bay window. She tugged a corner shade and let go. It snapped up to the window top like a speeding bullet, letting out a loud bang as it hit the top. Willow's terrified heart jumped straight into her throat and a cloud of dust tickled her nose. She opened the remaining shades with more care, and once opened they offered ample light to get a better look at things.

Beneath the sheets she found a formal gold sofa, several floral straight-backed chairs, tables with Queen Anne–styled legs, and various models of brass and ceramic lamps.

All the lamps were unplugged, but she found one with a bulb and plugged it into the wall socket. Nope. After trying two more lamps, she concluded the power didn't work.

She returned to her backpack and removed a pad from inside, writing down *electric.* Organization mattered if you had a goal. Even a weight-loss goal, she'd learned with her first big weight-loss success, which was the kind of thinking that helped her start her company.

Crossing the foyer, she entered the dining room and walked past a large, sheet-covered table with chairs and a brass chandelier, dripping with noticeable cobwebs.

She walked into the kitchen. After opening the dusty curtains over the sink, she turned the faucet. Cold, brown liquid sputtered from the spout. Letting it run for a minute with no noticeable change, she figured she'd found problem number two and would add contacting a plumber and cleaning supplies to her list. A dirty, dull, gold-patterned vinyl floor showed signs of wear, and curled away from the wall in one corner, not far from a rusted gas stove. Across the room sat a boxy refrigerator. She walked over and opened it, gagging as the stench from a few items left behind assaulted her senses. She slammed the door shut and hurried from the room.

No water. No power. Filth. She couldn't sleep here. Finding a place to stay would cut into her funds, but until she got some basic twentieth-century functions restored, what choice did she have?

But the cab driver had left. Damn.

She returned to the porch. Inhaling the fresh air didn't relieve the stinky scent from the refrigerator, but she worked hard to forget about it while using her phone to search the internet for a room. The Clemmens B and B, right here in Bitton and just over a mile away, had a room available.

Hell, in her slimmer days she used to run five miles as a warmup. She could walk a mile and a half.

After reserving a room online and paying for it with a credit card, she went back inside and started to list what she'd need to get this place cleaned up. For several hours, she got lost in the details of her cleanup on the main level, leaving the second story and attic for another day.

When finished, she locked up and briefly inspected the outside. Through the woods, she spotted the white cottage where Jilly had said she lived. How did a child so young deal with the loss of a parent? As she stared at the house, she wondered how long Jilly had lived there, and where she and her dad would live if Willow sold this property.

For a moment, grief slithered around her, pulling her to a sad place. Mostly for the little girl, but also for her own losses. She blew out a breath, releasing pity and turning to good old common sense to gain perspective. Jilly's father must've known someday the owner might come along and he'd have to move. She'd make sure the lawyer gave them plenty of notice, so they didn't get stranded without a place to live.

Her stomach growled. She hadn't eaten since the train ride.

She rushed back to the porch, grabbed her luggage and headed to the end of the long driveway. As she turned onto the main road, all the excitement that had driven her energy upon arrival dwindled with her need to sleep.

She walked slowly. Around ten minutes into her walk, a passenger van passed her going in the opposite direction. She recognized the driver as the man from the train.

Funny he'd be here. The address on his van had been in Bath. When he'd asked where she was headed, she hadn't told him Bitton. Must be a coincidence.

A minute later, the sound of an engine behind her made her glance over her shoulder. He must've turned around, because the van followed her. A coincidence or... Wait? Had he followed her cab here?

She picked up speed, walked with purpose. Same as she'd have done in the city at night, if someone nearby left her alarmed on a quiet street.

The engine sound moved closer. And closer. He pulled alongside her, his passenger window already rolled down, and stopped. "Hey there, Rosebud. Remember me?"

In Manhattan, she'd learned to be street savvy, but the friendly calm of this area could fool anybody into letting their guard down. She slipped her free hand into the pocket of her jacket and wrapped her fingers around her phone.

She forced a smile. "Yup. Nice to see you again."

He looked her up and down, then square in the eyes. "Need a ride?"

"No, but I appreciate the offer."

She glanced around. The area wasn't remote. There were houses and buildings. Just no people outside. A few years ago, she'd taken a class on self-defense for women. For what it was worth. She'd missed half the classes because work had been busy, but one move vaguely stuck in her head, good to use if someone tried to pull you into—

"I didn't expect to see you in Bitton." He smiled.

"No?"

"Nope."

"Did you follow me here from the train station?"

His smile slipped. "What? Why on earth would I... Look, Rosebud, I didn't follow you. I'm just a guy driving home from work."

"Could you stop calling me Rosebud, please?"

His brows lifted and he studied her for a moment. "I'm afraid we didn't have a proper introduction on the train."

Even if he wasn't a killer, he was kind of pushy, and she didn't like pushy people.

He stuck his hand out the window. "I'm Owen—"

"You know, I'm well versed in self-defense." The second the comment passed her lips, she wished she'd just shut up. She couldn't remember how to perform the one maneuver she might need to use, let along be considered well versed.

"Oh, are you now?" A slow smile crept across his lips.

She was tired. Hungry. And his smirk pushed the button on her slowly building irritation. She lifted her chin and held up her cell phone. "I don't want to have to call 9-1-1, but I will. Don't underestimate me, sir."

"Oh, trust me, I don't." His rich brown eyes twinkled with amusement. "But a lot of help calling that number will do you."

"Why?"

"It's 9-9-9 here for emergency calls."

Her face warmed. If he'd offered the ride with ulterior motives, why would he share such information?

What an idiot I am.

Sweat beaded on her forehead. Now she *did* want to run, mostly out of embarrassment.

"Look, I'm sorry." He frowned and did look like he felt bad. "Just teasing you."

"I see you're just being kind with your offer, but I'm fine on my own."

"Okay, then. I'll let you get on your way."

She forced a smile, so he didn't leave here believing all Americans were nuts.

The van did a three-point turn and he headed back in the direction he'd first been going, giving her a quick wave as he accelerated away. As he did, she remembered how he'd given her a business card on the train, definitely not something an attacker would do. *Yup, a big idiot.* She trudged forward and hoped she never ran into him again.

* * * *

Jeesh, women! Cute but paranoid.

He turned off the road and followed the driveway to the fork. For a second, he considered checking in on the house before the owner arrived, but he could do it after supper or tomorrow.

Swinging to the right, he followed the tree-lined dirt driveway leading to the cottage. A spot on the thatched roof above the white stucco exterior showed damage. Was it new or had he just not noticed it? Maybe he'd call Dad tomorrow, see if he could fit in a quick repair.

A good time to mention he needed part-time work. Sure, he'd have to eat humble pie. His past responses when Dad had tried to convince him to help carry on the business hadn't always been polite. Like one whooper he'd said at the cocky age of twenty-one. *Hell will have to freeze over before I'll become a roof thatcher.*

Owen cringed and wished he could do that moment over again. Back then, he'd been young, cocky, and rude to a man who worked hard to take care of his family. Despite the way his father constantly put down the things Owen enjoyed, the man didn't deserve that kind of snarky comment from his kid.

He parked and gathered his things. Henry trotted out from around the side of the house and, spotting the van, bellowed a war cry worthy of a Viking. Seconds later, Jilly appeared. Where one went, the other followed.

He kicked the van door shut with his foot. "How's my favorite girl and favorite dog?"

Jilly approached. "We're good, Daddy."

Henry let out a low "wooooooooo," a very PBGV greeting.

Owen had never heard of the unusual hound breed until he'd met up with Tracey one night at Rory's Pub during a break in his European tour schedule. They'd dated in high school for a while, going their separate ways after graduation. That night, some sixteen years later, he'd learned that Tracey's life had literally gone to the dogs. She not only raised this hound breed but also ran a successful grooming business and showed dogs for other owners at prestigious shows.

Henry reached Owen first. He patted the wire-haired dog on the head then swooped Jilly into his arms. At six, she was getting big for swooping. Still, he didn't care.

"Did you bring me anything?" She watched him seriously, her large chestnut eyes making him incapable of ever getting upset with her.

He lowered her to the ground. "Now why would I do that?" He reached inside his jacket pocket, slowly removing the other candy bar he'd purchased. He held it toward her. "You wouldn't want this, would you?"

Her mouth dropped open. "My favorite!" She squealed as she swiped the bar from his hand.

His heart lifted with a surge of love for his daughter, the joy on her face always a gift. Especially after what happened to her mother. "But wait and eat it after dinner."

"Did you get anything for Henry?" Jilly put a hand on her hip and waited. He'd swear she was six going on sixteen.

Henry wagged his tail and watched Owen with the same expectant expression.

"Nothing for Henry today. And don't give him candy. He could get sick. How about we stop and buy him a bone at the butcher on our way to dance class later?"

"Okay." She patted the dog's head. "Sound okay, Henry?"

More tail wags from the most agreeable animal on the planet. Tracey had called them "the happy breed." Henry proved her right.

They walked to the house, Jilly chatting away about her day.

He'd never take a moment like this for granted. After Tracey died, Jilly had cried herself to sleep every night. Once she'd been assured they could stay here, she'd been better. Worry over the latest news caused Owen's gut to flip-flop.

He reached for the solid door and turned the knob. "Nan inside?"

She nodded, and he noted the pigtails he'd so carefully tied for her this morning were still in decent shape. "Can I play on the swings until dinner?"

"Sure." He glanced down, happy to see she wore sneakers, like she'd said when he'd called her from the train. Last week she'd tripped running in sandals. Proper footwear fit under things a father wouldn't think about, but a mother would. "Yes. Don't go far. We're eating soon."

She took off, the dog at her heels.

He entered the cottage. "I'm back."

A delicious scent captured his attention. The sound of the oven door opening led him to the kitchen, where he found his ex–mother-in-law leaning over the stove, basting a chicken with her back to him. "Hi, Bea."

"How'd it go for this morning's meeting?"

"Good. Got a new client." He stole a cherry tomato from a salad on the counter. "Thanks for getting dinner started."

She shut the oven door and straightened. "It's no problem." She wiped her hands on an apron tied at her waist. "Glad to hear you drummed up some new business."

"Sorry again about the change in my workday." He went to the refrigerator and pulled out a beer. "I don't know what I'd do without you."

"Please, Owen. I don't ever mind." A quick flash of pain showed in her eyes. Tracey's suicide seemed to be a part of every conversation, without anybody bringing it up. "Being here for both of you is the least I can do."

"Well, it doesn't mean I can't say thanks." He smiled, wishing he could erase her pain. Erase Jilly's pain. Hell, they all shared the same ache, just in different forms. "I got an email from the lawyer who handles this land. After all these years, the owner plans to claim the place."

"Oh my." Bea frowned, age lines on her thin face deepening. "So you'll need to find a new place to live?"

"Eventually. Hopefully they'll take their time getting here. The owner lives in America. That should give me a little time."

She glanced out the window facing the swing set, her deep-set frown no doubt demonstrating the same concern for Jilly as Owen. "I wonder if that would explain something Jilly told me."

He took a long drink of the beer. "What's that?"

She turned to Owen while untying the back of the apron. "She ran into someone at the house this afternoon. An American woman."

Owen shrugged off his jacket and tossed it on the kitchen chair. The blonde he'd met walking down the road and on the train took on a new light. He leaned against the kitchen counter. "What else did Jilly say?"

"Not much." Bea chuckled. "Only that the woman took ballet and tap lessons when she was Jilly's age and she definitely liked Henry."

"Well, who doesn't?" They both laughed, then Owen said, "I doubt it's the home owner. The lawyer said he'd just spoken to the US attorney a few days ago."

"Then it wouldn't seem so." She tossed the apron on the counter and smoothed her knit top at the hips so it flattened to her jeans. "We worried this day would come. Gerard and I could make some room for you in our apartment, but…" She drew in a long breath. "Long term, two more people and a dog could be an issue in our small place."

"Don't worry. I'll figure something out." For only a split second, he let himself imagine Jilly without Tracey's favorite dog, who'd attached himself to Jilly since her mum died.

Bea turned to him and he forced a smile. No sense in worrying her. She motioned to the stove. "Fifteen minutes, the timer'll ring. Take out the chicken. Don't forget about dance class tonight. I've got to get home. Gerard and I are going out with friends for dinner."

"Have a good time."

Bea grabbed her purse and a sweater off the kitchen table. "Tomorrow I'll get Jilly from school and come over here. Take your time with the tour—if it gets late, I'll tuck Henry safely in your house with his dinner and feed Jilly at my place."

She turned and walked toward the door and he followed. "You're an angel, Bea. I couldn't do it without you."

She pulled open the door, and glanced over her shoulder, watching him with glistening eyes. "Anything for you two."

She smiled weakly and left as he called Jilly inside. Henry ran to Owen ahead of her, glancing back to make certain Jilly was close behind. What if he did have to get rid of Henry in order for them to find a new rental in their price range? Could he do it?

The weight of the thought nearly smothered him. Nope, it would be like her mother dying all over again.

Once the owner of the house showed up, he'd think about what he could do to delay a move. Anything was worth a shot for his daughter's happiness.

Chapter 5

Willow turned down the gravel driveway, where a white sign with painted flowers in each corner read *Clemmens Bed and Breakfast*. She approached the two-story building with a plain white stucco exterior and clay tiled roof.

Her feet ached, her bladder screamed for release, and her stomach rumbled like an approaching storm. She should've taken that ride from... What was his name? Her mind had been preoccupied when he'd said it, and now she couldn't even recall what letter it started with.

At the bed and breakfast's rustic, wood-stained door, a sign read *Entrance*, so she walked inside. Across the room was a mahogany desk surround holding a check-in plaque. She went over, taking note of the lobby's comfortable sofa, creamy walls, and homey decorations. Very Hallmark-store.

"Hello?" she called.

A pleasant-sounding woman sang from another room. "Be right there! I'm just trying... Hold on."

Seconds later, a short, slightly plump woman came out of a doorway behind the reception desk. "Good afternoon. Can I help you?"

"Yes. I have a reservation."

She frowned. "Oh? We weren't expecting anyone this afternoon. I wonder if Eddie—"

"I just made it online. Not long ago."

"Ah, I see. I thought maybe my husband took it and didn't tell me. He does that sometimes." She exhaled loudly and brushed a strand of light-brown-and-gray hair escaping her bun near her temple. "I'm exhausted. I've been in back doing some cleaning. Online you say?"

"Yes."

She turned to the computer. "Eddie usually does these reservations, but he stepped out. Now let me see…"

She slowly tapped the keyboard with her index fingers.

Willow waited patiently, then leaned forward and saw her last name on the screen. "There I am. Willow Armstrong." She smiled, hoping she wasn't being too pushy, but her physical needs beckoned.

"Oh, thank you, dear." She tapped a few more buttons, then glanced up. "I'm Edna Clemmens, by the way. It's very nice to meet you."

"You too."

"I hate all this technology." Edna's forehead crinkled as she stared at the computer screen for a moment, then poked at the keyboard again. "My Eddie, he loves it. Got us all set up with this system, but I miss the days when the phone would ring and I could talk to whoever wanted to book a room." She looked up. "Do you know what I mean?"

Willow's bladder screamed, "Hurry up," and she crossed her legs. "Yes. Things sure have changed. So my reservation is okay?"

"It is, dear. I see you paid when you booked."

A door opened somewhere in the house and a man yelled. "I'm back!"

"In the lobby. We have a guest checking in."

"Yup. I saw it online. Got the back room upstairs ready."

"Shall I get Eddie to take your bag?" Edna turned around and took a metal key off the rack hanging on the wall.

"No need. I can handle it."

"Then off we go."

They followed a hallway with cream-colored walls, each lined with wooden plaques with sayings such as, "Families are like fudge; mostly sweet with a few nuts," and "Find Joy in the Journey."

The first door they passed held a hand-painted sign identifying it as the Daffodil Room, with a bright yellow flower of the same name. Willow's stomach growled. "Is there a restaurant nearby?"

"In town, there's Rory's Tavern. A lovely pub. We just finished afternoon tea, but I can make you a little plate of food and something to drink if you want a snack before dinner."

"That sounds delicious."

She nodded and hurried past the Orchid Room, also with a hand-painted version of the flower near the room name.

Edna glanced back over her shoulder. "You're American?"

"I am."

"What brings you to town?"

"A property in town that belonged to my grandparents."

"Oh?" Edna paused and raised her perfectly penciled-on eyebrows. "What are their names?"

"Derrick and Sarah Armstrong? Did you know them?"

"Well, good heavens. Of course. Lovely people." She started walking again, taking Willow up a staircase to the second floor. "When Sarah died, it was such a loss for poor Derrick, but he kept himself busy." She shook her head. "Their house has been empty for a long time." She stopped in front of a door marked Rose Room and turned to Willow. "Would you look at that?" She motioned to Willow's neck and laughed. "Your necklace is a rose. Must be more than a coincidence."

Willow smiled. Whatever the reason, Edna knowing her grandparents seemed a sign things might be going her way.

"I'll get a plate of food together for you." Edna put the key in the lock, turned it, and pushed the door partway open. "Come down when you're ready and let me know if you need anything. Otherwise, welcome to Bitton." Edna scurried down the hall, yelling her husband's name.

Willow entered and dropped her bag. Soft pink walls. A white bedspread with a pattern of roses. Roses, roses, everywhere. In a vase on the nightstand. Decorating the edges of a mirror positioned over the white dresser. This was much better then sleeping in that dark, dusty house alone, with no power and dirty water.

As she crossed the bathroom threshold, she touched the necklace and smiled. Perhaps the power of the rose had guided her to the right place.

* * * *

"Unfortunately, I got here and found the house needs work." Willow sipped tea from a delicate china cup decorated with pink flowers. Perhaps the best tea she'd ever had.

A breeze came through the open casement window, filling the cozy sunroom with the crisp scent of autumn air. She patted the photographs her mother had saved over a lifetime, pressed to Willow's thigh in the pocket of her linen tunic.

"Well, fortunately for us, you found our place." Eddie, a barrel-chested man who'd just received a lecture from Edna about his high cholesterol, reentered the room popping the last of what appeared to be a cookie into his mouth.

"Oh, Willow. I wanted to show you something." Edna stood and went to a side table where she opened a drawer. She removed a stack of pamphlets, handing one to Willow and placing the rest on the center of the coffee table.

"This is everything you need to know about Bath's annual Jane Austen Festival. I hope you can find time to participate in some of the events." Edna returned to the seat next to her husband. "Eddie and I go to several of them."

Willow chewed a bite of sandwich and swallowed. "I'm only here because of the house. Everything depends on how much I get done. I'm scheduled to fly back in two weeks."

"If you can find time, you must come." Edna pushed a plated scone sitting on the table toward Willow. "All the money goes to a local charity, and we have so much fun. Ms. Austen was a woman ahead of her time, writing about arranged marriage versus doing so for love. Right, Eddie?"

Eddie sipped his tea then lowered the cup. "Indeed."

Edna nodded her satisfaction then looked at Willow. "Are you a fan?"

"Not really."

Obligation had played a part in why she'd married Richard, though. Her stepfather had introduced them at a private family function. Tall, polished, and charming, Richard could work a room and leave lusty-eyed ladies in his wake. And he'd worked his magic on her. Willow easily won her stepfather's approval when she and Richard got engaged. Their marriage had suited both men, from a business and political standpoint. But in hindsight, deep, passionate love had never entered the equation.

Edna motioned to a jar on the table. "Have some clotted cream with that scone, dear. They belong together, like salt and pepper."

Clotted cream sounded *extremely* fattening, as if the name alone were a warning from the FDA about what would happen to your arteries if you ate the treat. However, factoring in her walk and lack of food, she opted for a generous scoop. After spreading it on and taking a big bite, she held back a moan as the buttery dough and creamy spread tantalized her taste buds.

On her second bite, eating guilt crept into her belly. Always hiding around a corner, waiting to ruin her day. She used her palm to flatten her shirt at the waist, running her hand over her stomach. Always checking, even when thin. Gone were the days when she *couldn't* find an inch to pinch. Now there was definitely an inch, reminding her of her stepfather's nasty weight comments and her old, pudgy self. She lowered the plated scone.

"Isn't that so, Willow?"

She turned to Edna, shaking off the ache in her chest. "What's that?"

"Your grandparent's house. It's been left to you?"

"Oh yes, yes." She drew in a breath. *Steady girl. How could Charlie's meanness still bother me after all these years?* "I'm anxious to start cleaning the place up. Is there any place I can buy supplies?"

Edna motioned to her husband. "Eddie can drive you into town to get what you need."

His gaze lifted from Willow's scone, making her want to give him half of the treat. "I'd be happy to."

"I appreciate it." She turned to Edna. "Could I show you some pictures that belonged to my mother? I'm wondering if any of them might be my grandparents."

Edna's eyes widened. "So, you've never even seen photos of them?"

"No." Willow removed the pictures from her shirt pocket and handed them over. "My mother—their daughter, Chloe—always told me she moved to the States after they'd already passed. When I found the will, I realized she'd lied."

"I never knew Sarah and Derrick had a granddaughter."

"The home was originally left to my mother. The will said it went to me in the event of her death. When she passed in a car accident, I received some of her special things. The will was amongst them, but for some reason, she'd never told anybody about it."

"I'm so sorry she passed." Edna frowned. "I remember when Chloe left town. Her parents never talked about her much after that. Only to say she seemed happy in her new home."

Evidently, secrets had been kept on both sides of the Atlantic.

Edna pressed her lips tight while flipping through the photos. She held up a picture of a young couple getting married. "This is definitely them." She passed it to Willow. "Take a look. I can see a bit of your grandmother in you. You have the same jawline."

Willow studied the photo. She didn't have her mother's delicate facial features, and had always wished to know where in the gene pool she'd acquired her blond hair and high forehead. But here she'd found a connection in the determined jawline of a stranger.

"And Derrick..." Edna paused and looked off into the distance. "Often quiet, but always friendly. He worked very hard at his accounting job and was quite active in the church. That's how my family knew them. Goodness." She smiled with happy remembrance. "Derrick always walked around town. He loved to walk. And paint. He painted a beautiful oil painting of the church that still hangs in the pastor's office. Your mum was a few years older than me in school. She didn't always come with her parents to church, and I never got to know her that well. But your grandparents knew everyone at the church."

Willow devoured each word. Even though Edna couldn't identify any of the others in the photographs, Willow had learned more from this stranger than from repeated efforts asking her mother about family history.

A yawn escaped. "I'm sorry. This has been wonderful, but I've been up since yesterday morning my time."

"Go rest. You need sleep." Edna stood. "If you want dinner, Rory's starts serving at six-thirty. Maybe take a short nap."

"Good idea." She thanked Edna for the tea and went back to the cozy room.

Lying on the bed, she closed her eyes and conjured images of the life that once existed in her grandparents' home. Each tidbit Edna offered about a family Willow had never known existed nourished her soul. Unanswered questions bombarded her as she sank deeper into the mattress and drifted off to sleep.

* * * *

"Good night, baby." Owen pulled a blanket up to Jilly's chin and kissed her forehead.

"I'm not a baby." She scowled.

"You'll always be my baby girl, no matter how old you get. But maybe I can think of a new special name for you. How about Jilly Bean because you're sweet as candy?"

She giggled. "I like it."

"Then goodnight, Jilly Bean. I love you." He patted Henry, who'd already curled into a ball at the end of her bed. "'Night, Henry." The dog squeezed his eyes shut tighter, but his tail flopped once.

Owen left the room, closing the door halfway. After grabbing a few cookies from the kitchen cabinet, he went into the living room and flipped on the television. His phone sat on the coffee table and showed he had a voice message. He listened to the faint message, the connection poor.

Hello. I'm looking for the caretaker for a house at... My name is Willow Armstrong...about...power being turned on and a few... I'll be working there tomorrow...I'd appreciate it if... Thanks!

Willow Armstrong. She sounded like the American woman he'd met this afternoon. Rosebud. He chuckled at her reaction to what he'd called her. Most women would've liked a pretty nickname. Not her.

Using his phone, he typed her name in the internet search bar.

Sure enough, several photos of a blonde resembling Rosebud appeared, but the photos showed a severely slimmed-down version of the woman he'd met today. Her silky wrap-around dress clung to slim hips and the heavy pendant of her necklace looked like it outweighed her long neck. Shoulder-length, shiny hair framed intense blue eyes. Determined as steel. Like if she only held one match in her hand, she'd somehow set a field ablaze. Yes, this was her. Only now with a slightly fuller face and curves any man would stop and notice. He left the image search and clicked on the website.

Well, look at that. Founder and CEO of a firm called Pound Busters. On the "About Willow" page, he learned she'd founded and started the company that had gone from private to public in the past decade.

He clicked on a link to Willow's Five Commandments of Weight Loss. A small blurb on top said these were the five rules their founder followed to achieve her own success.

Commandment One: Balance is Best
Commandment Two: Believe, Don't Blame
Commandment Three: Consistency is Your Companion
Commandment Four: Fix, Don't Feast
Commandment Five: Motivate Your Mind

He'd never had to lose weight in his entire life, but if he did, those rules sounded as good as any.

He learned about her struggle with weight as a child and how she'd overcome it with a militant weight-loss regime during college. Her company had started based on this dieting premise, first with a Manhattan location, but it grew rapidly into a weight-loss empire followed by both celebrities and regular people alike.

So Rosebud had money.

"Daddy?" Jilly squeaked from her bedroom. "Can I have some water?"

He exited the search and put down the phone. So began the nightly ritual of Jilly asking for things before she finally went to sleep.

"Be right there."

He walked to the kitchen and filled the glass with a small amount of water. Many well-off Americans owned homes abroad. So why not Willow?

As he walked toward his daughter's room, he began to wonder if he could change Willow's mind about selling. Somehow convince her to keep the place for vacations.

Sure. It might work. Then he wouldn't have to move and could stay here as caretaker.

But how could he best show her what the Cotswolds and neighboring areas offered without appearing as desperate as he felt?

Chapter 6

Willow sniffed. Food. Bacon, maybe sausage?

She rolled to her side and pulled the covers to her chin. The scent lingered, taunting her until her stomach grumbled with need and she opened her eyes.

Bright sunshine seeped through the frilly rose-patterned curtains in her room. She lifted her phone off the nightstand. Seven-thirty a.m.? Her catnap had turned into twelve hours of sleep.

The list of chores waiting to be done today booted her in the ass. She dragged herself out of bed, still dressed in the clothes she'd changed into when she got here. After a quick shower, she dried her hair and tied it in a ponytail then slipped on a fresh pair of faded jeans and a white oxford shirt, the tails worn out so she could feel comfy and not stuffed in her clothes.

She followed her nose to the scent that woke her, ending up in the sunroom where tables had been set up along the casement windows and guests she hadn't seen before dug into hearty plates of food.

Edna stuck her head into the room. "Morning, sleepyhead. You missed dinner and must be starving. A full breakfast okay for you?"

"Yes, please. Sounds delicious."

She got seated and before she knew it, Edna hustled back in and lowered a plate in front of her. Two eggs over easy. Sausage and bacon. A halved tomato that looked fried on one side. Whole mushrooms. Toasted bread. And in the center a scoopful of rustic, brown baked beans. This ensemble of goodies served as a poster of Pound Busters *Don'ts*, but the company philosophy—while engrained in her thought process—went straight out the window, where years of her dieting logic had gone.

A half hour later, with her stomach satisfied, Willow went with Eddie to a DIY store where she purchased trash bags, packing boxes, and cleaning supplies.

He turned into the dirt driveway leading to her grandparents' house. "Now call me if you need anything. It's no bother to run over here for an errand or when you're done."

"Thanks. I plan to be here until the afternoon. Edna made me lunch."

"She's a good cook. I'm a lucky man." They reached the house, and he stopped the car. "Here you are. I've always thought this quite a lovely place."

With a clearer head, and through less-tired eyes, Willow stared at the two-story country Victorian. "It is beautiful." She pushed open the door. "Thanks for the ride."

She retrieved her supplies and waved as he pulled away.

Willow headed for the house, her step light and energized for the day ahead. New assignments sucked her right in, where she'd get so immersed in the details, the project would be completed long before the due date. Heck, her classmates in boarding school had voted her "least likely to pull an all-nighter."

Unfortunately, when she pushed open the door, the excited buzz faded with the old stench of the house. Probably made worse when she'd opened the refrigerator yesterday.

The cleanup here suddenly seemed more daunting than starting her weight-loss company. Smells and trash. Broken conveniences, like water and electricity.

She dug deep inside, retrieving the resolve that always pushed her through the day. She could do it. She *had* to do it. The sale of this house was a "do or die" moment. At least from a financial perspective.

After leaving the door open, she opened all the windows to get rid of the awful smell. She made a mental note to call the groundskeeper again if he didn't call or stop by soon.

She gathered her supplies and headed for the living room, plunking them in the room's center on a patterned cream-and-Wedgewood-blue area rug. A full turn around the room proved she had her work cut out for her. Wall shelves and an étagère held books and bric-a-brac, perfectly arranged as if someone had decided to step out for the day, not leave it for good.

She cracked open a garbage bag and packing box and set about her task. What she learned about her grandparents after an hour of work could be summed up in one sentence: they'd loved to read. Books about history, religion, popular fiction, self-help. It pained Willow to give them away, or worse, throw them out. After glancing through *The Years of Grace*, basically a guidebook on preparing to get married and raise a family, she tossed it in a box of things to donate. The topic, though, made her wonder how her grandparents had gotten along with her mother, who Willow remembered as more of a free spirit.

She rose from the floor and looked around, taking some pride in her accomplishments so far. Back in the foyer, she removed a bottle of sparkling water from her lunch bag. While taking a long gulp, she studied the dark wood staircase.

Photos lined the wall leading upstairs. She took her drink and walked up the first three steps, stopping at a landing. Family pictures of her mother and grandparents. As she moved up the steps, new faces appeared, all unfamiliar. Maybe more family she didn't know about?

Slowly, she made her way up the flight of stairs, pausing to study each photograph until she reached the top. She faced a long hallway, counting eight closed, dark wood doors, including one at the end of the hallway, possibly a closet or attic.

She opened the first door. Two nightstands holding brass lamps flanked the headboard of a four-poster bed. Framed photos, a Bible, and a hairbrush sat on top of a tallboy.

She crossed the hardwood floor, covered only by an oriental-patterned area rug, and pulled open a shade. Dust particles flittered in front of her face and she swatted them away as her gaze landed on a photograph on the tallboy.

Pictures. Eyes to the past. In her case, they were all she had left. She went over and lifted it. In this one, her mother—about seven or eight— stood between her parents, holding each of their hands. Even back then, the camera lens clung to her huge eyes, so unique and pretty they'd been her trademark during her brief modeling career.

A lump settled in her throat. After a lifetime of believing none of this existed, she finally held a photo that proved it had. These really *were* her grandparents. People who might have loved her without reservation, who knew she'd been born since they'd put her in the will, yet never met their granddaughter.

The photo blurred behind her tears, prompted by frustration and an ache for what could have been. Why did her mother leave here? Why didn't her grandparents reach out? If they knew they had a granddaughter, why hadn't they discussed it around Bitton?

What had gone wrong with this family?

"Hello? Anybody around?" A man with a deep voice and a British accent called from downstairs. "It's the groundskeeper."

Finally. "Be right down."

She tossed the picture on the dresser and hurried downstairs. As soon as her feet hit the landing facing the foyer, she stopped.

"What are you—" Heat rushed her cheeks. The man with the van she'd met yesterday stood at the door, his lean frame tilted against the doorjamb and his arms crossed. The same amused grin she'd seen yesterday crossed his lips. "Please don't tell me you're the groundskeeper."

"The one and only. Nice to see you again, Rosebud."

She laughed. "My God. How small is this town? Am I going to find out next that we're related?"

He stood straight and rubbed the back of his neck while still smiling. "I doubt it. I'd have been told by now."

"I'm Willow Armstrong." She approached him, hand extended. A more suitable greeting then yesterday's neurotic tirade. "Sorry. When you offered me a lift, I didn't quite hear your name."

He shook her hand, a good handshake, with a touch of tenderness. "Owen Hughes."

His dark chocolate eyes locked on hers. Kind eyes. How had she missed this? "A lifetime of living in Manhattan has left me streetwise but perhaps overly suspicious."

"No worries. I'm sure you were knackered from the flight."

"I was. I mean, if knackered means tired."

He chuckled. "It does."

"You were very kind to twice offer me a ride."

"When I bumped into you yesterday, had you just left the house?"

She nodded. "On my way to the Clemmen's B and B. My plan was to stay here, but this house isn't fit to live in."

"I imagine not."

His gaze trickled from her face all the way down to her clean white sneakers, the perusal making her breath shorten. A man hadn't looked at her this closely in a long time, although she hated when they did. Especially now, with the added poundage.

Just then, Owen's kind eyes met hers and his lips softened into a smile. "I think you met my daughter yesterday."

"Oh yes. Jilly said her dad worked as the groundskeeper." Willow looked away from him for the few seconds she needed to push away his intense scrutiny. She lifted her chin and smiled. "Yes, we had a nice chat. She's adorable. Seems very grown-up for such a little girl."

"As her dad, I'd have to agree on the adorable. And on the other, there are times I'd swear she's already a teenager. It's a world where kids grow up too fast." The shine in his gaze spoke to his love for her, but then his expression went neutral. "It's been a long time since anybody has shown an interest in what goes on with this house." His voice, for the first time, carried an edge. "You're thinking of selling the place?"

"Not thinking. I absolutely will." She lifted her brows and nodded her head, just so he'd understand she took her goals seriously. "But right now, it has no power."

"Yes, your message said."

"And the water is brown. On top of that, all my grandparents' things need to be moved out. Plus whatever else I find along the way. Did you know my grandparents? I mean, being the caretaker and all."

He shook his head. "No. I'm from town, but we hadn't met. I took over this job for…well, Jilly's mother, my ex. She'd done this job before she passed away." He said it quietly and offered nothing else about the circumstances for such a young woman to have died. "When I came to take care of Jilly, I agreed to take this job, too."

"I thought you owned a local travel company."

"I do both," he said quickly. "Anything else I can answer for you about the place?"

"Before I list with an agent, I'd like to take a look at the cottage. When it's convenient for you and Jilly, of course."

His jaw flexed. "Sure. It's through those trees. I'm taking a group to Stonehenge soon, but can spare a few minutes to show you outside the place. Our driveway and the one to this house are connected, but it's an easier walk through a path in the trees."

As they left the house and crossed the yard, she said, "How far is Stonehenge from here?"

"Not far. About an hour."

Another selling plus. They walked in silence and started down the worn dirt path where Jilly and Henry had emerged yesterday.

She glanced his way, studying him in more detail. He'd shoved his hands in the pockets of his khaki pants and his white oxford shirt opened to expose his Adam's apple. The shirtsleeves on the slightly wrinkled shirt were folded to his elbow and the ends of his hair curled at the shirt's collar in back. He seemed to be in deep thought and, for some reason, his silence bothered her. Maybe because he'd been so lively on the train.

"Would you need a hand with the house cleanup?" He finally looked her way and lifted his thick, dark brows.

"I might."

"Let me know." He pointed ahead. "Here we are."

Quaint and cozy summed up the white stucco structure. Henry peered out a window, howling at them.

Owen chuckled. "I heard you met Henry yesterday, too."

"I did. He's a real character." Her gaze drifted away from the dog to the roofline over the window. A straw roof?

"Well?" He motioned with his hand and stared at the place with pride. "What do you think?"

"It's cute. Kind of old."

He raised a brow. "There are a lot of old things in England. This was the original house built back in the mid-eighteen hundreds. Years later, someone bought the property and built the larger house."

"Eighteen-hundreds? I'm shocked they didn't modernize this place. I mean that roof..." She shook her head. "Very old."

"What do mean?"

"It's straw. One huff from the big bad wolf and it's a goner."

He laughed. "That's very funny."

She crossed her arms. "I'm not trying to be funny. From a resale standpoint, I'd imagine it's not a plus."

"From a resale point, it's classic. That there is a thatched roof, one of the historical treasures found in this part of England. One of the reasons people visit the Cotswolds."

She studied it again with a critical eye. "Still, the heating bills with that type of roofing must be enormous. A more modern roof material would surely save money."

He snorted a laugh. "You Yanks. Always want to pave paradise and put up a parking lot. Listen, Rosebud, thatching is one of the oldest-surviving building crafts and England's most common roof covering until the end of the nineteenth century. These roofs are extremely thermally efficient— warm in winter and cool in summer. Better than conventional materials."

"What about fire? Couldn't straw catch on fire easily?"

He shook his head with confidence. "Homes with thatched roofs are no more likely to catch fire than those with conventional roofs. Didn't you read up on the Cotswolds at all before coming here?"

"Only a little. My goals were just to get to my grandparents' house, fix it up, then sell it."

He stared at the house then he turned to her. "I think one of my tours is in order. Tourists come here from all over the world and you should find out why before you get rid of this lovely property."

"Oh, I'm set on selling it." She debated on telling him why, but then decided against it. Nobody here knew anything about the mess she'd left behind in the States. Keeping it quiet meant freedom from questions and judgment. "This trip is business, not pleasure. Now back to that roof, would you say it's in good condition?"

"It's seen better days."

"Do you know someone who could give me a professional assessment of the roof?"

He pursed his lips. "I do."

"Could you pass along their name and number?"

"I'll give them a call for you." He shoved his hands in his jacket pockets, and turned to the woods. "I need to get going."

"Sure." She followed him. "Thanks for showing me the place."

He nodded. They walked back, Owen quiet and staring straight ahead. She searched through their conversation, worried she may have offended him again. Then it hit her why he'd acted so uncomfortable at times: she was selling the place where he and his daughter lived.

"My goal is to sell both the big house and cottage, but if you'd like to buy the cottage in order to stay here, I can talk to the lawyer."

He stopped. "Me? Buy it?"

"Yes. So you don't have to move."

He shook his head and started to walk at a fast pace. "Buying a place isn't in my plans at the moment."

She hurried to catch up with him. "Go ahead. Make me an offer I can't refuse." She smiled when he glanced her way. "I need to sell as fast as I can, so I'm open to a good offer."

He slowed down, and she hoped the intense look on his face meant he was giving her offer due consideration.

As they neared his van, he stopped and faced her. "Thank you for the offer, but I'm not interested. I'll call the power company and someone about that roof." He shifted, glanced down for a split second. "You know, the offer stands for a tour if you'd like. It's on the house since we're neighbors. All I'd ask is maybe a review online if you like it."

She couldn't figure out why he'd offered the tour, but she felt bad refusing, especially after how she'd turned down rides from him. Twice. "You know, a tour sounds like fun."

He lifted his brows, almost surprised to finally get a yes. "Good. And if you want a hand inside, I can swing by when I have time."

"Sure. I could use a hand with some heavier things. I appreciate the offer."

"Happy to do it. I'll be in touch soon."

Willow returned to the house, happy to get this project fully underway. She'd consider her budget for repairs before she went any further. And maybe if she made progress by the end of the week, she'd actually take him up on the tour offer.

* * * *

Owen exceeded the speed limit hoping to reach his Stonehenge–Avebury tour group meeting at the Royal Hotel on time.

As he followed the road that ran along the River Avon, even the radio blasting a new Ed Sheeran song he liked couldn't stop him from thinking about Willow's assessment of the straw roof. Maybe some Americans didn't appreciate the history found in such landmarks. Most structures in the States weren't nearly as old as those in the UK.

He turned onto Upper Bristol Road and flew past the large residential houses made of limestone. He chuckled, remembering what she'd asked about the cottage roof. If Dad had heard her talk about replacing it, his lecture would've been longer then Owen's. Although Dad relished any excuse to offer a lecture.

Strange she'd go right to selling the place. A wealthy woman like her didn't need money.

If he'd been willed a house in a foreign country, he'd first learn about the area, not rush to sell. Money wasn't everything. Okay, maybe not entirely true. He could sure use a little more these days.

Willow, though, seemed determined to sell her property. Fast.

The entire time he'd been with her, he kept trying to find a subtle way to put his half-thought-out plan to work. A free tour for a review. Hell, what a witless offer.

His call moments ago to the power company showed they were busy, estimating the repair crew might be out in a few days. He hoped so. Any delay might keep Willow here long enough to allow him to help her fall in love with England. Fall in love with the Cotswolds. And maybe, if luck was on his side, she'd decide not to sell and his problem would be solved.

He turned down a side street to detour from the busier tourist areas and finally arrived at the Royal Hotel in Bath, only one minute past the time he'd been scheduled to get here.

He'd never considered himself manipulative, but right now, with Willow, what choice did he have? The idea he could get her to love the Cotswolds might be a long shot, but he'd do anything for his daughter's happiness and to stay in this cottage for a little longer.

Anything. Except beg her not to sell for his daughter's sake. She was fully entitled to sell her property, but if she decided on her own to stay, well, that was a different story.

Chapter 7

From her seat on the living room sofa, Willow popped the last bite of her sandwich into her mouth. She debated what to pack next. Her grandparents sure had collected a lot of stuff. Stationed over by the bay window, a walnut étagère filled with decorative knickknacks was next on her list.

She stood and tossed the wrapper in a black trash bag on the floor, filled with books, newspapers and other items in no condition to keep. On her way to the étagère, there was a knock at the door.

Peeking out the window, she spotted a white van with lettering that said *Western Power Distribution*. Owen had left only a few hours ago, but to get such a quick response must mean he possessed some real pull around town.

She opened the door to find a youngish man with a beard, wearing a fluorescent work jacket over black pants and a shirt. "Hello."

"Good afternoon, ma'am. Are you the home owner?"

"I am."

"I just received a work order to restore power at this address." Another man got out of the truck and headed for the door. "We were in the area and figured we'd take a look."

"Wonderful. It's been shut off for some time."

"That's what our records show. We'll need to inspect the wiring before we do anything. Old houses, they can have all kinds of issues." He looked around the foyer and reached out and touched a crack on the foyer wall. "Age catches up with wire and things should be checked to avoid possible fires." His coworker came up behind him and nodded. "Do you mind if we come in, take a look around?"

"Please. Just go where you need to."

He tipped his white hard hat and went off.

Rewiring a house would cost a fortune. Willow figured she'd need to invest some money in this place, but she'd hoped for as little as possible. Electricians weren't cheap. Besides electricity and the brown water, what other problems might be lurking?

She took her phone from her purse and Googled problems with old homes. Hazardous materials, termites, plumbing, foundation or structural problems... Her angst escalated.

She exited the article. This old house might need more work than she could afford or have time to complete. In her desperation for money, maybe she'd been hasty jetting off to England and should've taken time to evaluate potential costs to ready for sale. Or had the lawyers hire someone to do exactly what she'd flown here to do.

She sighed. Coming here had been a haphazard idea. Since she *was* here, though, the only choice was to move forward.

After assembling a cardboard box, she went to the étagère and devoted her attention to packing. She lifted a figurine of a woman in a billowy skirt, far too pretty to get rid of or even give away. Underneath, *Royal Doulton - Buttercup* had been imprinted on the base.

Had her grandmother handpicked this or was it a gift? After going through all the figurines and thinking about her grandmother with each one, she kept only a few as keepsakes of her grandmother's collection.

On the next shelf were more family photos, the largest an oval photograph of her grandparents framed in silver antique. Derrick's hair had thinned and Sarah's face showed wrinkle lines near her eyes and mouth. The couple smiled, but not with the same joy found in earlier snapshots.

Willow opened the back latch, removed the photo, and flipped it over. In lovely script, someone had written *Sarah and Derrick, 1975.* Seventy-five. Willow had been born in seventy-six, conceived and born in the US. Her mother's leaving could explain their sad smiles.

She added it to the pile of things she planned to take back to New York. All she had left to connect her to the one set of blood relatives she knew about.

Melancholy rushed her like a sudden fog. Since finding the will, she'd learned more about her family's past than in her whole thirty-nine years, but it left her thinking about all the moments she'd missed out on.

She lowered herself to the floor, concentrating on the next shelf to ease the pain. It held several crosses and angel figurines, speaking to the deep faith she guessed they had after what Edna had shared about them. When she finished wrapping the last one, she went to the bottom shelf holding an assortment of small porcelain dogs. A stubby-legged, curly-haired one reminded her of Henry and she laughed.

Gathering all the dogs, she carefully wrapped them in paper and put them aside for Jilly.

"Ma'am?"

She rose, dusted off her jeans, and went over to the workman and his coworker. "Any chance all you have to do is flip a switch?"

He shook his head. "I'm afraid you have some wiring issues. We can't restore power until you get an electrician out here to do some work. Once that's done and approved, we can make arrangements to get you up and running."

The balloon of her hopes for fast money popped, pricked by a small pin of reality. No matter. She'd get it done. "Okay, then. Thanks. I'll call you after the electrician does the updates."

He nodded. "Cheers. Have a good day."

She sat on the front porch steps watching the truck pull away. So what now? Maybe Owen knew an electrician.

Woooooo! Wooooo!

Henry burst through the woods and her tense shoulders relaxed. Next Jilly came running from the same path, a backpack strapped to her shoulders.

Just the sight of the two made her doom and gloom evaporate like a drop of water in the sun. Henry reached Willow first and wiggled around her legs. She ran her hands over his long torso, which only made him squiggle even more. "Hi, Henry. I missed you, boy."

Jilly stomped toward her and stopped short, panting as she spoke. "Henry won the race."

Willow laughed. "He has the advantage of four legs to your two. Did you just get home from school?"

"Yes. My nan picked me up." Henry ran inside the open door. Jilly shook her head and plunked her hands on her hips. "I'm sorry about him. Daddy is right. He *is* missing some manners."

"Well, he's cute, so he can get away with it. Would you like to come inside?"

"Yes, please. Nan sent me here with some tea for you. She said nobody visiting England should work through teatime."

"How sweet of her. And a good rule to live by." Was Jilly's grandmother Owen's mother or his ex-wife's? Willow stood and brushed off the back of her jeans. Motioning with her hands toward the door, she donned a mock formal voice with an English accent. "Won't you please come in and join me for some tea in the parlor?"

Jilly giggled. "Now you sound like you're from England, too." She marched inside.

As Willow entered behind her, a rustling noise came from the kitchen. Seconds later, Henry darted into the living room, prancing around the open space. Willow leaned over and patted his back. "Henry, you are one silly dog."

Her reward came with a tongue across her cheek, but as he did, she smelled something tasty on his breath.

Jilly lowered her backpack to the coffee table then removed a thermos and pretty floral teacups. "Nan made the tea with sugar and milk. Is that okay?"

"Exactly how I drink it. Hold on. I have something perfect to go with our drink."

One foot inside the kitchen, she figured out why Henry smelled of food. Half of the scone Edna had packed with Willow's lunch now sat on the dirty floor. She picked it up and tossed what was left in the trash.

"Well," she announced, returning to the living room. "I *had* something perfect. A scone, but Henry ate half of it."

The dog stood near Jilly, watching Willow with shining dark eyes while his tail swayed. Willow's annoyance melted, leaving her convinced this dog could get away with a murder rap.

"Oh, Henry." Jilly frowned at him. "He's often a very bad boy. Daddy says he knows when he's being bad, but does it anyway."

"Do you think that's true?"

The little girl shrugged. "Maybe sometimes, but my mum always said Henry is special."

"I can see why." Willow's heart ached for the child's loss. She wanted to reach out and hug her, but after knowing her such a short time, it didn't seem right.

Jilly reached inside her backpack again. "Oh look! Nan gave us scones."

Willow smiled. "Perfect."

They got everything ready, and after shooshing away Henry twice, Jilly sat beside Willow on the Queen Anne–style sofa. As they enjoyed their afternoon tea, Willow learned all about Jilly's school and her first-year teacher.

"Do you have a best friend?"

"Nicole. She lives down the road." Jilly picked slowly at her scone, then broke off a piece and fed it to Henry, who'd been smart enough to stay nearby. "There's one girl I don't like."

"Why?"

"She's mean. Her name is Ashley. She said I'm almost an orphan because my mother died." Jilly frowned and glanced at Henry when he whimpered, no doubt requesting more food.

Willow understood the pain behind Jilly's silence. The press had been brutal to Willow after the pizza video surfaced. "What Ashley said was mean. And not true."

"Daddy said to ignore her." Jilly stroked the dog's ears. He turned his head and licked her hand, making Jilly almost smile. "He told me that bad people always get what they deserve."

"He's right, but it's hard to ignore it when someone hurts your feelings. Isn't it?"

Jilly nodded, her focus still on Henry.

Willow watched the pair, the bond between girl and dog something more than just his being a pet. "When I was in first grade, two kids teased me because I didn't have a father." The nasty boys also said her mother talked funny because of her British accent, but she didn't want to focus on that.

Jilly looked up. "Where was he?"

She shrugged. "I don't know. I never knew him and my mom didn't tell me anything about him."

"Why do you say it that way? Mom, not Mum."

"We say it differently in the US."

"What happened to the mean boys? Did they get what they deserved?"

Jilly picked up her scone and took a bite, but watched Willow with her eyes opened wide, as if she were about to tell her the meaning of life.

"I'm not sure if they did. Like your dad, though, my mother said to ignore them. I did and they eventually stopped saying it. Sometimes kids do things to get a reaction. You know, they want you to get upset, for their own agenda."

Like Nikki Winslow, who'd taken far too many jabs at her weight since she started to gain. Maybe Nikki had been a mean girl while growing up.

"Oh, before I forget," Willow stood. "I have something for you."

Willow carried over a box holding the dog figurines, placing them on the sofa cushion between her and Jilly. "I thought you might like these. They belonged to my grandparents."

Jilly lifted one and opened the newspaper wrapping. Her eyes shone as she picked up one dog after the other. "Look!" She held up Willow's favorite of the bunch. "It's Henry." She ran a nail-bitten finger along the porcelain. "You mean they're all mine?"

"All yours, if your dad doesn't mind."

"I'll ask. Thank you, Willow." She stood and tossed her arms around Willow's neck.

Willow hugged her small frame, holding her tight, the way she'd wanted to when they'd spoken earlier about her mother.

Jilly returned to her seat. "So your nan lived in this house? How come you didn't visit ever before?"

How best to tell a child this age a story she didn't fully understand herself? She'd never shied away from honesty, so why start now? "I never actually met them. My mother moved away from England and went to the US when she got older."

"What's the US?"

"America. It's also called the United States, so we say US to shorten it."

"Oh." Jilly nodded. "So your mum moved there? Away from here?"

"Yes. After I was born, she never spoke about my grandparents. But last week I found papers that told me my grandparents left me this house after they died."

"Oh. Then this house must be special."

"Yes it is." Willow's heart warmed, not only at the insightful observation, but also for this young girl, who possessed wisdom beyond her years. Losing a parent could do that to a child.

"Maybe tomorrow, after school, you can come by and help me upstairs. I was going to pack up my mother's room and could use a hand."

"Can I bring Henry?"

Willow glanced at the dog, who sat staring at their half-eaten scones resting on the coffee table. "I'd be sad if you didn't."

Jilly drank the last of her tea and stood. "I'd better go. I have homework."

Together they repacked the backpack, including the porcelain dogs, and walked to the door. Henry followed.

"Tomorrow, same time?" Willow asked as she opened the door.

"Yes, but I'll have to check with Nan or Dad first."

"Smart girl." Willow winked. Jilly smiled so bright it reached her eyes, squeezing a little something inside Willow's chest.

Jilly walked off, Henry running ahead of her, but always with an eye on his mistress.

A dark wave of sadness rushed toward Willow, unexpected after all this time. Yet she never forgot. The hysterectomy needed to save her life had just been compartmentalized, stored away so it didn't take her down. Those damn fibroids just wouldn't stop growing. Maybe that's what led to her working so much, along with Richard's distance after the procedure.

The joy brought by Jilly and Henry faded. She shut the door, already looking forward to their visit tomorrow.

Instead of calling Eddie for a ride back to the B and B, she packed her belongings and left the house. A walk in the fresh country air and beautiful September day might offer freedom from her troubles in New York.

On her way down the dirt-paved driveway, she looked forward to returning to the B and B, a place starting to feel like her home away from home.

Chapter 8

Willow's phone alarm beeped, waking her exactly thirty minutes after she'd lain down for a nap. She showered and sorted through her luggage until she found a pair of so-called skinny jeans that she grabbed, along with a loose peasant top and black flats. Suitable attire for the pub Edna recommended last night.

About to blow-dry her hair, she stopped and studied the outlet on the wall, which didn't match the one on her blow-dryer cord. Of course. She hadn't packed an adaptor for it.

Willow headed to the lobby. No signs of Edna or Eddie, so she went to the sunroom, where she found Edna putting some used plates from the glass coffee table onto a tray.

"Hi Edna."

She glanced over her shoulder. "You're back. We missed you at tea today." Edna leaned over and picked up the tray. "Did you need me for something?"

"Yes. I forgot a converter for my blow-dryer. You don't have a spare one I could borrow, do you?"

Edna straightened. "Your what?" Her forehead wrinkled.

"Blow-dryer. To dry my hair."

"Oh, a hairdryer. Sure. Just one sec while I put these in the kitchen. I'll meet you back by the reception desk." She hurried off.

Willow waited back in reception, but before Edna even reached the room, her voice traveled down one of the hallways. "Tell me, Willow. How did it go at your grandparents' house today?" She rushed in, huffing and puffing. "Get a lot done, did you?"

"I'd call it a decent start."

"Oh good. Now let me get that hairdryer." She disappeared through the door behind the desk. A few seconds later, she exited, carrying one. "Keep it while you're here." She leaned on the counter. "I imagine most of their belongings were still there?"

She nodded. "There's a lot to be packed. Oh, I saw some pretty angel figurines. I know you said they were active in church."

"Yes. They attended St. Mary's, like my family. Had I mentioned your grandfather served as deacon?"

"Not before. So he was very involved?"

"Oh yes. Served on the church boards, too." She tipped her head, frowning. "And your mum never talked to you about them?"

Willow shook her head. "I grew up believing she'd moved to the States after they passed away." A fact filling her with increasing resentment.

Edna bowed her lower lip and her double chin popped. "It's really quite a shame. They'd have loved spending time with their grand—wait! I know who might be able to answer your questions!"

"Who?"

"Hettie McBride. A close friend of your grandmother. Goodness, they co-chaired so many of the church events."

Willow held in her glee. This could be just the break she needed to learn more. "Any idea where I can find her?"

"Edna?" Eddie called from another room. "Where did you put the cookies we got at the store the other day?"

Edna rolled her eyes and raised her voice. "Sweetheart, I'll be with you in a minute." She lowered it and said to Willow, "They're hidden. I swear. That man is going to kill himself if he doesn't start listening to the doctor." She cleared her throat. "Now let me think. Hettie isn't in Bitton anymore. She moved in with her son quite a few years back, but I don't remember where they went. How about I ask around?"

"That would be wonderful." Willow reached out and squeezed Edna's hand. "Thank you so much."

Edna squeezed back. "No bother at all." She glanced toward the kitchen as the sound of drawers opening and closing carried into the lobby. "Let me go see what he's doing. Enjoy your dinner."

Edna scurried off, hollering, "Eddie Clemmens. If you're hungry, have an apple. Don't you care about your heart?"

On her way back to her room, Willow smiled. Their loving arguing was similar to moments she'd witnessed with her mother and stepfather. The kind of arguing when you care. Willow and Richard had never fought like that and she'd taken it as a sign they had a good marriage. In truth, though, both were too busy to care. Their marital problems came into sharper focus, forcing her to see that perhaps it had died long before he'd cheated and fell in love with someone else.

As she dried her hair, she discarded further thoughts about her failed marriage and focused on the idea a woman named Hettie McBride might hold the key to unanswered questions.

Willow applied makeup, fluffed her hair to her shoulders, and studied the result. For the first time in two days, her eyes sparkled and she looked happy. The only setback? The fullness of her cheeks since gaining weight, making her reflection seem like a stranger each time she glanced in a mirror. Or was the stranger the skinnier woman who had driven her hard for so many years?

* * * *

Willow's taste buds watered as she closed the Rory's menu. A rather extensive offering compared to pubs at home.

Music floated in the air, song after song from the 1960s. Willow couldn't resist tapping her foot to "Be My Baby."

The young woman who'd taken her drink order a few minutes ago returned, her long legs doing justice to a pair of flared jeans. She carried herself with a gentle swagger of confidence, an attitude that suited her short black hair with soft spikes on top.

"Here you go, miss." She lowered a tall beer, with a frothy head skimming the top, onto the table. "I forgot to tell you my name is Bonnie. I'll be taking your order, too."

"Then I'll have the fish-and-chips, side of mushy peas." She'd never heard of the side dish but was feeling adventurous.

Bonnie scribbled on her pad. "Good choice. I'll put in your order. Cheers!"

Willow watched the waitress walk away, envious of her nice shape. Her own tight waistband squeezed her midsection, reminding her that ordering fried food wasn't the smartest move.

At some point, she needed to address her weight issues. How could the ability to control her weight, a huge part of her life for so long, vanish overnight? She'd lived and breathed by those five principles that ultimately became the Pound Busters' Five Commandments of Weight Loss.

The day she'd sat down and put her philosophy to paper, everything in her life changed. Nobody believed in her, but she'd held firm. Naysayers couldn't stop her. The five rules had saved her, drove her, inspired her to lose weight and even stay thin. And her regime worked, because it inspired others to do the same.

So what, though? Commandment One stated Balance is Best. So why shouldn't she eat fried food every so often? Balance, right?

She reached for the beer, taking a long sip that went down cool and smooth. Worries about the high-calorie meal vanished as she considered a new diet rule: when you are in another country, calories don't count.

Getting out her planner to get organized for the day tomorrow, she glanced around Rory's Pub. If Edna hadn't recommended it, Willow might have skipped past. The plain and uninviting exterior, some kind of poured concrete livened up with a golden-tan paint, wouldn't have made her wander in. Inside, though, possessed old-world, cozy charm. Rich, dark wood beams were set into white walls holding knickknacks in eclectic groupings, like dated brass instruments, sports paraphernalia, and paintings that all somehow worked in perfect harmony. A brick fireplace glowed and large picture window looked out onto the street.

When she'd first entered, she'd expected the place to be like bars in the US. Yet, as she sat here, even an outsider like her got a sense of a more relaxed vibe. Maybe because of the man wearing a suit and loosened tie sitting in the far corner, reading a newspaper and nursing his beer. Or the laughter of the two couples at a nearby table who sampled appetizers and drank from frothy mugs while they played a game of cards. The British seemed to occupy pubs in the same way Americans occupied coffee shops.

She flipped open the planner and started a chore list. First, she'd contact Owen about needing an electrician. The gross brown water she'd found on day one would require a plumber, too. Next, in big letters she wrote *COTTAGE*. The roof needed some work, but depending on what Owen's contact said, she might or might not do it. The main house would be her primary focus.

The distant expression on Owen's face when he'd talked to her about the cottage bothered her. When it came up, he'd lost his usual easygoing manner. But maybe she shouldn't read into it too much. If he wanted her to know something, he'd surely speak up.

After listing each room and the day she planned to conquer its cleanup, she put the planner away and took out her phone. An email from the Board of Directors of Pound Busters had arrived in the morning, New York time. Earlier, she'd ignored an incoming call from Nikki.

As she tapped open the email, she saw Abe Ginsburg cc'd and was glad to have her attorney involved.

Dear Ms. Armstrong,

This is to advise you that the board requires the presence of you and your attorney at our October board meeting...

Willow quickly closed it. Out of sight, out of mind, right? An email from Abe also sat in the inbox, from three hours after the board letter had been sent.

Keep your chin up, Willow. You're stronger than the whole lot of them.

Thank God for Abe and his wife, the closest thing she'd ever had to an aunt and uncle. When Willow was growing up, when it seemed like the whole world barely noticed her, the two of them would. They'd talk to her about current events, suggested books she might like to read, asked her about school.

"Here you go, miss."

Bonnie held a plate and waited for Willow to move her things before setting it on the table. "Can I get you anything else?"

"No thanks, I'm good right now."

"Cheers, then." The waitress smiled and left.

Using her fork, she broke into the crunchy, coated fish. One bite and satisfaction surged through her. Yes, she liked her new commandment and planned to follow it religiously while here.

She savored each bite. How many times in her life would she have passed on such an indulgence, selecting something like broiled cod instead? She scooped up another forkful. The flaky white fish, offset by the crisp-fried batter, definitely tickled her fancy. A true elixir for what ailed her soul, along with crunchy fries and buttery mushy peas.

For several minutes, she worked her way around the plate and let the joy of a good meal flow. Halfway through, she leaned back and finished off her beer while looking around. More folks now sat at the bar and the 60s music—a Frankie Valli tune—seemed louder than when she'd arrived. She searched for the waitress to order another beer.

Just as the trumpets escalated and Frankie belted out, "I love you, baby…" her gaze landed on Bonnie being serenaded by none other than Owen.

He sang loudly, placing both hands over his heart and making them thump. Bonnie stood near a barstool, swaying to the music and laughing.

Owen continued to sing and move his hips, looking pretty darn good in black Levis. At the next verse, he belted out, "Oh pretty baby…" then took Bonnie's hand and twirled her around. The bar crowd roared their delight.

As he un-spun Bonnie, she threw her head back and laughed again. "Owen, you kill me. Now let me go take my customers' orders." She crossed the room to a table near the door. Owen returned to the bar while the gang applauded him.

She watched him in his natural environment. Friends patted him on the back, enjoying a moment of comic relief. He was obviously well liked.

She sighed and returned to her dinner, giving up on the idea of ordering another beer.

A few minutes later, Bonnie walked over with a beer in hand.

Willow laughed. "You must be a mind reader."

She smiled. "Don't I wish. It's from Owen. He claims nobody should have an empty pint with their fish-and-chips."

Willow chuckled. "Good words to live by."

She glanced to the bar, where Owen sat with his back to her, the sleeves of his oxford shirt rolled to his elbows and tails out. A thin leather jacket hung off the back of his stool. She'd been about to ask Bonnie to thank him, but he chose that second to turn around. He gave her a big smile and lifted a brow.

She waved and mouthed, "Thanks."

He saluted her with two fingers to his temple and turned around.

Willow looked up at Bonnie, who watched Owen with a slight smile. "I caught your dance number."

Bonnie shook her head. "He's always doing things like that. Such a clown." She took the empty beer glass. "A real charmer, that one is."

Was he? Willow hadn't noticed. Well, maybe a little. He did have those kind eyes and captivating smile. "He seems to know everyone."

"Owen was raised here, but moved away for a while. Now he's back to raise his daughter."

"I met her. Jilly's a sweet girl."

"Hey, Bonnie. You've got some thirsty clientele over here." A slightly plump man with white hair and a noticeable slur in his voice yelled from the bar. Bonnie looked his way, and he winked and blew her a kiss.

"Cheeky bastard," she whispered to Willow. Her voice rose and she waggled a finger in the direction of the customer. "Don't be such an arse, Reggie, or I'll cut you off right now."

The man's full cheeks puffed. "What? You wouldn't do that!"

"Okay, then. How about I call your wife to come get you?"

His face flashed beet red and he turned around. Bonnie laughed. "I've got to rule this place with an iron fist. Otherwise they'll take advantage, you know?"

Willow laughed, thinking about her staff at the company. "I hear you. It's the same in the US."

"Holler if you need anything else, love."

She left and Willow returned to her food. Taking a bite, she glanced over to Owen's seat, now empty.

Just as she shoved a chip in her mouth, someone behind her spoke quietly into her ear, "Never thought I'd find you here, Rosebud."

She coughed, nearly choking on the chip. Owen walked around, took the seat across from her, and pushed her water glass closer. She took a drink and cleared her throat. "With only three restaurants in town, the odds were pretty narrow. I do have a name, you know."

He laughed and leaned back, slinging his arm over the back of the empty chair next to him. "What's the matter, Willow?" He said her name easily, like he'd known her forever. "You don't like nicknames?"

"Can't say I've ever had one." She ate another chip.

"They aren't meant to hurt. Not the special ones, anyway." The deep and fluid timbre of his voice held a soothing quality. His gaze dropped to her neckline, where she knew the necklace dangled; then his eyes slowly lifted and met hers. "I think the name suits you."

Willow's cheeks burned. It wasn't that he took the time to give her a nickname. More like the idea he somehow believed the beautiful flower suited her. A woman who, in her mind, was the opposite of delicate and flowerlike, who didn't deserve a name as graceful as Willow.

"Shall I go? I'm interrupting your meal." He started to get up.

"No. I don't mind if you stay. And thanks for the beer." She pushed her remaining fries toward him. "Want some?"

He lowered himself back in the chair. "No thanks. I'm waiting for an order at the bar. The food is good here."

"So is the entertainment. I enjoyed your show with Bonnie. You guys dating or just friends?"

"Dating?" He laughed. "She's probably fifteen years too young for me, don't you think?"

Willow shrugged. "You wouldn't be the first man to date out of your age group."

"I guess not. Well, she's a friend, that's all."

"It looked like fun. You're quite a performer." She picked up her napkin and wiped her fingers. "Oh, the power company came by."

He raised his dark brows. "That was fast."

"I thought so, too. Figured you pulled some strings."

"Nope."

"Anyway, they said I need the house rewired. Do you know an electrician?"
He thought for a moment. "One of my mates from school runs a local
business. I'll call him for you, see if he can stop by."

"That would be fantastic. I mean, I love the B and B, but it's costing
me money. Sooner I get the house livable, the sooner I can stay there while
finishing my cleanup."

He nodded and didn't say anything, but his furrowed brows suggested
he overthought what she'd said.

"I saw Jilly and Henry today."

"Did you now?"

"She came over with a thermos of tea her grandmother made."

Owen's face warmed. "Bea. She's my former mother-in-law and a true
saint. I don't know how I'd do this with Jilly if it weren't for her."

"Your parents aren't in the area?"

"Oh, they are." He looked at her plate for a second and his jaw tensed.
"They didn't approve of my divorce. At least Dad didn't. But they help
occasionally. I—never mind." She almost asked why they didn't approve,
but he said, "Hey, tomorrow I thought I'd come over after lunch to help
you. Is that okay?"

"You don't have to—"

"I want to. Really. I don't say things I don't mean."

She stared into his dark eyes, filled with warmth and sincerity. "Sure.
I appreciate the offer."

"Great." He stood, gave her a quick smile. "Cheers then."

"Goodnight."

One thing remained certain. Owen Hughes was an enigma. Cheery
and well liked by everyone on the surface, but every so often, she'd sense
more in his quietness. Or the slight tenseness on his face. What went on
during those moments? Maybe tomorrow she'd find out.

Chapter 9

"Excuse me, Edna?"

Willow stood in the doorway to the room behind the reception desk, waiting while Edna talked to a woman wearing a formal gown from centuries ago. Edna kneeled on the floor beside the woman, folding the hem. She slid a pin along the silky fabric and looked up at Willow. "Hello there. Come on in."

She entered, giving a smile to the other woman. "Sorry to interrupt. Eddie said he'd drive me to the house, but I can't find him."

"He just went upstairs, but he'll be right back down. This is my friend, Kathleen." She motioned to the curly-haired brunette, wearing dark-rimmed, modern-styled glasses and an eighteenth-century bonnet, the contrast a little odd. "Kathleen, this is Willow, our newest guest. Her grandparents used to own that lovely house down the road that's been empty for a long time. You know, where Tracey Hughes lived." Edna shook her head and tapped Kathleen's leg. "Can you turn a little?"

Edna hadn't mentioned she knew Jilly's mother before this, but in a town this size, she surely at least knew of her.

"Hello." Kathleen tipped her baby-blue bonnet at Willow. "A pleasure to meet you." She gently lifted the skirt of her delicate white dress, which had added feminine touches of a satin blue belt and dotted little flowers of the same color, and did a half turn. "My new dress for the festival. What do you think?"

"It's beautiful." Willow's black yoga pants and oversized pullover seemed way underdressed right now.

Edna slipped another pin into the dress hem. "The Grand Promenade is in three days, and then a week later is the Regency Costumed Masked Ball. It's my favorite event. Willow, you should come to the ball."

"Oh, I couldn't. I mean, I don't have a dress—"

"I have several dresses," Kathleen said. "I'd be happy to let you borrow one."

"That's very kind. Thank you." Willow couldn't imagine taking time from her schedule for a ball, but she didn't want to offend, either. "Let me think about it."

"Looking for me, Willow?" Eddie appeared behind her. "I'm ready whenever you are."

She thanked Kathleen for the dress offer and left with Eddie. On the way to the house, even *he* talked about the festival. In the span of just over a week, the festivities also included readings from Austen's work, presentations on clothing and accessories of the time period, and ballroom dance workshops.

Once at the house, she thanked Eddie for the ride, and told him she'd walk home again this afternoon.

Soon as she got inside, she went to the living room and admired its uncluttered and cleaned-up state. A sign of progress. But more important were fond memories of yesterday's tea with Jilly, which cemented a history of her own in this house. A history she'd been denied thanks to her mother's silence. Fast as the thought appeared, she let it go. It was foolish to cling to anger over what could've been.

She continued to the kitchen, a room she'd need if she ever planned on staying here. At least she would if she ever got power restored. It might be smart to see how long the B and B could house her.

She entered the room and stepped onto linoleum flooring, dulled by dirt and wear over time. A tiled backsplash needed cleaning, and the countertops still held a dated toaster and a Westwood mixer.

She boxed up everything on the counters, hoping an antique store might want these relics. For a few hours, she scoured the counters and floors until her arms ached.

When her stomach growled for the third time, she glanced at her watch. Half past twelve. Lunchtime. She wiped off her dirty hands with some baby wipes while inspecting her work. Cleaner but not any newer.

As Willow grabbed her sandwich, a car pulled into the driveway. She stepped out onto the porch just as Owen's van came to a stop. He waved then got out, holding a bag.

She squinted into the bright sun. "I figured you'd smarten up and change your mind. This cleaning is dirty work."

He approached and stopped in front of her, grinning. Reaching up, he gently brushed her chin with his finger. "I can see that. You've got a smudge right there."

Her cheeks flamed. "Oh, thanks." She pulled a tissue from her jeans pocket and wiped. "Did I get it?"

He tilted his head to inspect her and when his warm eyes met hers, she got a little jolt. "Yup."

She turned to the door and motioned him inside, wishing to put distance between his sweet little gestures and her ridiculously overt feminine reactions. In the business world, a man would never have dared to do such a thing, nor would she have allowed herself to react.

"I'm taking a lunch break."

He lifted the bag he carried. "Good. I was going to eat, too."

She followed behind him, vowing to watch her reactions to his nice guy gestures. It wouldn't be smart to get close to anybody here. "Why don't we eat in the living room?"

He shrugged off his light jacket, tossed it on the staircase banister, and entered the living room.

"Have a seat." Willow took one on the sofa and he sat across from her on an upholstered chair, resting his lunch on the table.

He glanced around the room. "You've been busy."

She removed her sandwich from the wrapper. "When I set my mind on something, it usually happens."

He lifted a brow while taking out a bottle of soda and twisting off the top. "That doesn't surprise me."

"I did my first entertaining in the house yesterday. Tea with Jillian and Henry."

"So you said at Rory's. She had fun, too. Naturally her sidekick came along." He chuckled softly and took a sip of his drink. "If you don't want Henry in here, just say the word and I'll tell Jilly."

"Are you kidding? He's always welcome. Although I will say, he's a little devil. He ate half the scone Edna packed for me."

Owen raised his dark brows. "Only half? Generous of him to leave you some." He smiled. "Henry keeps us all on our toes. Tracey—Jilly's mom—she bred these dogs." He removed his sandwich and unwrapped it. "She also handled them for other owners in shows. Can't figure out how she ever got them to listen. Henry's mind is definitely his own."

"He's adorable and loves Jilly."

Owen took a healthy bite of his sandwich, nodding at her as he did. He chewed, and swallowed. "That was the only reason I agreed to keep him." Willow had only seen Owen exhibit warmth toward the cordial canine. "You sure it's the only one?"

He grinned. "Don't you dare tell a soul. Better my daughter think Henry walks on thin ice with me. It'll keep her more vigilant about making him mind his manners."

"I won't say a word." Willow sensed that dog could do anything and Owen wouldn't separate the two of them. "Tell me how you got into the travel business."

While they ate their sandwiches, he told her how a semester in college spent in Italy made him fall in love with the idea of a career in the travel business. Willow loved listening to him talk about the places he'd seen, people he'd met. His dark eyes sparkled with passion, proof of his love for the work he used to do.

Owen reached into his bag and removed a candy bar, the same type he'd eaten on the train.

"Is that your favorite?" she asked.

As he tore off the paper, he looked up. "Jilly's favorite and they've become mine. Why?"

"You ate one on the train when we first met."

"Good memory." After splitting the bar in half, he leaned forward and stretched one half to her. "Here. Try it."

"I shouldn't."

"Sure you should. Look." He pointed to the inside of the treat. "This has two layers. Crispy cereal bits on the bottom and fluffy nougat on the top. Then it's coated in Cadbury chocolate."

"It's tempting…" She patted her gut, reminded about the last number on the scale. "I've been eating a lot since I got here so probably sh—"

"Come on, Rosebud. You look perfect and should enjoy eating when traveling. It's one of my travel rules." He placed the bar on the lunch bag in front of her. "Now eat it or you'll insult me." He grinned as he took a bite from his.

She looked perfect? When had anybody last said that to her? Even if someone had, she wouldn't have believed them. But Owen's kindness seemed genuine, so she kept her resistance to herself.

"One bite." She lifted the bar and brought it to her mouth. The slightly warm chocolate and nougat melted against her tongue as she chewed. She took a second bite and moaned. "Oh yes. This is very good."

Owen leaned back and threw an arm over the back of his chair, a satisfied smile on his lips. "See. What'd I tell you?"

She held up her palm. "Can't talk now. I have to finish this." She took another bite and enjoyed his hearty laugh.

"While you finish, I should let you know I spoke to my electrician friend." Owen crumpled up his empty sandwich bag. "Said he'd try to stop by later today."

"Okay. Everything is taking longer than I planned, but not much I can do about it."

"Nope." His eyes shifted away for a split second. "You can't plan everything."

Owen, so at ease, and yet every so often, he'd clam right up.

"Oh, thanks for those little ceramic dogs you gave Jilly. She played with them right up until bedtime."

"Not a big deal. I figured she'd like them."

He studied her, the power in his dark eyes wielding an intenseness that took hold of her. "It was a big deal to her, though." His voice softened. "You made my daughter happy yesterday. Those moments mean a lot these days."

A glimmer of sadness showed in his gaze before he pulled it away, concentrating on crumpling up his candy wrapper and stuffing it with the rest of his lunch garbage.

Willow wished she could offer something to ease his pain. "Well, she made me happy, too."

He offered a sad smile and drew in a deep breath. "So what's on the list to get done, boss?"

"Could we start by getting the old fridge out of the kitchen? It seriously stinks, and I can't move it alone. Oh, if you know someone who can help get it to a dump, I'm happy to pay them."

"I've got a mate with a truck. I'll give him a ring. What else?"

"Want to help me pack up what's inside the kitchen cabinets this afternoon? I cleaned in there this morning and guess it's time to empty the cabinets."

For the next hour, they worked hard, removing the refrigerator, then each going through the cabinet contents. Owen worked the upper ones and she found a spot on the floor to deal with the lower-level ones.

As she reached inside the last one, Owen said, "Take a look at this."

She stood and walked over, watching him study a photograph.

He handed it to her. "It came from the utensil drawer."

It was an old Polaroid photograph of her mother with a young man. A date in the corner showed September 1975, when Mom would have been around seventeen, close to eighteen. Hip-hugging bell-bottoms flowed down her mother's slender legs and two long pigtails fell against her gauze shirt, right near her chest. The guy appeared about her age and wore baggy jeans, a white T-shirt, and a dark leather jacket. His long hair fell below his chin. He cocked his head with a certain swagger, the kind of confidence her mother appeared to like in a man.

She glanced up at Owen. "This is my mother."

He leaned in to see the photo. "Huh." He glanced at her then back at the picture. "There's a slight resemblance, but I can see features of your dad's in your face, too."

"Him?" She pointed at the boy.

Owen nodded. "Oh, isn't that him in the picture?"

"I-I don't know. I never knew my father."

He frowned. "Oh, guess I assumed because of the message on back."

Willow turned the photograph over. *Dear Chloe, I will love you forever… Sean.*

She stared at the teenager, searching his face. Turning to Owen, she said, "You think I look like him?"

"There are some similarities in the shape of your face and his, around the nose and chin. Probably coincidence."

"Probably…" But as her gaze drifted back to the photo, she focused only on the young man, trying to see him through unbiased eyes. The nose. The chin. Were they hers? "Do you know where this was taken?"

"The Roman Baths, right in town."

"So that means my mother lived in England in September 1975." September '75 Mom had been in England. Eleven months before July '76…when Willow was born.

The date. The idea this man once loved her mother. And what Owen saw…

"Excuse me a second." She went to an oval mirror in the hallway and wiped away the dust. Again, she studied the teenage boy more carefully. Dirty-blond hair, slender and strong profile. She looked up. Yes, similar to the face she saw every time she looked in a mirror.

Her throat grew thick. Given all the pieces set before her, could Sean be her father? Why would her mother tell her she got pregnant after she arrived in the US, while modeling? The timeframe just didn't add up.

Owen came up behind her and gently touched her shoulder. "Are you okay?"

She met his gaze in the mirror and swallowed the hard lump in her throat. "Yes."

"You don't seem fine."

"My mother..." She drew in a deep breath. "She told me my father was American, conceived after she left England. She also told me my grandparents died long before I was born, but I know now it's not the truth. Makes me wonder about *everything* she ever told me. The date on this photo suggests she conceived me one month after this was taken. I suppose she could've, but it's becoming clear she wasn't exactly the pillar of honesty." The fog of confusion drifted over her, too many facts and not enough answers. "If only I knew the exact date she left England."

Owen nodded. "Are there any records you could check?"

"Probably." The woman Edna had mentioned. Of course! "You're from Bitton. Edna told me about a close friend of my grandmother's. A woman named Hettie McBride. Edna didn't know where she might live now. Would you?"

"Matter of fact, I knew Ronald McBride. Played cricket with him in school. Hettie's his grandmother. She lived with his family, but after we graduated, I heard they moved. Not sure where. How about I check around, see what I can find out?"

"That would be a great help." He stood close, his nearness comforting to Willow. Grateful she didn't have to face this moment alone, she twirled around and touched his forearm. "Thank you, Owen."

He gave a no-biggie shrug. "Happy to do it."

She stored the photograph in her purse, filled with hope that this would lead her to her birth father.

* * * *

"She's coming soon." Owen chuckled, watching Henry hanging his head out the van's passenger window, his usual vigil as they waited for Jilly to get out of school.

Henry whined for a bit. Owen ignored him, instead thinking about Willow. Finding a connection to the man who might be her father qualified as a pretty big deal. Tonight he'd check the internet to see if he could find Ronald.

He'd pegged Willow as a woman with no problems. Head of a company. Earning a salary that most likely allowed her to live quite well in Manhattan.

Yet something seemed off.

Why all the worry while here about spending money on improvements with her wealth? And why the rush?

His phone rang. He grabbed it from the van console, glancing at the display. "Hi, Dad."

"Hello, Owen," he said, his tone curt. Dad always sounded a little annoyed by life in general. "Your mother said you'd called looking for me?"

"Yeah, any chance you could stop by my cottage and take a look at the roof?"

"Got a problem?"

"Not me. The property owner is in town and wants a professional to tell her if the roof needs work. There's an area that's in need of a repair. She'd pay you."

"Sure." He paused. Owen braced himself, certain what would come next. "A few years back you would've been able to help her."

Boom! Every single time. "Twenty years ago, Dad. Not a few years," Owen snapped, but right away softened his tone. "And I can tell it needs some work, I just think you'd be able to give her a more thorough answer."

"Well, I can't come tomorrow," he said, almost defensively. "Next day, okay? Early morning, before I get working."

"Sure. Thanks." He drew in a breath, remembering to be nice. "How you feeling?"

"Back is a little sore. I thank God every day I have your brother there for the heavy lifting."

Another dig. A lifetime of digs. Often mean comments that tore away at Owen's self-esteem during childhood. "I'm glad you have someone there for you." Owen again considered helping his dad part-time. He could save some cash, making it easier for him and Jilly to afford a place that took dogs. But at what price to his pride and the self-esteem he'd salvaged after moving away from here?

The shrill school bell sounded before he could ask. "I'd better run. Jilly's about to get out of school."

They hung up. No. He'd never work for his dad. Never. Leaving him with one option. To work hard to get Willow to love the Cotswolds, even if a love for this place didn't exist in his heart.

Somehow, he'd have to get her on a tour. But how? Guilt slowly wormed through him, catching him off guard. Maybe it was wrong to convince her to like England just to get her to keep the land.

Jilly exited the building and her gaze landed on the van. "Henry!" She ran over, her pink backpack bouncing on her shoulders.

She went straight to the passenger door, arms outstretched. Henry leaned further out the window and licked her face to the point that she squealed.

The sound of happiness. Owen's heart swelled. He got out and opened the sliding door. "Hop in, honey. I've got to get back to helping Willow with her house."

Jilly got inside and the dog leapt from the front seat to the bench seat near Jilly. "I'm supposed to help her today, too. She invited me yesterday. She's my new friend."

"So I've heard."

Bea could probably use an afternoon off from watching his daughter. He quickly called her with the change of plans and they left the school grounds.

Glancing in his rearview mirror, he could see Jilly staring out the window. "What'd you learn today?"

"Nothing. We should bring Willow some tea. She liked it when I did yesterday."

"I guess we could stop and pick up something. I could use a cup of coffee. How 'bout we get her coffee?"

"Can I have some?"

"No." One time he'd let her try a sip and couldn't get her to bed later. "But if we stop at Josie's Café, she has hot chocolate, too." She frowned and he added, "How about we get biscuits, too?"

"Yes!" She shouted and smiled. "And one for Henry, too?"

"Sure." He laughed. Always something for Henry.

"Do you think Willow will be glad to see me again?"

"I have no doubt." He glanced back, catching a glimpse of his daughter's smile. "You like her, don't you?"

She nodded. "Willow is a pretty name."

"It is. Very pretty."

"I like her hair. It's blond and soft."

Owen did too. The day he'd first seen her rushing to the car of the train, the frazzled blonde garnered his attention. In part because of her determination as she joined the line, standing firm when anybody tried to sneak in front of her. But also he'd noticed the bounce of her hair and the way it fell along her long neck. Joining her hadn't been planned, but it was one of only two seats remaining and an easy choice.

"Right, Daddy?"

"What, Jilly-Bean?"

"Her hair. It's like Mum's."

"Yes." He braced himself for an upset, ready to pull over if she cried.

"And I love her eyes. I wish mine were blue."

He breathed a relieved sigh. "Willow's are nice"—*Mesmerizing, actually*—"...but nothing is as gorgeous as your brown eyes, my love.

And don't you forget it. Did you notice Henry has big brown eyes, too? So you two match."

At the sound of his name, Henry looked over and bellowed a low howl. Jilly leaned across the seat and patted the dog's head. "Hear that, Henry? We match."

"Here we are." He pulled in front of the shop, parked, and turned around. "There's a famous singer from Northern Ireland who wrote a song about a brown-eyed girl."

"A whole song?"

"Yup. Want me to sing it?"

"Yes, please."

Owen sang a verse and the chorus from Van Morrison's "Brown Eyed Girl," savoring Jilly's delight.

But a new worry crept up on him. Was her quick attachment to Willow a good or a bad thing? After all, the American wouldn't be here for very long.

Chapter 10

Willow sat on the living room sofa, staring at the photo of her mom with the mysterious young man.

Sean possessed mesmerizing eyes and a confident grin, making it easy for Willow to understand why her mother might have fallen for him. But she couldn't understand why her mother left behind this kind of love. Willow squinted at the picture, wishing the people could come alive and spill everything.

There had to be something in this house that might give her more clues. *Of course!* She dropped the photo on the coffee table and raced upstairs. Her belly trembled with each step. If the truth remained hidden somewhere in her mother's room, was Willow ready to hear it?

She slowly turned the crystal knob, pushed open the door, and stepped inside. Moving through the room, she pulled sheets off the furniture, tossed them in a corner, then looked around.

A pink shag rug. Posters of Led Zeppelin, Queen, and David Bowie. A twin bed with a dainty white-spindle headboard and a tie-dyed bedspread. A bookshelf holding stuffed animals. This room showed the story of young girl evolving into a teenager.

She walked to the closet and opened the door. On the floor sat a cardboard box and she opened it to find dolls of varying sizes. She stretched on tiptoes and lifted a plastic container off the shelf, filled with small things: postcards, old nail polish, hair clips. She put it on the floor and from the shelf removed a chocolate brown hat, decorated with a white ribbon tied where the crown met the floppy brim.

Heaviness bombarded her chest, a wave of sadness making it hard to breath. If only she could've seen this room through her mother's eyes. Learned why she'd saved those postcards, or found out her favorite Queen songs. The closet blurred behind her tears, but she blinked them away and put on the hat. She took a pretty red-and-white sheer scarf off a peg and wrapped it around her neck. The soft silk caressed her skin like the gentle touch of her mother's hand. Her heart twisted into a ball of grief, blended with the bittersweet joy over finding this part of her mother's childhood intact.

Dresses stuffed the small clothes rack. Long and short. Wild patterned prints and denim. All vintage by today's standards, but stylish at the time. She smiled, thinking of the *Vogue* and *Harper's Bazaar* magazines always on her mother's nightstand, along with weekly shopping trips to Bergdorfs.

Strange how many clothes she'd left behind when she moved, though.

The thought nagged at her as she went over to a nightstand next to the bed and pulled open the top drawer. Hair clips, headbands, a pack of gum. The next drawer held a teen publication featuring David Cassidy called *Jackie Magazine.*

She lifted a gold box of cigarettes marked *Dunhill Slim Size.* Willow chuckled. What kid didn't try cigarettes? She removed one, imagining her mother smoking these with her friends.

Willow put the pack away, stood, and went to a walnut-veneer desk. On the wall to the right of it hung a calendar. American Cities 1975. Her mother must've liked America, given that she moved there.

Pinned open to December, the monthly photo showed a collage of three pictures taken in New York City; the Rockefeller Center Christmas tree, the Empire State Building on a snowy night, and a winter-scape near the Central Park pond. All sights Willow had seen many times, often with her mother. Yet, Mom had never hinted they were places she'd dreamed of seeing while growing up in England. Not once.

Red felt pen lettering stood out on various dates. A shopping trip to Bath on the 9th. A Christmas party at Rachel's on the sixteenth. December twenty-seventh showed the last entry and it simply read *L.*

Willow repeated the date over and over. Nothing of special significance popped out and *L* meant nothing to her. Was it someone's initial? A place? Someone's birthday? Or could it have meant leave, as in leaving home for good?

Then a thin thread drew an unexpected parallel to the date... Willow had been born seven months later.

Meaning her mother *had been* pregnant with Willow while living in England.

Numbness pounded her. The deep deception slashed open a new wound, leaving her stunned and grappling with a way to process this new reality. Willow sank into the desk chair, the truth slowly taking form until it spun into the rage of a tornado. With each passing second, it picked up speed as she reflected upon lies she'd been spoon-fed over a lifetime. So many lies.

Willow yanked open the desk's middle drawer and pushed around pens and pencils as her irritation escalated. A small key made her pause and she removed it, but with no clue what the key went to, she dropped it and slammed the drawer shut. She tugged open the side drawers and searched each one. Slamming them shut, she glanced around the room. Where would a teenage girl hide something from her parents?

Her gaze landed on the bed. She took three quick, long strides, dropped to the floor next to the mattress and slipped her arm beneath the bedspread to the space between the mattress and box spring. Running her hand along the bed length, she found nothing and plopped on the mattress, one step from giving up. A trunk stuck out from behind the bedroom door.

She rushed over and grabbed the handle on the end, dragging it away from the corner. Although it felt light, something inside shifted as it moved. She kneeled and worked the two brass locks. No luck. She stood to run downstairs for the hammer in the kitchen and stopped.

Her heart raced as she hurried back to the desk and removed the key. Once it was inserted it into the trunk, both tabs flipped open. Her heart pounded in her ears as she slowly opened the trunk.

Two items sat in the bottom. A centerfold picture of pop star idol Andy Gibb and a red, leather-bound diary.

She took the diary and plunked onto the floor. Taking a deep breath, she opened page one, dated November 1974, more than a year before her mother left. She skimmed the first few entries. Mundane comments, typical of a teenager. She impatiently flipped to the last page, about three-quarters of the way through the book. Drawing in a deep breath, she started to read.

December 20, 1975

After school, Sean took me to our favorite place in Bath for a Christmas celebration. Mum and Dad thought I'd gone to work, an excuse I used to stay out later. We exchanged gifts. He gave me a beautiful bracelet and I gave him a sketch I'd made from a picture of the two of us. He said he loved it. He said he loved me. Only, this time, I didn't say it back. It would hurt him all the more when I left.

Leaving soon is all I can do. I will never forgive my father, for making my only choice adoption. This baby grows inside of me. There's a connection. I could never give it to another family. But I simply cannot tell Sean the truth, either.

The truth? Willow's muscles went limp. Had she ever really known her mother? Secrets appeared to be a way of life for her. Things hidden from a daughter she said she loved. Even kept from a man who loved her. The man who might be Willow's father. Had her mother lost all sense of decency? Being a party to betrayal of the worst kind—lying to the people who loved her the most.

Fury escalated and quickly exploded. She threw the diary and it hit the wall then landed on the floor. *"Liar! LIAR!"* Willow collapsed on the bed and buried her head in her hands.

Willow's temples throbbed. Her whole life had been a sham. Raised in her stepfather's world of moneyed Manhattanites, she'd been the proverbial square peg in a round hole. With her mother's ease in lying, everything she'd ever said could be up for grabs as fake.

Raised by a liar, Willow had been able to pull off the biggest charade of all... Transforming from the chubby little girl who'd been told to get good grades because she'd have nothing else to fall back on into a skinny, successful businesswoman.

Didn't that make her a phony, too? A fat girl hiding inside the body of woman who struggled every single day with her identity?

The stress of the past two years rolled toward her like a tsunami, leaving her to drown in the knowledge that the one person who had truly loved Willow had lied about *everything*.

She lay down on the bed and curled to her side, knocking the hat off. Every muscle ached, as if she'd had the crap beaten right out of her. Control, once everything, had been slowly stripped away, leaving her with the terrifying prospect she'd never gain her life back again. Did it even matter? It wasn't even a life she felt proud of any longer.

She drew her knees to her chest and closed her eyes, almost wishing she'd been kept in the dark.

* * * *

Owen cracked open the house door, having knocked twice and gotten no answer. "Willow?"

"You said she was here, Daddy."

Owen stuck his head inside and glanced around. "She was when I left."

Henry squeezed into a spot near Owen's legs, poking his long snout into the door opening. Owen leaned over to grab his collar, but as his finger grazed the band, the dog scooted inside. Before Owen could blink, the canine bolted halfway up the staircase, howling loud enough to wake the dead.

Jilly pushed past Owen. "I'll get him."

"Hold on, Jilly—" She took off as fast as her furry friend and hollered his name as she stomped up each step.

Owen debated following them. It was still Willow's house and barging in would be considered rude. But he had to retrieve his belongings. At least they'd made so much noise, Willow wouldn't be taken by surprise.

"Daddy, she's up here."

He walked up the stairs, following the sound of Jilly's animated discussion about her school day. When he reached the room, he stood at the doorway.

Willow sat at the head of the bed with her legs crossed, her blond hair mussed on one side. A sheer scarf draped her neck. His gaze traveled the scarf's length to the lopsided opening of her oxford shirt, which offered a glimpse of her cleavage. He shamefully enjoyed a peek a little longer than seemed right.

"Do you like my hat, Daddy?"

Jilly sat on the bed facing Willow, her legs crossed the same way. She wore a floppy brown hat too large for her head. Henry lay on his side between them, chewing on something.

"It's gorgeous, baby. Where'd you get it?"

"It's Willow's mommy's."

He glanced at Willow. She offered a short smile and nodded, but a sadness resonated in her rich blue eyes. Owen wished he could read her mind.

Jilly continued to babble like a gentle brook about her school day while Willow listened intently. The way adults should listen to kids, but rarely did.

When Jilly finished, Willow smiled. "Gosh, that sounds like a fun game. Maybe you can teach me how to play." She glanced at Owen. "Sorry, I didn't hear you knock. I was out cold. Maybe I'm still jet-lagged."

"It can take a little time." A force tugged at his chest. Sympathy for her. Something he didn't want to feel. Not if he were to keep a distance while trying to convince her to keep this place and him as caretaker.

"Good thing Henry woke me. Right, good boy?" Willow rubbed the dog's stomach and his tail batted the mattress.

Owen walked closer to them. "For a dog that doesn't often come when called, he sure seems to understand a lot of English."

Willow laughed, but Jilly just shook her head. "Daddy, you know Henry just can't help himself. It's his breed."

"Your mother made excuses for him, but I wish he'd listen better." He reached over and petted the dog, because he could never be annoyed with him for long. He met Willow's gaze. "Sorry we woke you. Do you want to keep cleaning or head back to the Clemmens? I can give you a ride."

"But, Daddy." Jilly frowned. "We brought Willow a treat and she promised I could look in her mum's room today."

"It's true." Willow nodded. "I thought Jilly might want to play dress up." Her voice quieted. "Plus, I could use a break."

Her mother's room and clothes. Sadness explained. "Sure. You two ladies have some fun while I get our afternoon snack ready."

"Yay!" Jilly clapped. She jumped off the bed and grabbed Willow's hand, guiding her off the bed and toward the closet.

Owen turned to leave and remembered the call he made while waiting at school for Jilly. "Willow." She turned, raised a brow. "My dad is a thatcher. I've asked him to take a look at the cottage roof. Should be out in a day or two."

"Oh, thanks."

"Excuse me." Jilly's tiny hands wrapped around one of the silky long dresses hanging in the closet. "Can I wear whatever I want?"

Willow glanced at Owen for a second, then looked back at Jilly. "It has to be suitable for our afternoon snack time. Nothing too racy."

"What's racy mean?"

"We'll know it when we see it." Willow gave Owen a little smile and turned back to the clothes. "Now what about something like this one?"

Owen loved watching Jilly with Willow. His daughter had returned to herself, filled with the kind of energy and happiness she'd had around her mother. No matter how much love she got from him, Bea, and Owen's parents, it would never fulfill what had been taken from her when her mother died.

All he wanted was Jilly to feel protected and happy, his goal to shield her from further change. But now, with the cottage about to be sold...

Panic seized him. "Willow?"

She turned from the closet. "Hmm?"

"Why don't you take a day off tomorrow? Let me show you some of the sights?"

Before she could say anything, Jilly grabbed the hem of a silk dress with a plunging neckline. "You should. Daddy is a good tour guide. Is this racy?"

Willow smiled down at her, then slowly lifted her head and looked back at Owen. "Okay. If Jilly recommends I do it, then we're on." She returned her attention to his daughter. "And yes, it's racy."

Owen went down the hallway. At the top of the stairs, he paused as Jilly's faint voice carried down the hallway. "Do you miss your mum?"

"All the time."

Willow stated it very matter-of-factly. She always spoke directly. Never offensive, but no curtseying around an issue for her.

Jilly replied, "I don't know anybody else who lost their mum. I'm glad you're my friend."

"I'm glad I am, too," Willow said, her voice softer.

Once downstairs, he busied himself getting their snack together, while the idea of Jilly growing closer to Willow niggled in the back of his thoughts. Just as he finished arranging the hot drinks and biscuits on the living room coffee table, the sound of footsteps made him look up.

Jilly and Willow entered the living room, their arms opened wide, shouting in unison, "Ta-da."

Jilly wore what might have been a bright orange minidress to an adult, but it hung to her ankles. At her waist, the extra fabric had been cinched by a belt around her torso, creating a billowy effect. She still wore the floppy hat, and had added some long, beaded jewelry.

"How do I look, Daddy?"

"Gorgeous, princess! You look simply gorgeous."

"What about Willow?"

Willow plopped her hand on her hip, pursed her lips, and threw back her head, tossing her blond hair over her shoulder. She lifted her fingers in a peace sign. "What do you think? Am I the poster child for peace, love, and rock n' roll?"

The bohemian, paisley-print, silky dress hugged her curves and the V-neck showed just enough of Willow's cleavage to make a virile part of him squirm. Her sparkling eyes boosted the ensemble and the dramatic pose oozed confidence, and yet he swore he sometimes saw that self-assurance waver.

He couldn't stop staring, or even put a clear sentence together as all his manly instincts ground his speech to a halt.

Willow frowned. "Oh, God. Is it that bad? I mean, it's a little tight, but—"

"No! Not bad at all. Are you kidding me?" His neck warmed. "It's that good."

She arched a brow. "Oh, sure. Now you're just saying that."

"Come on, Rosebud." He rubbed the back of his neck. "Truth? You left me speechless."

"Is speechless good?" Jilly asked.

"It's real good." His gaze met Willow's and her fair skin blasted pink. "Great, in fact."

She smiled. "Okay, let's not lay it on too thick." She laughed while shaking her head. "I'm fine with good."

Relief he couldn't explain washed over him. "I'm done setting up here and would consider myself a lucky man to have my afternoon tea with two gorgeous ladies."

As they sat around the table, Jilly took a biscuit. "Daddy, why do you call her Rosebud?"

"It's a nickname, like Jilly-bean." He motioned to Willow's neck, to the necklace he'd seen her wear every single day. "See? It's a rosebud."

Jilly went over and took a close look at the necklace while Willow waited patiently. She returned to her seat, shaking her head. "My daddy is silly sometimes."

"Yes, he is." Willow's gaze shifted to Owen, her smile making a little something swell inside his chest.

Chapter 11

Owen turned left onto New Bond Street, parked along the curb, and hurried to his office. He reached the building and took the steps two at a time to the second floor. At the top of the stairs, he entered the office door and crossed into the small reception area.

Margo stopped typing and glanced up from her computer, watching him over the rims of half-framed reading glasses. "I can't remember the last time you got in before 8:30."

"Miracles can happen." And he sure needed one today. Eddie would be dropping off Willow soon for their full-day tour and he hoped he could pique her interest in the area by the end of it.

"I just emailed you next week's tour schedule."

"How's it look?" Owen inhaled the awakening scent of coffee and went straight to the pot.

She returned to her work. "We've got full tours almost every day."

"Great news." Maybe he'd start turning a profit on his investment soon. He stirred in cream, lifted his mug, and went over to Margo's desk, taking a seat in the chair across from her. "I'm off on a personal mission and I'd like your advice."

Margo turned to him and puffed her full chest, making the buttons on her tight blouse buckle. "You want *my* advice? Well, I'm arse over elbow."

He chuckled. Margo's colorful vocabulary after working in the office of a construction firm had followed her here, but she never used it around customers. "No need for sarcasm. I'm a bit uncomfortable with something I'm doing."

She leaned back in her chair. "This day is starting to get interesting. Go on."

"Remember I told you the owner of the estate I live on is here, and wants to sell the place?"

"I do."

Owen rubbed the back of his neck. Saying this suddenly sounded ridiculous. "She's a nice woman—"

"Oooh, a woman?" Margo slipped off the glasses and rested her elbows on her desk. "You never told me that. Older? Younger?"

"Around my age, I'd guess. But that doesn't matter. What I want to ask you is if what I'm about to do seems wrong, and—"

She let out a hoot. "I see. A little one-on-one time with the landlady, eh?" She grinned.

"No! Good Lord, Margo." His neck burned beneath his collar. Now he'd have to keep that quite pleasant image out of his head while with Willow today, especially after yesterday's dress-up moment. "Please, let me finish."

She chuckled. "Sorry, boss. Just teasing, you know?"

"I know. Here's my dilemma. She's never been to the area and, I thought, if she got to know what it has to offer, she might not want to sell. If she doesn't sell, maybe Jilly and I won't have to move anytime soon. Give her more time to adjust to…well, life as it is now."

Margo's head bobbed. "Oh, I see. And what do you want from me?"

"I-I don't know. Like I said, she's been very kind to Jilly and Henry. But do my motives seem…" He sighed. "A bit underhanded?"

She pursed her lips and thought for a short moment. "It's really about not having to move Jilly, right?"

"That's right. Plus keeping the dog. Not all places will accept animals. Otherwise, I'd never interfere in someone else's decision. Bea suggested I just tell her my concerns about Jilly, but I can't use guilt on the owner. That feels all wrong. In fact, maybe by trying to sell her on the area, I'm manipulating her into staying."

Margo shrugged. "Nonsense. I don't think what you're doing is a big deal. You're just showing her around. Frankly, it might be nice for her to see things before she sells. Go out. Have a nice day. Let the cards fall where they will."

Owen's guilt lessened and he permitted himself to feel a little better. "Okay, then. Thanks for listening." He stood to go to his office.

"Is she pretty?"

He looked back. "What?"

"The landlady. Is she pretty?"

Owen's face heated. "I guess she is. I really hadn't noticed. Why do you ask?"

"Because, you haven't been out with a woman since you started here and a guy like you should have lots of dates."

"Okay, Yente." He grinned. "When I need a matchmaker, I'll let you know." He went to his office, yelling to Margo, "I'm doing a little work before I leave."

Owen got settled and turned on his computer. Last night, he'd begun a search for Ronald McBride on the internet to help Willow, but Jilly's bedtime antics waylaid his efforts. By the time he returned to the living room, he'd forgotten what he'd been doing and got wrapped up in a television program. When Willow had mentioned that Hettie was her grandmother's close friend, the quiet desperation in her eyes had driven a path straight to his heart.

He typed the man's name in the search bar. Several appeared, a few on Facebook, so he went in that direction. The first had to be in his seventies, not Owen's schoolmate. The second, though, lived near Bristol and a recognizable photo of Ronald, a few pounds heavier, gave Owen hope he'd found his man.

He tried to Google search a phone listing, and located it as unlisted, so instead he sent a Facebook friend request. All he could do for now.

For the next fifteen minutes, he returned some emails. Outside in the lobby, the door opened then closed. Willow's voice carried into his office, although too low for him to hear what she said. He shut off the computer, gathered his cell phone and wallet, and left his office.

Willow stood in front of Margo's desk, wearing black flats, a full skirt, and a white top that just skimmed the glorious waist and hips that were still burned into his mind from yesterday's asset-hugging outfit. Her blond hair fell to her shoulders and curled at the tips.

"You don't say." Margo smiled at Willow. "Some day I'd love to visit New York City."

Owen cleared his throat and Willow spun around. She wore makeup today. Owen hadn't even noticed it missing all the other times he'd been with her, but now it enhanced her natural glow.

"Good morning." She smiled, something about her more relaxed than usual.

Margo cleared her throat then arched her brow in a clear display of innuendo he hoped Willow hadn't seen.

He focused on Willow. "Good morning. You're early."

"Eddie was anxious to drop me off so he could get to his appointment in town. I can wait."

"Yes. Take your time, Owen." Margo's cat-who-ate-the-canary smile scared the hell out of him. "I don't mind keeping Willow company."

"No need. I'm set to go." He stepped to Willow and guided her by the elbow to the door, opened it, and motioned with his hand. "After you."

Willow stepped out into the hallway.

Before he could scoot out, Margo called his name. He glanced over to find her staring at him with that same scary grin. "What?"

"She's *very* pretty. Like you hadn't noticed."

Heat blasted his cheeks. "You know where to find me if you need me. Otherwise, I'll be back late afternoon. Cheers."

He left fast as he could, before Margo said something else to make him feel like a schoolboy with a crush. Which he wasn't.

* * * *

Owen tooted at a driver that drifted into his lane and glanced over to Willow. "We're not far from Stonehenge."

"Great. I can't wait."

Owen's earlier preamble about the day's activities sounded as intriguing as a travelogue. After Stonehenge, they'd also visit Avebury, Castle Combe, and Lacock National Trust. Not that she knew what those were, but as she looked out the window at the shamrock-green fields, excitement for today's adventure brewed inside her.

They approached a traffic circle and she grabbed the armrest.

"No sounds while we drive the roundabout this time." He stared straight ahead, but grinned. Last circle, she'd yelped loudly when she thought a car in the opposite lane was about to hit them head-on. Owen had swerved, almost causing an accident. "Pay attention and you'll see it's not that difficult to drive on the left."

"Says you." She crossed her arms.

He shook his head and maneuvered the traffic circle like a pro, blending with the large volume of cars merging into it and effortlessly taking their exit. "See?" He glanced at her and winked.

"I find Manhattan traffic less intimidating."

He chuckled, always so at ease. His relaxed attitude reminded her of the English countryside. Untroubled. Peaceful. Easy to be around.

They flew past a sign for Stonehenge. "Exactly how old is this rock formation?"

"It was built in several stages, the first five thousand years ago. The stone circle, what most people think when they hear Stonehenge, was from the late Neolithic period about 2500 BC."

"Amazing when you think about it. I read that the Celts built it?"

"At first it was thought Druids or Celts, but carbon dating showed the stones were a thousand years too old to have been built by them."

He turned into the welcome center lot and they parked. After purchasing their tickets, Owen suggested they walk to the site and bypass a small shuttle bus. Along the way, he talked about burials found on this site and other things of interest.

Willow listened, but her gaze focused on the magical formation. Built in the middle of nowhere, the extraordinary stones jutted from the earth. Robust. Tall. Fearless. Their presence softened by a blanket of endless green grass, where sheep grazed and wildflowers danced with each gentle breeze. Emotion swelled in her throat. The majestic site, in a matter of seconds, held her captive with its magic.

They reached a footpath leading around the ancient formation. Willow couldn't tear her eyes away from the circle, dumbly awestruck as if she'd just spotted a celebrity. Closer, the sheer size could humble even the most vocal critic. She slowed down, taking in details. How could any ancient civilization have moved stones this size, mounted them in the ground? Could the magic of the stones fix her floundering life?

Owen placed a hand on her back, guiding to the path's side and stopping. "Pretty awesome, huh?"

"I'm searching for words and can't seem to find them." Awareness of the heat of his hand briefly stole her attention. She turned to him, noting his concentration as he looked straight ahead. "Do you still find it amazing? I mean, you've probably seen it so many times."

He shrugged, then turned and met her gaze. "I used to. This part of England is rich with history and scenery you'll find nowhere else in the world, but I got tired of it. Guess I've got a little wanderlust in me. It's why I worked for bigger tour companies over the past twenty years."

"Where have you gone?"

"Most of Europe. Russia. Japan." He dropped his gaze to the ground and a flash of sadness pained his expression. "I came back here to be with Jilly, and I'm happy to do it, but there are days I miss the adventure of exploring new places. Hell, I'd be lying if I said I didn't." He nodded and started to walk again so she followed. "But she means everything to me so..."

A father's love for his daughter. Jilly was one lucky girl. Willow rode a brief wave of resentment over her mother's choice to keep Willow's father from her.

They moved around the stones, both quiet, immersed in their own thoughts.

"If you think it's crowded today, during both the winter and summer solstice, tens of thousands of visitors flock here. It's quite amazing." He pointed straight ahead. "Lots of groups come here for spiritual reasons. I'm guessing that's what those people are doing."

They neared the group of maybe twenty-five people or so, all sitting in lawn chairs arranged in a semicircle and holding hands. A man wearing a tie-dyed shirt stood in front of the others. Upon a closer look, every person seated wore the same patterned shirt and they all appeared to be in their sixties or older.

The man in front let out a shrill whistle, immediately quieting the others. "Want to watch?"

She nodded, suddenly aware Owen stood shoulder to shoulder with her.

At that moment, the ringleader raised his arms like a conductor. "Okay, everyone. Are we ready?"

A man in the first row with thinning white hair, dark-rimmed glasses, and a full white beard raised his hand. "What song is it again, Bob?"

Bob lowered his arms. "Bernie, it's 'Amazing Grace.' Remember when Arlo Guthrie sang it at Woodstock? You were supposed to practice before we got—"

The man named Bernie laughed and the others joined him.

Bob shook his head and remained straight-faced. "Okay. Ha-ha. You got me. Now let's sing!"

The group launched into an a cappella version of the well-known song. People passing by stopped and listened.

Willow got lost in uplifting lyrics, more poignant in this magical setting. Being lost, then found. Her eyes watered. In a way, her entire life she'd been lost. Empty. Wandering. In search of something to define who she was, where she belonged. Who was the real Willow? The teenage girl who ate away sadness she could never quite explain? Or a weight-obsessed woman, who could achieve any mission she set out to accomplish? In either case, this trip seemed to have brought her home.

A lump lodged in her throat as she scanned the gently rolling fields, the sheep, the powerful stones. Home? This could be where she should've been raised. A tear slid down her cheek. She brushed it away and blinked her eyes dry.

Owen chuckled, breaking the spell that had been cast over her. "Well, would you look at that?" He pointed just past the singing seniors. "It's one of my mates from my former tour company. Mind if we go say hello?"

"Not at all." Talking to someone new gave her a reason to think about anything besides her vacant lot in life.

Together they walked to a grassy area not far from the singers, approaching a younger man with sandy-brown hair and a beard. He watched the performance with a smile on his face.

"Blimey, if they'll let you in the country, they'll let in anybody," Owen said loudly.

The man glanced at Owen, then his eyes widened and he smiled. "Hey, dude. I've been thinking of looking you up, but I've been busy with this tour."

The two men shook hands and Owen introduced Willow to Julian Gregory, a tour guide he knew from his last job, who sounded American.

They chatted about their old tour days, Julian mentioning he'd be moving to the US, where he planned to write a travel series for his fiancée's employer, a publisher in upstate New York. "I met her on one of my Tuscany tours last year. I'm pretty sure I met up with you in Siena that trip."

"And you didn't share that with us? Holding out on your friends?"

He laughed. "Never. I was with these guys." He thumbed to the travelers wearing tie-dyed shirts. "They go by the name of the Woodstock Wanderers. Thanks to them, I let someone under forty on their tour and found the love of my life."

Owen congratulated him, patted him on the back, even said he might visit him in the States someday. Willow listened, but her mind drifted. Had her grandparents and mother visited Stonehenge? Or any of the other places she'd be seeing today? This trip unearthed as many questions as it had answered.

They said their goodbyes and continued down the path.

Owen pointed to an area without any other tourists. "Want to go sit for a minute? Sometimes quietly enjoying a place becomes its own little journey."

"Sure." She loved how he expressed himself. "That's a nice way to put it."

"Well, that's because I'm giving you the deluxe tour." He winked. Taking her elbow, he guided her to a spot and they lowered themselves on the soft grass.

Owen stretched his long legs out in front of him and leaned back on his elbows, staring at the stones as if he'd never seen them before. "This really is a fascinating place. Some think it might have been a burial place, others a celestial observatory of some kind."

"Both could make sense."

"Then again, it could've all been done as a Neolithic team-building exercise." He grinned. "You know, like they might do on *The Office*."

She laughed. "Maybe I'll try this at my office."

"If you do, please send photos."

They sat quietly for a long moment. Then Owen said in a softer voice, "But others think it might be a place for healing. Beyond physical repair, but the healing we sometime need inside of us."

She turned to him and found his dark eyes searching her face. "What do you think?"

"I don't know." He shrugged. "But now, I'd forgotten how when I come here, something about this place makes me reflect on myself. My life. My choices." He frowned. "That can be its own form of healing."

She nodded, curious to know more about his life and choices. "I think you're right."

They both stared out to the stones, silent again. Did Owen search for a piece of himself lost somewhere along the way, just like her?

* * * *

"Ready for the next stop?" Owen reached across the aged-wood table in the George Inn for their check.

Willow grabbed it before he could. "It's my treat. Lunch is the least I can do to repay you. I mean, this personalized tour, complete with your charming accent, is worth lunch at a minimum."

"Am I charming you, Willow?" He cast a sly smile and wiggled his brows, making her cheeks get hot. He stood. "I'll be right back."

Yes. He'd charmed her all day. The deep timbre of his tone and the delightful conversation between them left her wanting to know more about the real Owen Hughes. Several times at lunch, while they'd talked about her company and life in New York, she'd touched his hand. Or had he touched hers? Were they flirting?

He strolled toward the men's room. Confident. Nodding at the bartender. Smiling at a waitress who he'd stepped aside to let pass through.

Before lunch, they'd gone to another stone formation at Avebury, and then he'd shown her around the Lacock National Trust, a village dating back to the thirteenth century. She'd loved the quaint streets lined with lime-washed, half-timbered and stone houses that made her feel like she'd stepped out of a scene from Harry Potter or a period film, like an Austen novel. Then she'd learned both were filmed in the richly preserved historical town.

Owen had proved quite knowledgeable speaking about the medieval cloisters, the Abbey, and a handsome 1sixteenth-century stable courtyard that had half-timbered gables.

As he came back to their table, their gazes met. This time, he seemed blind to the activity around him and only focused on her, or was it her imagination?

She stood before he got to the table. "Where to now?"

"A place called Castle Combe. About fifteen minutes away."

They headed to the van and got back on the road. Willow checked her email from her phone, catching another from the Pound Busters' board that she didn't open, afraid it would ruin this beautiful day.

They pulled into a parking lot and headed on foot down a hill toward the town. A few other visitors mingled around them.

Soon they came upon a quaint cottage with a roof thatched just like the one on her property. "Would you look at that? Another house needing a roof update."

He laughed hard and something about it made her happy.

As his smile faded, he motioned straight ahead. "Here we are."

The road narrowed at the start of the town. Rows of cozy homes lined both sides of the winding street, many with aged-stone facades and roofs made from split natural stone tiles. Other houses had exteriors of washed limestone and timber, with stone foundations. Rich green vines crept to second-story windows and baskets filled with red and purple flowers hung from doorways. The occasional car would drive by, but it didn't steal the seductiveness of yesteryear found in this picturesque setting.

Owen stood behind her. His voice landed close to her ear. "What do you think?"

"It's...enchanting."

He placed a hand on her shoulder, a gesture so natural she sank into it. Together they silently admired the village.

She glanced up at Owen. Again, his face carried awe, despite the lip service he paid to not being so enamored with the tourist attractions of the region.

He looked down at her, his handsome face close, his hand relaxed. "They call this the prettiest village in England."

"I can see why." Her heart beat faster, his proximity now and throughout the day putting all kinds of intimate thoughts in her head. She cleared her throat, hoping it would clear her head, but it didn't. "Based on your vast travels, what do you think?"

His smile faded and hand slipped from her shoulder. "Yes, it has an allure all its own." He motioned with his hand. "Shall we see the rest?"

"I can't wait."

They walked and made small talk. In the back of her mind, though, the side of her that loved to calculate business risk reeled with excitement.

Castle Combe, Stonehenge, and Bath were the types of things that would make her house quite marketable to an investor.

Her elation vanished, quickly replaced by a sense of loss at having found this wonderful place, only to have to leave it so soon. If she weren't driven by the desperate need for money...

But she was, and even if she left and never came back, she'd never forget this day. She'd never forget Owen, either.

Chapter 12

Willow yawned as she hoisted the heavy trash bag off the kitchen floor and lugged it outside, thinking about what the electrician who'd just left had said. *This wiring is decades old. Electric wiring isn't something you want to take for granted.*

No, she shouldn't. No matter what the price or the fact she had to wait for his supervisor to slot her in, this had to be done.

She yawned again. Yesterday's sightseeing had left her exhausted. Sleeping in might have been smart, instead of getting here early to start cleaning a room filled with junk on the second floor.

She tossed the bag inside a can and glanced up at the gray sky. The first dull day since she'd arrived. A car door slammed.

Going back through the house, she went out to the porch. Lettering on the side of a white flatbed truck read *Master Thatcher* and a phone number. Next to it stood a man she could've easily picked out of a crowd as Owen's father. Same tall frame, same strong chin, same friendly eyes. Add a few age lines to Owen's face and speckles of gray to his dark hair and you'd have a match.

She waved. "Hello. Are you Mr. Hughes? I'm Willow Arsmstrong, the owner."

A slow grin spread across his face, the resemblance to Owen's warm smile uncanny. "What's this 'Mr. Hughes'?" He stuck his keys in the pocket of his baggy tan pants and approached her while smoothing out his well-worn navy T-shirt.

He extended his hand. "Please. Call me Frank."

Despite the hard callus of his skin, his handshake was gentle.

"I just stopped by the cottage and took a look at that roof."

"Would you like to come inside and talk? Join me for a cup of coffee?"
"A cup of coffee sounds wonderful."

She ushered him inside and they went into the kitchen, where she'd set up a card table and chairs found in a closet upstairs.

While she poured two cups from the thermos Edna had brewed her this morning and handed one to Frank, he filled her in on the state of the thatched roof on the cottage.

"In short," he said, after a very long-winded analysis of the condition, "You do need a few repairs."

She sat across from him at the table. "Any idea how much it'll cost to fix?"

He withdrew a pad and short pencil from his pocket of his pants, scribbled for a minute, then pushed the pad her way. "Somewhere in this range."

Her stomach went queasy. Another large expense.

"If the roof had been maintained over the years, it wouldn't be so bad. Owen should've talked to me about the roof when he moved in." Tense lines pulled at the corners of Frank's mouth and he shook his head. "Too busy starting up his new travel business when he knows well enough about roofing matters. He could've earned a nice living in this line of work, but he's got more pride than common sense."

Based on the prices Frank charged, she figured the statement true, but Willow had no desire to take sides in this family matter. "If I decide to do this work, any idea when you could start?"

The taut lines of his anger softened. "We've got a tight schedule, but I might be able to fit you in a few weeks from now. I mean, since Owen knows you. Usually we have a longer wait."

A few weeks? She'd never get home when she'd planned, not if she stayed until both places were ready to list for sale. "That's very kind of you. I need to get back to the States at some point."

She refilled their coffee and asked more about his business, learning Frank ran it with Graham, Owen's younger brother. Pride shone in Frank's eyes as he discussed Graham's work with him, a far cry from his reaction to Owen's new venture.

In the middle of a funny story about his oldest grandson, someone knocked at the front door before it opened.

"Hello?" Owen yelled.

"In the kitchen," Willow replied.

Owen reached the kitchen doorway and stopped, a stone-cold expression on his face. "Hi, Dad. Did you stop by the cottage yet?"

"I did. You must've already left to take Jilly to school." Frank lifted his coffee and sipped while watching Owen over the rim. He lowered the cup. "You could've told me about the roof problems sooner."

Owen's jaw tightened. "Yes, well..." He glanced down to his hand, where he held Willow's jacket. "Good morning. I'm just returning this. You left it on the van's back seat."

She took it and tossed it on one of the chairs. "Thanks. I forgot all about it." She stood. "Let me get you some coffee."

Owen glanced between the two cups. "No thanks."

"Stay." Frank quickly stood up. "Time I left. I've got to meet Graham at a big job over on Sandy Lane. You let me know what you want me to do about the roof, young lady." He tipped his head. "Nice meeting you."

He walked past Owen and gave him a quick nod. A second later, the front door closed.

Owen exhaled and walked over to the counter and leaned against it. He met her gaze, smiled slowly. "Did you have fun yesterday?"

"I did. I'm exhausted. Can you tell me what just happened here?"

"Regarding what?"

"With your father, Owen."

"Oh. That." He shrugged. "We don't get along too well."

"I'm sorry. Why?"

He raised his dark brows.

"Sorry." She softened her tone. "If you don't mind talking about it. He seems nice."

"He is nice. To everyone else." Owen stuck his hands in his jean pockets. "If you must know, it seems I'm the biggest disappointment in his life."

The obvious pain in Owen's eyes touched a place inside of her also wounded by insensitive parents. Frank's angry comment about Owen's travel business were not the words of a proud father.

"I'm sorry. I know that must hurt."

"I'm fine."

She walked closer to him. "Listen, I've seen firsthand how parents can hurt kids. Not physically, but by their words."

"Why? Was someone like that to you?"

"Yes. My stepfather, Charlie. He..."

She stopped, the confession about her weight leaving her face, neck, and ears impossibly hot. Why let embarrassment stop her? Owen could see her size.

She inhaled and stared at the tile wall over his shoulder. "My mom married Charlie when I was five. He never missed a chance to remind me

I was fat. Subtle ways, but hurtful nonetheless. 'Are you eating again?' or 'You'll never get a boyfriend at your weight.'" Willow swallowed a lump forming in her throat. "I hated him for reminding me. Like I didn't know I weighed more than other girls at school? Jesus, I knew it every single day of my life." The worst of the admission over, she looked Owen in the eyes and saw nothing but sympathy. "Anger over his comments drove me to get skinny. So driven, I sold hundreds of thousands of customers on my weight-loss plan. But as you can see, I'm no longer driven."

"Willow, don't—"

"Please. I know what I am and always will be. Even when I'm skinny, a heavier version of me is waiting inside to come out." Embarrassment over the confession lingered, but at least she felt something. For months now, she'd been numb. "So, Owen, I understand how parents can make us feel like shit simply by making us believe our feelings don't matter."

Owen straightened and gently placed his hands on her shoulders. "You listen to me, Willow. I don't know what you see in the mirror, but, for God's sake, you're crazy if you believe you've turned back into a chubby little girl." His gaze burned into hers. "You're—you're gorgeous, smart, and great company. And your curves would turn the head of any man worth his salt."

Heat burned her cheeks. She wanted to believe every word. How many times had she encouraged members of her program to believe in themselves, because loving yourself was the first step toward any kind of self-improvement? Great. Now she could add hypocrite to her list of flaws. "Stop. You don't have to say that. Honestly, I'm okay."

He snorted a laugh. "Just like I am. Listen, I found your weight-loss company on the internet with your photo when I learned you owned the place."

"Oh, so you knew all about my business when I brought it up at lunch yesterday?"

He dropped his hands and shrugged. "I did. I didn't want you to be mad."

"No, I'd have done the same."

"My reason for confessing is because I saw a photo of a bone-thin version of you. Through my eyes, that version can't hold a candle to the gorgeous lass who stands before me."

Letting go of the image engrained in her brain for decades seemed impossible, but she couldn't deny Owen's attention had a way of making it fade away. "You're very kind to say so."

"Kind?" He tossed up his hands. "It's the truth. Are you going to argue with me? You shouldn't, because I always win."

She laughed. Owen's gift to others came in the form of the smiles he created. "Okay, you win. I will own the beauty you see, at least for the moment. Now, will you tell me why you think you disappoint your father?"

"It's simple. We've never shared the same interests. If I played cricket, he wanted me to play soccer. If I wanted to sit inside and read, he'd tell me books were for wimps. My brother, Graham, is more like him. Problem solved when I went off to the university. I majored in history and literature." He shook his head, a reluctant smile forming. "It drove the old man crazy, but for once I did what I loved and didn't give a damn what he thought. It's been a lifetime of growing apart, I guess. Working in the tour business, I didn't see him much."

"And now you're back."

He nodded. "Back for a good reason. Unfortunately, it's near him, although I like seeing more of my mum." He drew in a deep breath. "Okay, confession time over. Besides returning your jacket, I stopped by to tell you that Ronald McBride accepted my Facebook friend request. I sent him a message, explaining how I'm trying to locate his grandmother and why. Soon as he replies, I'll let you know."

Another step in the right direction, all thanks to his help. She touched his arm. "Alone, I'm not sure I'd have ever found Hettie. I honestly don't know how to thank you."

"Seeing the relief on your face is enough thanks. Is there anything I can do for you to help out around here? Tomorrow I have some time."

"I might need some help in the attic."

"Morning okay?"

"Perfect. Hey, I'm seeing more sights this afternoon. Edna and Eddie are taking me to Bath for afternoon tea at the Pump Room."

"You'll love it. If you have time, make sure they take you to the Royal Crescent and The Circus, both beautiful examples of the architecture in Bath. Guess I'll see you in the morning."

He turned for the door.

"Owen?"

He stopped and glanced back.

"I really did have fun yesterday. You were nice to take a whole day to show me around."

"Happy to be of assistance." He tipped his head like a gentleman of class. "And I had a good time, too."

She followed him out and waved from the porch as he pulled away.

The revealing moment she'd just had with Owen swirled inside her head. She rarely spoke of her childhood memories. Even when interviewed by magazines in her role as the CEO of Pound Busters, she chalked up her obsession with weight loss to a chubby childhood alone, but never dared revealed the painful incidents she'd shared today.

Another mask she hid behind. Not the fat versus skinny mask, but something deeper. A mask to hide pain caused by external sources, the power of them embedded so deeply inside that they controlled the very way she saw herself.

Yet here, in Bitton, she felt comfortable. Like she belonged "as is."

Chapter 13

"Come on up." Owen stood in the attic, right near the door opening, and motioned with a wave of his hand to Willow. "I promise, there are no ghosts."

"Very funny. Seriously, you checked everything?" Willow put one foot on the first step. "It didn't sound like you walked around up there much."

He raised his brows. "Okay, Rosebud. Want to tell me exactly what's going on here?"

"It may sound silly, but when I was ten, a bat attacked me in our attic. To call it terrifying would be an understatement."

"It attacked you?"

"Okay, it flew around my head and I screamed. Can you check for bats?"

He stared at her for a second then smiled. "Sure."

His feet padded on the floor overhead. She leaned against the hallway wall when it struck her how idiotic she must sound, terrified over something that happened so long ago. His opinion of her mattered more than when she'd arrived in town.

"Would you look at this?" Owen said loudly from upstairs.

"What?" She froze. "A bat?"

"No." He laughed, the happy sound rolling gently to her ears. "It's a bat-free zone. Come on up and see what I found."

Willow climbed the stairs and found him by a window, studying a painting displayed on an easel.

He glanced her way. "This is signed by your grandfather." He motioned for her to join him. "Seems he was a painter."

"Edna mentioned that." She approached, studying the oil painting. A city view done from a country hillside.

"It's Bath." Owen stepped aside and she joined him in front of the easel. "Your granddad was talented."

The details were painted with a loose brushstroke using pure but intense colors and giving the viewer a sensory effect of the scene. An impressionist style, void of pure linear definition and with a more unfinished style. "His work is incredible."

"There are more canvases against the wall." Owen walked to the other side of the room and she followed.

A lineup of vibrant oil paintings told a story of England spanning the seasons. A snowscape of a rotting fence gate with low rolling hills in the background. Flat fields of spring green, fighting with frosty patches of snow while half-naked tree branches sprouted lime buds. Summer wild flowers growing against an old stone wall in a quaint village. And the vibrant earth tones of autumn leaves as a backdrop to a wood post sign that read *Cotswold Way.*

Owen came to her side and motioned with his hand to the autumn painting. "Oh, that's why these locations look familiar. They're all painted from the Cotswold Way."

"What's that?" She looked to Owen, who'd crouched down and studied the painting closely.

"A walking trail. Been around for decades." He moved on to the next painting, giving it the same intense study. "Around ten years ago the government made it a national trail."

He waved toward the first painting he'd been staring at so carefully when she first came up. "That one, with the view of Bath, is probably from a spot on the trail."

Willow examined the paintings while Owen walked over to a box and opened it. As she did, a rush of excitement bubbled inside her over the treasure they'd stumbled upon, the artwork personal and close to her grandfather's heart. She imagined him sitting by the light of the window and painting from a photograph or outdoors at a spot on the trail.

Owen laughed. "This doesn't surprise me." He held up a magazine. "Come look at what I found in these boxes."

She walked over and took it. *"Walk Magazine?* I've never heard of it."

"Probably because you're not a Rambler."

"What are they?"

"An association for people who enjoy walking and other outdoor pursuits. They act as a watchdog to keep the walking paths in proper condition, have fundraisers, provide information on the trails. I actually met with them four months ago because we started doing walking tours of the Cotswold Way in the summer months."

"People hire you to have them walk somewhere?"

He nodded. "Many pursue the path on their own, but it's become popular to hire guides. My company maps out a route, books hotels for each overnight stop, transports luggage there. This way when you reach each town everything you need is there. We offered about two tours a month over the summer season. All the tours were booked solid."

She knelt beside him and rifled through the opened box of magazines, discovering her grandfather's Rambler membership paperwork about halfway down. "Oh look, he was a Rambler."

Owen nodded, preoccupied with another unopened box.

She stood and went back to the painting lineup. What were her grandfather's favorite towns along the walk? Which trail did he think gave the best views? As an older man was he able to still walk them, or only up until a certain age?

The weight of disappointment wiggled straight to the core of her chest. She'd never know the answers. Again, she stared at his artwork, vivid representations that brought each location to life. At least through his eyes. Yes, through his eyes...

She glanced over at Owen, who opened a plastic trash bag. "How long is the trail?"

He glanced over his shoulder. "About a hundred miles." He pointed to another stack of magazines. "Can I toss these?"

She nodded and turned back to the paintings, each one suddenly screaming a message to her.

Come see us, Willow. Walk in your grandfather's shoes.

"I'm thinking, if my grandfather loved walking the Cotswold Way so much, maybe I should walk it, too."

He dumped the box of magazines into the bag then glanced to her, his dark brows furrowed. "You could. There are some shorter walks from town to town. Maybe less than twenty-five kilometers."

"No, not just to one or two towns. I mean, everywhere my granddad walked. From these pictures. What better way to experience the family roots my mother denied me? It's only a hundred miles."

"Yes, but that distance will take you some time." He lifted the trash bag. "At least a week, week and a half."

"So? I'll extend my stay. It'll be perfect. The electricians need to do some work, so I'll schedule it around when they're here."

Owen drew his dark brows together, and though he didn't say a word, his frown spoke for him.

She laughed. "What's wrong? You don't like my idea?"

"No. I think you'd enjoy it. But how about I get one of my guides to go with you?"

"Thanks, but it's not necessary." Willow pulled her phone from the pocket of her jeans, and started to take photos of each painting. "Can you help me identify where these were taken? I'd like to incorporate some of these locations into my route."

He dropped the trash bag and it clunked on the floor. "Why don't you reconsider that guide? I don't know if a woman alone is always safe. I mean—"

She lowered her phone. "Owen, I run around New York City all by myself. Surely, in this beautiful countryside, nothing bad could happen."

"I'm not saying it does, but it could."

She laughed. "Don't be a mother hen. Besides, I don't want to walk with a stranger."

He came to her side. "How about if I walk with you?" The shine in his eyes held so much hope it teased her heart.

She took his hand and squeezed. "You are very sweet to worry about me, but I'll be fine on my own." She let go. "Besides, you have work to do and Jilly to take care of. But can you help me plan my route and suggest some places to stay?"

"Yes. I'd be happy to." He offered up a stiff smile, one she read as reluctant agreement.

"Great. Now let's finish up here before you have to leave. I'd like to treat you to dinner or lunch for all your help, if you have time."

He smiled more genuinely this time. "Sure."

They worked silently, tossing out old paints and half-used canvases, saving brushes and clean canvases that someone might be able to use. Willow buzzed with a surge of energy eluding her for over a year.

All because of the Cotswold Way.

* * * *

"I made it." Edna plunked into the empty folding chair beside Willow at the Bath Central Library, where a group of about fifty or so waited for tonight's Jane Austen reading.

Even Owen liked to partake in the festival fun. Right before leaving her house earlier today, he'd invited her to attend tonight's event, where and he some fellow local actors would perform scenes from Austen's works.

Edna leaned over and stuffed both her shopping bag from the store located below the library and her purse beneath her chair. "I forgot to mention, in the morning Kathleen is dropping off a dress for you to wear to the masked ball. You're coming, right?"

"When is it again?"

"Friday night. Do come! It'll be fun. I'll help you put up your hair, plus the dress she gave me will look stunning with your eye color." Edna patted her knee. "You really shouldn't miss it."

This past year, she'd turned down invite after invite to social events. Dressing up for a party at her current weight could be painful. Over time, though, the excuses had sounded flimsy. So what if she'd needed a larger black party dress? Each refusal had disappointed her friends.

She turned to Edna. "Sure, I'll come."

Edna squeezed Willow's forearm. "Oh good. Try on the dress tomorrow and we'll see if it needs to be hemmed."

A stout woman with short dark hair and large wire-rimmed glasses stepped in front of the rows of chairs. "Welcome to our Jane Austen Festival reading. I'm Jeanette Stockman, your host for tonight."

The fifty or so people seated in the brightly lit room clapped.

"This year, instead of a reading, we have a group of local theater performers who've agreed to perform for us. The theme for this year's selection from Ms. Austen's work is love, courtship, and marriage. There's a deeply passionate side to Jane Austen's works and tonight we've chosen passages from *Pride and Prejudice*."

Willow whispered to Edna, "Owen Hughes, the caretaker at my house, is one of the performers."

Edna's penciled-on coal-colored brows lifted. "Oh my," she said a little too loudly, making a few heads turn. "He's a perfect Darcy."

The announcer stepped aside, adding, "For the first selection, the part of Elizabeth Bennett will be played by Julia Parker and Fitzwilliam Darcy is performed by the very dashing Owen Hughes." She raised a brow and many of the women in the audience smiled.

Very dashing. Yes, darn him. Not only dressed in Regency clothing, she imagined. Even in his modern-day attire, he seemed gallant.

A pretty brunette with her long hair twisted into a loose bun, tendrils brushing her cheeks, stepped into the performing area and sat on a bench while looking off to the side, her spirits clearly broken. Her plain Regency-style dress reminded Willow of those seen in the parade yesterday.

Hurried footsteps sounded on the carpet behind them and Owen appeared in the center aisle between the folding chairs. Dressed in a short-waisted coat, cream-colored pants, and sideburns firmly in place, he took long strides to the front, his chin held high and gaze fixed on Elizabeth. Dashing barely scraped the surface of how handsome he looked, and his sense of purpose commanded the audience's attention.

Owen and his fellow actor played the parts to perfection. Willow discovered an admiration for the author, who portrayed a man in love but unable to express himself. And more than anything, Owen's acting abilities left her stunned.

The scene ended and the audience erupted with applause, including one wolf whistle. Both actors took a bow, and on his second one, Owen's eyes landed on Willow and he winked. She nearly melted right into her seat.

Full of surprises, wasn't he?

They enjoyed the remaining performances. At the end, the entire group of actors came out and took a collective bow. As the crowd dispersed, Willow and Edna stood to greet Owen, who, according to Edna, approached them with his mother, Ginny.

Edna touched his arm. "Oh, Owen. You should be on the telly." She turned Ginny and after quickly introducing Willow, she said, "You sure raised a good one here."

Owen's mom glanced at him and beamed with pride. "Thank you, Edna. I'm always proud of my oldest boy."

Willow turned to Owen. "I think Edna's right. You should be television. You were great."

He shrugged. "Thanks. I used to perform in secondary school, then some at the university. Just a hobby. Not a big deal."

"Not a big deal?" Ginny shook her head. "You're always so modest, Owen."

Edna looked at Ginny. "Will I see you at the masquerade ball?"

"Not this year, I'm afraid."

Edna reached out and put a hand on Willow's shoulder. "I've convinced our newcomer to join us."

Willow laughed. "Yeah, I'm not sure what I'm getting myself into."

"It's fun." Owen turned to her. "If you're going to the ball, you should learn some eighteenth-century dances. Want me to teach you?"

"Oh, no way." Willow held up her hand. "I don't dance."

Every horrible memory of attending dances in high school released a barrage of insecurity. Wallflower. Always the fat girl, watching her thinner classmates moving with ease on the floor. "I'll get dressed up, but just want to watch."

"Tsk. Tsk." Edna frowned. "You'll have more fun if you fully participate. And Owen is probably a wonderful teacher."

"Don't they need someone to serve the punch or work the coat room?" Owen laughed. "You're always so funny, Rosebud."

"Who's being funny?"

He smiled and shook his head. "Seriously. It would be my pleasure to teach you. How about tomorrow, after I get back from a tour?"

All eyes were on her and she wanted to shrink inside herself. Dancing required grace and she possessed none. "I'm not a great dancer. In fact, I'm not one at all."

"Skill doesn't matter. It's fun."

"Fun. Sure. Fine. I'll give it a try, but after I break your foot, can we call it quits?"

He belly laughed this time. "Yes. But only once my foot is broken. Tomorrow it is then. I'll let you know the time."

And just like that, she would be forced to turn into a Regency-period ballroom dancer. Her inner wallflower groaned.

Chapter 14

Willow savored the last bite of her breakfast sausage just as Edna hurried into the sunroom. She placed two breakfast plates at the table of a new couple from Germany, then started excitedly suggesting places they should visit in Bath. Always so eager to make her guests feel at home. A true gem.

Willow exited the article she'd been reading about another woman who'd walked the Cotswold Way alone. The author claimed the trail changed her in ways she hadn't expected, but all for the good.

Changes for the good. She liked that sound of that.

She rose from the table. Passing by Edna as she stepped away from the new guests, Willow touched her arm. "Thanks for breakfast. Delicious, as always."

"Thank you, dear. Don't forget. Kathleen will be here any minute with your dress for the ball."

"I'll just brush my teeth before she comes." A ball. It sounded so Cinderella, making Willow laugh. "Will she bring a pumpkin and some mice, too?"

Edna stared blankly for a long moment; then she smiled. "Oh yes, Cinderella, going to the ball. I see."

"Be back in a few." She turned to head to her room.

On her way there, it struck her how her Manhattan friends would laugh at the notion of her attending a Regency-period ball. A strong, get-the-job done CEO like herself, dressing as if she'd stepped out of a *Masterpiece Theater* production.

What had she gotten herself into?

Yet, something about the prospect of the ball left her curious. Just like last night's reading at the library from *Pride and Prejudice*. After the performance, back at the B and B, she couldn't fall asleep. She'd gone on the internet and had watched the movie version, finding the premise captivating.

Once inside her room, she picked up her toothbrush and added a blob of toothpaste. While she brushed, a parallel between her life and Jane Austen's grew clear. Willow had been raised in a world of wealth because of her mother's marriage, but she'd never felt comfortable. Always on the outside looking in at people who judged others by social norms that, to Willow, often seemed silly and exclusive.

Jane's world held a narrow definition of how women should behave. In a similar fashion, the modern world cared about how a woman looked. While growing up, not only did Willow have to hear about the importance of being thin and dressed well, but expectations bombarded every single female in today's world, from women's magazines, television, and movies.

As she rinsed off her toothbrush, another reality hit her like a pie to the face...

She'd grown a business empire from those suppositions.

A wave of self-disgust tumbled toward her as another admission became clear as glass: skinny did *not* equal happy. No matter what society tried to tell you.

She stepped out of the bathroom and her phone rang. The display showed her attorney's name so she answered. "Hi, Abe."

"Hey. Is it a good time?"

"Sure, but I've only got a few minutes. Everything okay? I mean, it's the middle of the night in New York."

"Insomnia. It gets worse with age. Figured I'd use the time to give you an update. Things have quieted down with the board since you left, but I don't trust them. I'm still trying to find out your options to buy back the company, but I thought of another tactic if that doesn't work."

"I'll try anything that lets me keep my company." She ignored a voice reminding her about what she'd just realized.

"What if I can convince most of the board members to vote in your favor?"

"That'd be great. But will they? Nobody in their right mind would want to contend with Nikki afterward. She rules that place like Stalin did his armies."

"You're not kidding. But I ate lunch with two of the members the other day and learned not everybody is thrilled with her, so a door might be open for you. Possibly to include a new board president."

"Wow, they'd fire her? Wouldn't that be a twist on things. Well, I trust you, Abe. If you think it might work, go for it."

"How's it going with the house and property?"

"The good news is that I think the house could be a small gold mine."
Willow plopped onto her bed. "This area is gorgeous and the house has
the potential to be a truly beautiful place to live."

"I sense a but."

"It's been neglected for a long time. It needs an electrical wiring
overhaul and a plumber because the water isn't working right. Oh, the
deal also includes a cottage that needs some work on the thatched roof."

He laughed. "So you own a thatched-roof house, too?"

"Yeah, who'd have thought? I'll tell you a secret if you promise not to
breath a word to anybody in Manhattan."

"My lips are sealed."

"I'm going to a Jane Austen ball in a few days."

He laughed a little too long. "That doesn't sound like the tiger lady
of weight loss."

"No. It doesn't. I have no idea what I'm getting myself into. Oh, I may
be here about a week longer than I planned." She didn't bother to tell him
about her walk on the Cotswold Way, at least for now, but offered her new
return date. "I'd better run. Time for my gown fitting."

"Okay, Cinderella."

She laughed. "Good one. Talk to you soon."

A gown fitting. A hundred-mile walk to follow in her grandfather's
footsteps. The second she boarded the plane to come here, a metamorphosis
had begun. Good and surprising changes. Where would all this end?

* * * *

"Good news!" Owen smiled as he stepped inside the foyer of Willow's
house. "I've found your grandmother's friend."

"You mean Hettie? Ronald got back to you?" Willow's stomach dipped,
part excitement over getting some answers, the other nerves over what
she might find.

"Ronald says she's in a nursing home. Actually, it's a residential care
facility. She's faced some physical hindrances as she's aged, but her mind
is sharp and she might be able to answer your questions."

"Is she far?" She took Owen by the arm and pulled him further in then
closed the door.

"Bristol. It's about thirty minutes from here."

"Gosh, I can't thank you enough. If you get me the address, I'll see if
a cab can take me over—"

"Don't be foolish. I'll drive you."

"But you've done so much for me already. I don't want to bother you."

"No bother." He stuck his hands inside his denim jacket pockets. "We can figure out when later, because it's time for our ballroom dance lessons."

"Oh, right."

He shook his head. "Good try, pretending you forgot."

"Can't blame me for trying. Where are we doing them?"

"The cottage, where we'll have electricity for the music. I came to walk you over."

"And they say chivalry is dead."

"Not when I'm around." He raised his dark brows. "You ready?"

"One sec." She went to the living room and grabbed her purse off the sofa. When she returned to the doorway, he stood outside on the porch waiting, staring out to the trees.

"Ready."

He turned, a soft smile sweeping across his face as he waved a hand toward the steps. "After you."

As they started across the lawn, he said, "Jilly and Bea made us dinner. Then the four of us can practice after we eat. "

"The four of us? Are you afraid I'll be so bad you'll need more people to show me?"

"No." He cast her a frown. "These are group dances. Tonight we will learn an English Country Dance and it starts with steps in a group of four."

"It already sounds complicated. Maybe I should just observe."

He chuckled. "Willow, Willow, Willow. What goes on in your head?"

"Fear of humiliation."

"Now, if I may quote..." He held up a finger and shifted to a very scholarly sounding voice. "In the end, we only regret the chances we didn't take."

"Uh-huh. Did you make that up?"

"Nope. Saw it on a poster the other day."

"And I'll bet you were dying for a chance to use it."

He smiled, but didn't answer, and reached for the cottage's storm door. They entered the living room, a spacious area with a comfortable rolled-armed sofa and two chairs. The ensemble faced a brick fireplace holding a wood-burning stove. Dog toys scattered on the dark beige wall-to-wall carpeting gave the place a lived-in look.

"We're here," Owen said loudly.

Henry howled from somewhere in the house, and seconds later he charged into the room with Jilly behind him.

"Willow!" Jilly threw herself into Willow's arms.

She hugged Jilly's small frame, overwhelmed someone could be this happy to see her. A flash of what she may have missed by never having a child of her own threatened to steal the warm moment, but she fought it and hugged Jilly even tighter.

"Hello, Willow." A woman of average height with an easy smile and short dark hair streaked with gray approached. Willow released Jilly but took her hand. "I'm Bea, Jilly's grandmother. I'm so glad we finally get to meet."

"Me, too. Thanks so much for sending over both tea and Jilly in the afternoons. It's been a nice break from cleaning."

"My pleasure. Why don't we eat? Dinner is ready."

On their way out of the living room, Willow passed several photographs hung on the off-white walls. Most pictures were of a woman Willow didn't recognize, all taken during dog shows. In each one, the dogs were the same as Henry, some with different coloring. Probably pictures of Jilly's mom.

Did it hurt Jilly to see pictures of her mother in plain sight each day? Willow quickly reconsidered. If Jilly were her child, she would still want her memory kept alive.

She crossed a threshold into the kitchen. Pine cabinets. Slate-gray stone floor. Copper-bottomed pots hanging over the stove. And the delicious scent of the roast on the dark countertop filling the air, making Willow's stomach growl.

Bea lifted the platter of sliced meat. "Owen, could you grab the bowls?"

"Sure." Owen took a bowl of mashed potatoes and one of peas and put them on the table. "Go ahead and have a seat, Rosebud."

She looked at Jilly. "Where should I sit?"

"Next to me." Jilly hopped into one of the seats. "This is my spot. You go where my mum used to sit." She motioned to the chair on her right.

Willow caught Owen and Bea exchanging a look between them. But Jilly smiled happily, unaware of the adults' discomfort. Willow swallowed down the lump in her throat. "Thank you, Jilly. It's a real honor."

"Henry is allowed to sit by me." Jilly put down her hand and the dog ran to her side, sniffing at her fingers. "As long as he doesn't beg. Right, Daddy?"

"Yes. And the other rule is you're not allowed to feed him from the table." Owen used a sterner voice than usual, and yet she felt certain an infraction by either dog or daughter would somehow be overlooked.

By the time they finished the meal, Willow had counted three times a piece of Jilly's roast "fell" to the floor. Owen never said a word.

After dinner, Willow helped Bea clean up in the kitchen while Owen took Jilly to help him push back some of the furniture in the living room for the lesson. When she learned Bea liked to paint, she offered her the supplies from the attic.

A few minutes later, Owen came inside the kitchen. "Time to tango, ladies."

"Wait? We're learning to tango?"

"Bea, did I mention Willow's a real wiseass?" He grinned, took the dried pot from Willow's hands and stored it in a drawer. "Now let's get this show on the road."

She followed him out of the kitchen. Furniture had been moved, and the only obstacle on the floor was a shaggy dog, plunked dead center.

"Come on, Henry. You're in the way." Owen led him by the collar to a dog bed, where he sat and stayed put.

Owen turned to Willow. "Ready?"

"As I'll ever be. Don't say I didn't warn you. You may end up with sore shins or a few broken toes."

"Funny, I've never known you to be prone to exaggeration." He grinned. "Come on. It's like square dancing in the US. You've done that, right?"

"Yes, I have the horror of several gym classes seared in my memory."

"Don't be scared, Willow." Jilly came over and took her hand. "It gets easier. Daddy gave me a lesson last night. I got better the more I practiced."

"Is that so? Then Dad is a good teacher?" She glanced at Owen, who she swore blushed.

"Yes. Very good. He was…" Jilly drew in her bottom lip then glanced at Bea. "What was the word, Nan?"

"Patient." Bea nodded to her granddaughter. "Your father is very patient."

Owen clapped. "Okay. Enough talk about my stellar abilities. Down to business. Jilly, sweetheart, you partner with Nan and I'll partner with Willow. We're going to do a line dance."

Willow listened to the instructions and refrained from further sarcastic commentary. If Jilly could do it, surely she could put on her big-girl panties and give this a whirl.

Owen led her through the six-count step, taking her hand and following at her side. He spoke to her softly, as if she were a timid animal, one step from fleeing at the slightest provocation. It wasn't his voice that created a distraction, though. More like his guiding hand touching hers and those dark eyes, so kind, so inquisitive…

"Now step." Owen lifted his voice.

He went left. She went right, and bumped into him.

"Sorry!" She let go of his hand. "See? I'm not good at this."

"Nonsense." He tilted his chin to his chest and whispered, "I think you weren't listening carefully." Then he winked.

Heat blasted up the back of her neck. "I was listening." Owen raised a brow. "Well, sort of."

They tried a few more times alone. She did slightly better, so they squared off with Jilly and Bea. The movements were, indeed, like a square dance. Not that it helped her any. Owen worked the group with patience and it didn't go unnoticed by Willow that both Bea and Jilly caught on more quickly.

"Now, ladies, stay where you are. Let's try it with music."

Owen started a CD that played an upbeat violin jig. He hurried back to his spot. "Ready?"

They all nodded, but a stampede of butterflies cut a path through Willow's belly.

They began. Willow did the first few moves correctly, her eyes never leaving Owen's reassuring gaze. But when he turned in a direction she didn't expect, she overcompensated her adjustment and bumped into Bea, bringing them to a halt.

They all laughed, including Willow, but her shoulders stiffened. Self-consciousness. A lifetime trait due to her size and the very reason she'd avoided overt physical displays. Any day of the week, she could stand at a podium and talk to hundreds of people, but she sure as hell wouldn't want to dance in front of twenty. Behind a podium she could safely hide, but this dancing left her exposed in the worst way pos—

"Willow? Want to try again."

She looked into his eyes. "I guess." What she wanted was a glass of wine to loosen up. Maybe even two or three.

"You're doing fine."

"You truly are graceful, Willow." Jilly kneeled at the dog bed, petting Henry. "Remember when we met? You told me your name meant graceful."

A perfect teaching moment on irony for young Jilly, but when Willow glanced at the sincerity in the young girl's eyes, shame nibbled away at her for being so gutless. "I do remember, sweetheart. Maybe I need to try harder."

Three more times they tried. Three more times, Willow crashed into someone, missed a step, and then, finally, she stepped on Owen's foot. Any goodwill she'd mustered to try harder evaporated.

Owen glanced at Bea and Jilly. "Do you two mind having a seat while I work with Willow for a moment?"

"How about I get some cookies while you two practice a little more?" Bea extended a hand to Jilly. "Come on, big girl. Help me out."

They vanished into the kitchen. Willow watched as Owen did something to the music and then he returned to her side and took her hand. He led her to the center of the living room.

He faced her and took her hand. Placing it on his shoulder, he slipped one hand on the center of her back and wove his fingers through her other.

"This is regular dancing. I thought we were—"

"Shh. No talking, Rosebud. My God. If you were a twig, you'd snap in half. Relax. Get out of your head."

"I'm not in my..."

Owen leaned back, watching her with that heart-melting grin that always seemed ready for use.

"Okay. Maybe I am. A little."

Trumpets suddenly played, followed by Frank Sinatra's smooth croon. Gershwin. She loved this music.

"Deep breath," Owen said, his tone comforting. "I'll do the driving."

It took a minute to shake off the tension and do as he asked, but when she finally sank into his arms and relinquished control, he guided her like she was a marionette and he the puppeteer.

"What's distracting you?" His low, husky tone fell close to her ear while his hand pressed more firmly to her back.

Right now? Your touch. Your intense eyes. "Nothing."

"Do you really hate dancing that much?"

"I don't know." Yet a truth too embarrassing to share settled in her bones. She'd never felt totally comfortable in her own skin. But the roots were deeply embedded and hard to pull away from. So why? Why would this strange feeling still bother her?

She shut her eyes while he guided her. All the discomfort possessing her when they'd started wasn't new. It developed over a lifetime, worsening in high school.

Then a bomb dropped in Willow's mind out of nowhere.

A sliver in time, stored in the stockpile of small pains she'd accumulated in bits and pieces. Her friend's sweet sixteen party. That day, Willow had worn a black velvet and chiffon dress. She'd never felt prettier. While waiting in the foyer to leave, she'd heard her mother talking in the upstairs hallway.

"Be nice for once, Charlie."

"What?" He'd huffed a laugh. "I only said it's too bad she can't wear a dress a few sizes smaller. Jesus, it's not like I said it to her face."

But unwittingly, he had. And it still stung, all these years later....

"What do you think, Willow?" Owen tipped his head back and the painful memory returned to storage, where it could haunt her anytime she started to feel good about herself or her body. "Do you want to stop, forget the lesson?"

"No." It was now or never. Charlie be damned. "Sorry for the attitude. I'm just kind of self-conscious. That's all."

"No need to be sorry. Do you like this music?"

"I love Gershwin." The lyrics to "I've Got a Crush On You" wound around them, as fluid as the way he moved her.

Owen drew her close and whispered, "Get lost in the music with me."

Willow closed her eyes, concentrating on the sweet caress of Sinatra's voice and Owen's unwavering yet gentle hand. The more she gave in, the easier moving became. Owen's voice vibrated against her as he hummed the tune, leaving her unguarded, giving in, but not lost.

When the song stopped, he held her close for several long seconds. Then he leaned back and his dark eyes bore into hers. "See? You *can* dance, Willow."

A warm feeling started, found in the way he'd said her name and the depth in his gaze as he studied her, making her entire body burn with a desire to dance in Owen's arms all night. Weightless, happy, and supported. His lips parted, their eyes met, and she wanted to kiss him more than she'd ever wanted to kiss any man before. His hand slid along her spine, to the back of her head and she parted her lips as he leaned close—

"Here are some cookies, Daddy." Jilly burst in the room, her voice intrusive as an explosion. She carried a plate of cookies, her grandmother right behind her. "Nan said we could have two different kinds."

They quickly stepped apart, but it didn't stop Bea from offering a slight smile at them.

Bea took the plate from Jilly, put it on the coffee table, and took her granddaughter's hand. "Come to the kitchen for a glass of milk, too, Jilly."

As they returned to the kitchen, Owen left Willow's side and shut off the music. The magic spell cast over them broken, Willow excused herself to go get a glass of water, but she wished that moment between them had gone on just a little longer.

Chapter 15

"You okay?"

Startled by Owen's voice, Willow jerked her head around to look at him in the van's driver seat. "Yes. I am. I'm glad Hettie agreed to see us today. How far are we from Bristol?"

"About ten minutes."

Ten minutes until she'd face someone who *might* have all the answers her mother had hidden. Willow took a cleansing breath, but it did little to calm the whirlwind bouncing off the walls of her stomach. Much as she wanted answers, a slow reality that they might not be what she wanted to hear sank in.

Owen gave her a short smile then turned back to the road, not an ounce of tension visible anywhere on his body. But he was quieter than usual since he'd picked her up. Was he aware of the elephant in the car, thanks to a near-hit of their lips last night?

Sinatra had set the mood, but it was all Owen's doing that her dance tension slipped away and she'd melted into his arms. Yup, all his doing. Had she imagined the attraction between them last night? Been mistaken that they'd been about to kiss?

"You seem quiet," she blurted out, unable to stand one more second of not knowing. "Anything wrong?"

"No." He glanced her way and smiled, but it didn't have his usual sparkle. "Are you anxious about talking to Hettie?"

"Hell yeah. You know the expression 'Be careful what you ask for'?"

He chuckled. "Let's hope this works out better than that."

Hope. It was all she had left.

Soon they parked along the street in front of the retirement home, a weatherworn, three-story brick building with mature shrubbery near the entrance. Once inside, they were directed to a cheery lobby with tangerine sofas holding lime-green pillows and light beechwood tables. They sat side by side on the sofa.

After a few seconds, Owen stood. "Come on. Let's square off and practice our dance steps again."

"You're joking."

"Dead serious." He offered his hand.

"I guess we can." She slipped her hand into his and stood. "They probably have good medical care here, in case I break one of your toes."

He shook his head but the corners of his lips lifted. "We'll use imaginary dancers in our foursome."

"And you don't think that'll be more of a challenge?"

"Confidence, Rosebud. Confidence."

He reminded her of the count and they started to dance. The music came à la Owen as he hummed the instrumental they'd used last night.

"Has anyone told you that you have a good voice?"

He stopped humming and placed a finger on her lips. "No talking. Dance."

With a twinkle in his eyes, he resumed the tune and they performed the steps. Several staff members and residents gathered round to watch. The audience made her self-conscious, but Owen hammed it up for them and his attitude somehow made her relax. The steps came easier today, and she even made it through without a mistake. When they finished, he took her hand and they bowed to the lobby audience.

"Look at you." He squeezed her hand. "You did it."

As their eyes met, Owen's had that same heated glow she'd seen last night. His voice dropped. "I'm so proud of you."

Had she just seen pride, or something more?

"Excuse us." A voice behind them snapped the magic in half.

Owen dropped her hand and turned around.

"Are you Owen Hughes?" A young male staff member stood behind the wheelchair of a white-haired woman wearing a plaid skirt and button-down sweater.

"Yes. Mrs. McBride! I'd recognize you anywhere. You look wonderful."

"Oh, Owen. Still the same. Now, please call me Hettie. I caught the end of your dance number. Quite good."

"Thank you. This is Willow."

She smiled at Willow. "Hello, Willow. Are you the young lady related to Sarah and Derrick?"

She took a step closer to the chair. "Yes, I am."

"Nice to meet you."

"You, too."

"I wasn't sure I understood everything Ronnie told me about why you needed to speak to me."

Owen glanced around and asked, "Do you mind if we sit over there and talk?" He motioned to a table with four chairs.

"Not at all."

The orderly left, telling them to contact him when they were through. Owen moved Hettie's chair near a table while they sat around it.

Hettie and Owen talked about old times. Willow listened politely, but her head ran amok with how to raise the issues she came here to discuss.

Hettie finally turned to Willow. "So how can I help you, young lady?"

She took a deep breath and said, "Sarah and Derrick were my grandparents."

Hettie's white brows furrowed as she scrutinized Willow carefully. "Grandparents? They didn't have any…" She studied Willow's face again and her eyes opened wide. "Oh my goodness. Are you Chloe's daughter?"

A tidal wave of relief rushed over Willow. "Yes! Then you knew my mom was pregnant?"

"Sarah told me." Hettie frowned. "She remained close-lipped about it with others, but we'd been friends since childhood. Chloe's last year at their house, she'd changed. Then she left…" She looked toward the window staring out into a courtyard, but her eyes glistened. "A very sad time for my friends. Very sad."

A sad time. Sure, it wasn't personal. Yet it reminded Willow she hadn't been wanted from the start.

Hettie reached out and laid her frail hand over Willows. "I'm sorry, dear. If Sarah and Derrick met you, I'm sure they'd have put aside their worries about Chloe's out-of-wedlock pregnancy. They were just so, well, traditional. Things were so different back then."

Willow patted her hand. "I'm sure their daughter's ordeal was very hard on them. Do you remember exactly when Chloe left home?"

"Strangely enough, I'll never forget because we'd celebrated my sister's fortieth birthday the day before. Two days after Christmas in"—she shut her eyes briefly—"1975."

The calendar marked with an *L* on a date after Christmas, confirming everything Willow suspected. "Any idea where my mother went?"

"At first Sarah and Derrick suspected foul play and reported her missing to the constable. A few days later, one of Chloe's friends told them she'd run away from home. To London, of all places. They worried so much about her alone in that big city."

"She must've left London before the summer. I was born in July in Manhattan."

Hettie nodded. "Years later, Sarah learned from another friend of Chloe's that she stayed in London a month. She'd gone off to America with a man she met in London. How she found money to cross the pond and ended up in the States they never knew." Hettie closed her eyes and swallowed while shaking her head.

Willow placed a hand over her forearm and slowly rubbed. "It sounds like you were very close to my grandparents. They were lucky to have a friend they could trust."

Her eyes opened slowly but her sadness lingered. "They were good people. They deserved better from Chloe."

Anger swelled inside Willow. Her mother. A woman who cared so little about her own parents she'd denied them a granddaughter. Who didn't care enough to grant her daughter a life knowing them, too.

Since the car accident that took her mother's life, Willow had conveniently forgotten all the selfish and self-absorbed traits her mother possessed. Beauty had gifted her a certain kind of power. Even Willow wanted to be in the path of her popularity. Mom didn't think much about others. If she had, she might not have let Charlie's verbal abuses continue toward Willow's appearance.

She took Hettie's frail hand. "I wish more than anything I could have known them, too. Being at their house, I'm seeing the things they loved and did. I know they knew I existed, or I wouldn't have been in the will, but what I wouldn't give to spend a day with them."

"I'm sorry you are going through this. Knowing my friends, Sarah wanted to reconcile their differences with Chloe, but that Derrick made a mule look agreeable."

"Well, it's history now."

Hettie's eyes brightened. "Did you find Derrick's paintings and Sarah's collectibles?"

"I did. I've packed some to take back to the US with me."

"They'd be happy you did."

"I'm hoping you might know a few people my mother kept photographs of." Willow reached into her purse and removed the small stack.

She laid a picture in front of Hettie. "Do you recognize the girl with my mom?"

Hettie took the photo with her age-spotted hand. A smile crossed her face. "Oh yes. That's her cousin."

"Cousin?" Willow's heart leapt. A tremor of excitement pulsed through her veins. "Do you remember the cousin's name, or where she lived?"

Hettie pulled in her lips and didn't answer right away. "She's Derrick's brother's daughter. Right now I can't recall her name, but they lived in Kent. The family visited here frequently."

"So I have an uncle?"

Hettie shook her head. "I'm afraid his brother passed before Derrick."

Disappointment wound through her. "But I still have my mother's cousin. My second cousin."

"Yes." Hettie's gave her a sad smile. "I wish I could remember more. You can always check the Kent records for the name Armstrong. Maybe her cousin still lives in the area."

"Yes. Yes. I will. Since my mother passed, I thought I had no family left." A hard lump lodged in her throat. "Learning this, it means everything."

Owen reached out and rested his hand on Willow's back, where he rubbed in a slow circle. She shifted her gaze to his, comforted by the deep understanding lingering in his eyes. She swallowed and forced a smile.

She returned to the photo pile. "Here's another. Do you know who that boy is with my mother?"

Hettie's forehead wrinkled then she nodded. "Oh, yes. Sean. I'm surprised to see him with Chloe."

"Why?"

"Because Derrick got along with everybody, but Sean's father and he had some big falling-out. Business related, I think. But those two wanted nothing to do with each other."

Willow's heart banged against her ribs. "Do you recall Sean's last name?"

Hettie's lips pursed, accentuating the age wrinkles around her mouth. "Sean,...oh, what was it? His father, Mickey, worked at the local butcher." She tapped her fingers on the table.

Willow bit her tongue so she didn't scream for answers.

"I'm sorry. The memory works pretty well, but every so often it fails me."

"That's okay. Maybe it'll come to you." Willow patted her hand, despite the letdown unfurling inside of her. "On the back of the photo, he wrote that he loved my mother."

Hettie turned over the photo and stared at the message. "Funny, Sarah never told me that. In fact, she refused to tell me who got Chloe pregnant. Only shared about them pressuring Chloe to give the baby up for adoption."

Willow swallowed. Give *her* up for adoption.

A logical choice, but it still stung. "Do you think that's why my mother ran away? To keep me, not give me up?"

Hettie shrugged. "It had to be. Like I said, Derrick was stubborn, but so was Chloe." Hettie stared at her folded hands. "People can be so foolish about their pride. All I know is my friends were never quite the same after losing her."

"No. I imagine not." Willow leaned back in her seat. "So many lives not what they could have been. All because of one woman's choices."

They were all quiet, deep in their own thoughts, when Hettie blurted out, "Bloody hell. I can't remember his last name." Owen raised his brows, but Hettie didn't seem to notice. "He spent time with Willy Donnagan, a boy who lived on my street." Her eyes widened and she looked at Owen. "Ronnie might remember. By the way, did you know he has two daughters now?"

"Does he now? How old are they?"

Hettie started to talk about her grandchildren, and Owen gave her his full attention, even asking further questions about them. Such a good guy. Willow had been lucky to stumble upon him on this journey.

She pulled out a small pad and wrote down the information Hettie provided. If she found these answers to the puzzle of her life, she'd find the rest.

A few minutes later, Owen made eye contact with Willow, tipping his head to the door. She nodded.

He stood and went around the table. "It was nice to see you again, Hettie." He pulled a card from his wallet. "If you remember anything else, I can be reached here."

She took the card and read it. "Okay. Nice to see you too, Owen." She looked at Willow as she got to her feet. "My dear, I hope you find answers. Your mother never should have kept this from you, but I'm certain my friends would've been proud of you."

Willow went to Hettie and hugged her tight. "I'm glad we met and appreciate you taking time to talk me."

"Oh, my dear. I have nothing but time these days." She took Willow's hand and gave it a squeeze. "There's something special about you, just like your mother."

Willow's eyes watered. "Thank you, Hettie. I'll never forget meeting you."

They motioned to the orderly, who came over and rolled Hettie to an elevator. A few steps from the door leading out, the orderly yelled for them to wait.

Hettie waved them over, so they hurried to her chair.

"It's Cooke. Sean Cooke. With an *e*." She beamed. "Everything else on my body is going, but the old noggin never fails me."

"Cooke, with an *e*." Willow wanted to scream her joy, but instead gave Hettie another hug. "You've been a huge help."

"Let me know what you find."

They promised to visit again. As soon as they got outside, Owen took Willow's arm and drew her close. "Are you all right?"

"I think so. In a short amount of time, everything I've ever known as true has changed. Now I know part of the story. My mother's diary said she wouldn't tell Sean about the pregnancy for some reason, but did he suspect?"

"Only one person can tell us."

She nodded. "Sean Cooke."

"We can check on the internet for his name."

We. Owen had joined her crusade. She stared into his serious, dark eyes. "Your help with this is immeasurable, Owen. It's been a rough couple of years. These are the first signs that maybe my luck has changed."

"Why have you had a bad time?"

"It's hard to know where to begin. For starters, I'm the founder and CEO of a weight-loss company and..." She let go of his hand waved hers in front of her body. "My weight gain has become an issue." Her cheeks burned with the confession. "And—"

"Your weight is perfect. Stop talking like that. You're special, like Hettie said."

She wanted to believe it. Wanted to believe this handsome man found her beautiful, even perfect. But she didn't. His intense gaze scrutinized her, making it hard to confess the messy state of her life.

She trusted Owen, though. "How about we get in the car and start back to Bitton? I'll tell you all about my shitty year while you drive."

* * * *

"After the pizza incident, the board members publicly announced they may fire me." Willow's voice cracked.

For the first time, Owen spotted weakness in Willow's stoic exterior. Not when she disclosed her husband's infidelity or public belittlement. Not when she discussed the theft of both company and personal funds. Only every single time she mentioned her weight, her cheeks flushed and her voice lost its usual confidence.

Owen glanced her way. "Was the pizza worth it?" He grinned, hoping she'd smile. "I mean, there's nothing like good pizza."

She blurted out a laugh. "You know, it was a damn good slice."

He soaked in her joy momentarily before she returned to that practical and straightforward woman he'd met a short time ago.

"The night the pizza debacle aired, I had to do something. I went looking for an old bank passbook, figuring I could use the money to go to a spa where I might lose this weight. Then maybe, just maybe, the board would let me stay. I found the money—all I have. Funny. Years ago, I'd been too upset to look at my mother's belongings, but never did I dream there'd be a will from her parents. Finding I owned this house changed everything."

Owen swallowed back his shame. His first impression from the company website made him believe she owned a fortune. But she'd lost not only her money, but so much more. He felt sorrier for her than he did himself.

His silly plan to encourage her keep the property in England had busted wide open. He'd been a fool. A selfish fool. At least she didn't know what he'd been up to.

He glanced to the passenger's seat. "The sale of this house, then, will help you get back on your feet."

"Yes." She stared out her window. "And walking Cotswold Way alone may seem illogical to you. Maybe it is." She shifted in the seat and turned to face him. "But doing so just feels necessary. My gut is just telling me to do it. I—I need to feel strong again. Walking those hundred miles, it just might do the trick."

She offered a weak smile, but it traveled to his core. Gut calls meant everything. Owen had trusted his instincts his whole life. Even if it meant losing his father's love. "I understand. But I won't lie. I'll be worried about you out there alone."

The lines of her face softened. "Oh, Owen. That is so kind." She reached over and rested her hand over the top of his, sitting on the gearshift. "I appreciate your worrying, though."

He stopped at a traffic light, where he turned and stared into her pretty eyes. Determined eyes. Their intensity so powerful he willed them to give him strength, too. If she could do this, why didn't he feel strong enough to keep his daughter protected and happy? No matter where they lived?

"Then alone on the trail it is. How about I give you a few tips so you can gear up for it properly?"

"Tips would be fantastic. Hold on." She moved her hand to go into her purse, leaving him already missing her warmth. She withdrew a small pad and pen. "Okay, what are they?"

Owen talked about the terrain, footwear, finding a good walking stick, and more. More than anything, he wanted her to have this success and would do everything to make it happen. But that didn't change his own need to keep track of her on the walk. If not for her, for his own peace of mind.

Chapter 16

Owen pulled into his former in-laws' short driveway, cut the engine, and got of the car. On his way to the door of the detached brick house, he got lost in thoughts of his duplicity. His hidden agenda to convince Willow to keep the house made him a real cad.

Before he could knock, Bea pulled open the door. "I heard you pull in. Figured we could spare ourselves Henry's excitement over the doorbell ringing. Come on into the kitchen. I've something about to come out of the oven."

He stepped inside. "Smells good. Cookies?"

She nodded as she walked down the short hallway to the kitchen. "Jilly wanted some."

Owen followed her, stopping at the opening to the bright galley kitchen.

"How was the trip to Bristol?" Bea removed a tray from the oven and set it on the stovetop. "Did Willow learn anything new?"

"She did. Seems Hettie had been close to Willow's grandparents. She was able to share some wonderful stories about them." Earlier, he'd told Bea how Willow wanted to talk to her grandmother's friend, but it didn't seem right to divulge the more personal reasons behind the venture. "Thanks for taking Jilly. Where is she?"

"Upstairs watching a show in the guest bedroom. She played outside earlier but it started to sprinkle." Bea glanced to the window over the sink as she took a plate from a cabinet and put it on the creamy marble countertop. "Now it's stopped. Weird weather day." She grabbed a spatula, slipped it under a cookie, and plated it. "Everything okay? You've got that look."

"I have a look?"

Bea paused and tilted her head. "Well, yes. You just get—well, you're missing that relaxed glow we're used to seeing."

Owen leaned against the counter. "You're not wrong. I do have something on my mind." He stole a hot cookie off the plate and warm chocolate burned his fingertips. "I'm in a situation and not sure what to do about it."

"What's the problem?"

He told her about Willow's misfortunes in New York. "In short, I feel horrible about the way I tried to get her to like it here so she wouldn't sell."

"You're too hard on yourself, Owen. You've always been that way. Even when Tracey told you she wanted a divorce, you blamed yourself." Sadness flashed in her tired eyes. It struck him how Bea always looked tired since Tracey died. "We both know it was my daughter's problems that broke things down between you."

"Maybe. I think we both played a role in it." Even as the marriage ended, he wondered if he'd tried hard enough. Tracey never made it easy, though. "Still, this thing I've done to Willow just feels wrong. My motives were so calculating."

"Don't be ridiculous." She finished plating the cookies, and glanced his way. "You're not calculating."

"Normally, I'm not. But this time I may have been." He blew out a heavy sigh. "Willow's had a terribly rough time and here I was, only thinking about myself."

"No. You were thinking about your daughter." She dumped the cookie sheet in the sink and turned back to him. "Big difference."

"It's a gray area, Bea." An urge came over him to tell Bea the real reason his actions bothered him. "Fact is, there's something about Willow I just can't shake."

Bea smiled gently. "Yes. When I walked in on you two dancing to Sinatra I could tell."

Heat brushed Owen's cheeks. He dropped his gaze to the white-tiled floor and rubbed the back of his neck.

"Guess you caught us." He glanced up. "Willow is smart. Feisty, but not over the top, and plain fun to be around. I swear, she lives and breathes courage."

"And she's pretty."

He laughed. "Yeah, I kind of noticed."

"Good. I'm glad you did." She touched his arm. "Ask her out on a date. Go enjoy yourself. I haven't seen you do much for yourself since you came back to town."

A true statement. He'd dated plenty of women during his travels, but since returning here, his focus had been Jilly. He patted Bea's hand. "Maybe I will."

"Good." She turned to the sink and began to clean. "Now that you know her, why don't you tell her the truth about the cottage and what it means to you? Willow adores Jilly. Maybe Willow can find a way to make it work so you don't have to leave, but she can still get what she needs. Explain how you're short on cash, that you invested in your business and how, until it starts showing a profit, you're just strapped for cash."

"No way." He pushed away from the counter and paced the small kitchen. "I can't guilt her into accepting less for the property." He went to Bea's side near the sink. "She needs every cent she can get."

He stared out into the back yard, wracking his brain to find a way to solve both their problems that didn't leave a pit in his gut. "I'll have to find a place to live that fits in my limited budget. And if we can't keep the dog, then we can't keep him."

"What?" Jilly's quiet voice came from the doorway. That second, Henry darted into the kitchen and ran to Owen.

Owen ignored the excited dog, his mind racing to backtrack whatever Jilly might have heard.

Bea's face went ashen, but somehow she managed a smile. "All done with your show, honey?"

"Yes." Jilly approached Owen, her frown deepening each passing second. "We're moving?"

Lie to her. Lie!

Words got stuck in his throat. The truth sat on one shoulder, poking him with a reminder of the inevitable. On the other side sat a lie, short-term an easier way out. Honesty mattered, though. An important trait he wanted to teach his daughter.

He crouched down and took her by the shoulders. "There's a chance we may have to, sweetheart. If Willow sells her property, our cottage is part of it and will go to the new owner."

"But you said we might have to get rid of Henry." Her lower lip quivered, matching the shaking in his gut. "I—I don't want to."

"Neither do I, honey, but not all places take dogs."

Tears spilled down Jilly's cheeks. Owen hugged her and mentally beat himself up over every decision he'd made since returning here. Dumping his savings in a new business had been impulsive. Selfish. All to avoid Dad's offer of work.

Jilly sobbed louder, a sound that sliced right through his heart. Honesty stank.

"Baby, I will do everything I can to keep Henry. Please. Don't cry." He brushed away some wetness on her soft cheek.

The sobs stopped, but the tears didn't. "But—but Willow." Sniff. Sniff. "She's my friend. Can't we ask her not to sell it so we can stay?"

Her glistening eyes showed signs of hope, their power piercing his heart. "Sweetheart, I can't do that to Willow. She's..." He paused and searched for the right words to frame this so a six-year-old would understand. "Willow has problems and needs money very badly."

"But, Daddy, she loves Henry and me."

Owen swallowed the big, fat lump in his throat. "Listen to me, Jilly. Daddy promises to find us a place to live. I'll do everything possible to include Henry in our arrangement. Okay?"

She stared at the floor, nodding as a stray tear rolled along her cheek.

"You have to make me a promise. Can you?"

"Yes," she said quietly, still avoiding his eyes.

"Look at me, Jilly."

She lifted her glistening eyes.

"You cannot ever tell Willow what you just heard."

"Why not?"

"Because..." He drew in a breath. "It isn't fair to her. She does care about you, and Henry. But we cannot make Willow feel bad about selling this place. It belongs to her and..." He drew in a breath, calculating the impact of his explanation. "Basically, she let us borrow it for a while. Now we might have to return the cottage. We *will* be okay. Do you understand?"

He waited, and she finally quietly said, "Yes. I don't want to make Willow feel bad."

"Good. Then we keep this secret and do everything to make Willow happy while she's here."

"I will."

Owen pulled her close and hugged her tightly, with every bit of love he possessed for her.

Henry slipped in between them and began licking Jilly's cheek. His daughter giggled, easing the tension in the room. But it didn't lift Owen's pain over possibly disappointing her.

When the dog settled down, Owen took Jilly's hand. "Just remember, I always love you and am going to make sure this works out for us."

About time he asked his dad for some part-time work. The idea sank into his gut like the liver his mother used to make him eat, but this kid's happiness meant everything.

Henry put his paws on the counter to sniff the cookie plate. Jilly let go of Owen's hand and went to the dog, gently tugging his collar to get him down. A little boss lady at such a young age, but she already showed an ability with dogs.

Owen stood. "Jilly-bean, go pack your stuff. Time for us to head home."

As she ran upstairs with Henry bringing up the rear, not a trace of upset showed on her sweet face.

* * * *

Willow pedaled to the front of Rory's Pub, enjoying the crisp scent of fall in the air and a gentle breeze on her skin. If only she'd opened the storage space beneath the staircase when she first arrived, she'd have had seen this bike sooner. A little polish, air in the tires, and voilà! Easy transportation to get around town.

This morning at the house was her most unproductive to date. She'd been too excited to think straight after yesterday's visit with Hettie. Instead of packing or cleaning, she selected a painting by her grandfather to bring to Hettie as a gift when she went back to visit, as Owen had promised they would. She'd discovered the locations on the back of each painting and made a list of the places to incorporate them into her journey.

She hopped off the bike and searched the street for a bike rack. With none found, she surveyed the relatively quiet streets, opting to lean it against the pub's exterior wall, not too far away from the door. This quiet, friendly town didn't exactly seem crime ridden.

She entered the pub, pausing a second to let her eyes adjust from the bright sun.

"Willow!"

Bonnie waved from the bar, where several customers sat on stools and a sporting event blared on the television stationed on the wall.

Bonnie grabbed a menu and approached.

"Hi there." Willow smiled, happy to be remembered. "Nice to see you again."

"You, too. Here to join us for lunch?"

"Yes. The food here is delicious."

"Wonderful. The bar or a table?"

The tables were empty except for one couple near the fireplace. "The bar is fine." She walked over and slipped on a stool a few seats away from the others.

Bonnie placed a menu in front of her and went behind the mahogany bar. "How's the house cleanup coming along?"

"I'm slowly getting there."

"Good for you. Drink?"

"I'll have a beer."

Bonnie nodded and glanced to her side. "Take a look." She patted the menu. "Back in a sec."

Willow studied the menu, selecting the pizza in spite of the bad karma from her last slice.

While she waited for Bonnie, she looked over her notes on locations to visit during her upcoming hike. When Bonnie returned, Willow ordered. She'd been eating anything she wanted on this trip, but her clothes fit the same. Perhaps obsessing about her recent weight gain sabotaged her efforts to lose it.

A minute later, Bonnie placed a beer in front of her. Lowering her voice, she tipped her head to the right. "That woman sitting down there, she's an estate agent. You might want to talk to her about your place, find out what it's worth."

"That's a great idea. I'd planned on searching for one soon. Thanks."

"Gotta look out for our repeat customers." Bonnie winked and walked off.

Willow considered going over to the woman, but didn't want to interrupt while she finished her lunch. Instead, Willow sipped her beer and tried to focus on a map of the Cotswold Way. Her eyes kept drifting to the realtor. A conversation with her would bring her one step closer to getting the house listed.

The excited buzz over things actually coming together didn't last long. Listing the home also meant the end of her visit.

Her newly blossoming heart wilted. She'd found joy these past weeks. England meant family, people she didn't know but somehow innately believed she would like. Heck, everyone in this country seemed friendly. Then there was Owen. Sweet Owen. Handsome Owen. Who had more faith in her than she did herself. And Jilly, a little ray of sunshine, whose conversation and energy made the minutes together both fun and meaningful. She'd miss them both greatly.

A few minutes later, the men at the end of the bar cheered and Willow glanced in their direction. The estate agent waved and smiled. As Willow returned the greeting, the woman rose from her seat and came over.

"Hello. Bonnie tells me you're renovating the empty house down the road."

"Yes, I am."

Sticking out a hand, the middle-aged brunette smiled. "I'm Hope Jenson. Bath Realty."

"Willow Armstrong." She liked Hope's firm grip as they shook, a sign she had backbone. Dressed in simple fitted trousers, tucked-in white blouse, and navy blazer, she looked and acted professional.

"Do you mind if we talk a little about your place?"

"Not at all."

"How is it you own the house? It's been empty for years."

Willow told her about her grandparents' will. "The place needs work, but I'm in the process of updating the electric and plumbing."

"That's a plus. That house might sell to a single owner, but developers love places like this. They often turn them into a multi-owner dwellings. If you're interested, I can swing by to take a look at the place."

"I'd love that." A professional eye on the place. Exactly the boost Willow needed after uncovering one problem after another since her arrival.

"When I finish here, I have an hour to spare before another appointment. Or we could do another day."

"Today's perfect."

They kept each other company while finishing up their food. Forty minutes later, she tossed her bike in Hope's back seat and they drove over. As they finished a tour and headed down the main staircase to the first level, Hope nodded her approval.

"This place will be quite profitable for you, Willow. It has character and lots of room for many options." Bonnie stepped into the foyer and they faced each other. "The figures you've been quoted could be on the low side. I'll check a few comparative sales, and stop by to see the cottage when the current tenant agrees. If it's in decent shape, it'll yield you even more money. Would you be interested in listing with me?"

Willow stuck out her hand. "Absolutely."

Hope made a few suggestions for things to do before showing to potential customers, gave Willow her card, and said she'd be in touch.

Everything Willow hoped might happen when she'd boarded that plane at JFK looked like it would come true. Solving one of her problems, at least.

* * * *

"Hello, Sunshine." Owen's lively voice traveled through the B and B's phone.

"Hi. What a surprise." Willow leaned on the reception desk. "Why didn't you call my phone?"

"Edna called me. She has a couple who want to get on a tour tomorrow. When we finished business, I asked if I could talk to you."

"I see. Did you have a good day?" Today's full tour schedule had kept Owen busy from morning until dinnertime, and she'd found herself missing him.

Edna glanced over from the other side of the desk and smiled. A knowing expression that made Willow blush. Edna gathered the mail and walked down the hall toward the kitchen, leaving Willow thankful for some privacy.

"A long one," said Owen. "I'm going to bed soon. I forgot to ask on the way back from Bristol—can you handle one more dance lesson tomorrow night?"

"I need a lesson? Even after my superb performance at the nursing home yesterday? I thought I did pretty well."

"You did," he said right away, and his voice dipped into a huskier tone. "Maybe I just want to see you again."

Her belly warmed as her head fumbled for a response. "Oh, well in that case, a dance lesson sounds great." Oh, God. She would never master the fine art of flirting.

"Plan on eating dinner here, too. How was your day?"

"Busy. I found a bike at the house, cleaned it up, and treated myself to lunch at Rory's. Now you don't have to drive me everywhere."

"Who says I mind?"

"I just don't like to impose all the time. I'll still nag you for the occasional ride."

"Good. Hey, before I forget. My mate with the truck said he can swing by tomorrow to help us get rid of the old fridge. Does around noon work?"

"Definitely."

"Also, Hettie called me. She remembered hearing from someone at church a while back that Sean Cooke resettled in Painswick. I figured it's a place to start."

"Painswick? I'm almost certain my granddad did a painting from that town. Is it along the Cotswold Way?"

"I believe so."

"What a coincidence. Maybe I'll find Sean on my walk. It's like I'm meant to follow that path. Don't you think?"

"I wouldn't read too much into it."

"Well, I am. I've been mapping out some locations along the trail, based on the paintings in the attic. Painswick will definitely be a stop. Speaking of which, any chance I can take you out to lunch tomorrow after we load the refrigerator? I want to pay you back for taking me to see Hettie."

"You don't have to, Rosebud. I'm happy to help."

"I want to. Besides, I figured, if you don't mind, you could help me plan my route, since you have some experience in doing this."

"Sure." His tone held a smile. "I'd be happy to."

"Oh, guess who I met at Rory's today?"

"The queen?"

She chuffed a laugh. "No, but wouldn't you be shocked if I said yes."

"Blimey, I'd call the press."

She laughed. "I met Hope Jenson, a real estate agent. Have you heard of her?"

"Yup. I know Hope."

"She came by the house to give me an estimate and thinks I can easily get the price I'd been hoping for on the house. She'd like to look at the cottage, but I told her we needed you to agree on the time."

"Oh. Anytime is fine." His tone shifted, a bit stiff.

She'd seen this reaction before, always at the mention of her selling the cottage. Of course he'd worry. He had a daughter under his roof. "You know, Owen, I'll make sure I negotiate a deal that gives you plenty of time to find and move into a new place."

"I appreciate it, but don't you worry about us." His mood shifted, back to the upbeat tone he usually carried. "What did Hope think of the house?"

Maybe he didn't have any issues with moving and she'd imagined it. "As a matter of fact, she gave me some suggestions on a few simple, cheap updating tips to make it more appealing. I'm going to make a run to the DIY store soon."

"Well, you can't do that on your bicycle. I'm certain Bea's headed that way in the morning. Why don't I give her a ring, see if she minds some company? Around eleven she's swinging by the cottage to let the dog out. She won't have to go out of her way to pick you up. So, Rosebud..." He cleared his throat, almost sounding nervous. "I know it's last minute, but would you like to be my date for the Austen Festival ball? Then afterward, maybe we can go out and have a late supper."

"Oh, yes. I'd love to."

Jilly's sleepy voice yelled for him in the background. He sighed. "Hold on, honey." In his normal voice, he said, "I'd better run. Talk with you tomorrow."

As she hung up, she could feel the smile on her face. A date. Her first in a while, but knowing she'd have it with Owen made the outing all the more sweet.

She went over and sat at the small desk in the lobby holding a computer left on for guests. After typing in *Sean Cooke, Painswick* she hit Enter and held her breath. One listing appeared under Cooke's Foreign Car Repair, located on New Street. *Free collection and delivery. General Repairs and Servings. Member of Good Garage Scheme.*

She tried to imagine him, an older version of the confident young man in the photo. By next week at this time, maybe her guessing would be over. The elements of her life, once a puzzle with barely any pieces, were finally beginning to take form. So what if it took this long to happen?

Chapter 17

Willow lifted the roller from the tray of buttery yellow paint and stretched on tiptoes to reach the upper kitchen wall. She swept her arm with care, slowly spreading gorgeous rays of sunshine on the tired walls, lending them new life.

Hope had been right. Fresh paint spruced up the room.

Jilly's voice carried from the foyer, where Willow had left the door open for her. "I'm here."

"In the kitchen."

Jilly's fast footsteps echoed through the house and stopped when she reached the kitchen.

Willow glanced back over her shoulder. "What do you think?"

Jilly eyes went wide. "Pretty!"

"I think so, too."

When Willow had extended the invite for Jilly to come over and help paint, Bea had warned her that Jilly's help might cause more mess than assistance. Besides dirty sneakers, Jilly wore black leggings ripped near the knee, and an oxford shirt that fell to her calves, the sleeves rolled multiple times, leaving only her small hands sticking out. Good preparation for any paint mishaps.

"Yellow is my favorite color." Jilly came over and stood on near some newspapers, inches away from the paint can lid.

"I love it too." Willow lowered her brush and took Jilly's hand, guiding her away from disaster. "Come see what I bought for you."

"You got me something?"

"Yup." She kneeled on the floor and went inside the bag from the store.

"Nan said painting is messy work and made me wear one of Daddy's old shirts. At least, she hoped it was old."

Willow laughed. "It will be when we're done." She pulled out the small roller brush. "Here you are. This is your very own brush. Here's what we're going to do this afternoon. See this wall? I outlined it, almost like a coloring book."

Jilly nodded, her brows set in deep concentration.

"Now we've got to fill in the rest of the space, like this." Willow showed her how to dip the brush, ushered her to the wall, and demonstrated how to make strokes. "What do you think? Can you do that?"

"Watch." Jilly did what she'd been shown perfectly.

"You're a pro." A big beam spread across Jilly's face. "Now let me get mine."

They worked side by side and talked about having their dance lessons again tonight.

"You did very well last time," Jilly said in that grown-up voice of hers that made Willow's heart smile. "Even Daddy said so."

Willow must've come across as so insecure even a six-year-old felt a need to boost her self-esteem. So much for being a good role model. "I'm not usually so afraid of new things, but dancing just isn't my thing."

"But you did try. Nan says you should always at least try," she said matter-of-factly and returned to painting.

"Nan's right. I can learn from both of you. Hey, where's Henry?"

Jilly dropped her arm to her side, getting a blob of paint on the shirt's tail. "Nan wouldn't let him come. She said he's a busy bee and would probably make it hard for us to work."

"I love Henry, but she's probably right. Sometimes grandmothers know best."

Not that Willow would know, but standing in the kitchen of her own grandmother, she figured it was good karma to say so.

"Daddy took you to Bristol yesterday?"

Willow glanced over and a dot of paint had landed on Jilly's cheek. "Yup. He did."

"Did you have fun?"

"We always do. Your father is the best company."

"He makes me laugh." Jilly smiled and walked to the paint tray, dipped her roller in the pan, and returned to the wall, letting bits of it drip on the tarp.

Willow stopped painting and grabbed a cloth to wipe the mess, before someone stepped in it and left footprints all over the house.

After a few swipes of the roller, Jilly turned to Willow. "Are we painting in here because you want to sell the house?"

"Yes." Willow got on her knees and wiped. "An estate agent said people who might buy the house would like it better if I painted a few rooms."

Jilly lowered her brush. "But why don't you move in?"

"Well, I live somewhere else, sweetie. The whole reason I came over from America was to see the house and get it ready to sell."

Before she could tell her about the plans to keep in touch, she turned to see Jilly's face scrunched into a sad mess and tears flowing down her cheeks.

Willow dropped the cloth and scrambled on her knees to Jilly's side. "What's wrong?"

"I don't want you to leave."

She put her hands on Jilly's shoulders. "Look at me, sweetheart."

Jilly stared at the ground, her lower lip quivering.

Willow had to make this right. "I'm going to make you a promise. Even after I move, the two of us will still be friends. We can write letters, send cards. We can talk over the computer using Skype." Who was she kidding? She'd miss this place, too. "Maybe I'll even visit here again one day."

Jilly's willpower broke with a loud wail and her tears spilled in a downpour. Willow drew her closer and hugged with all her might.

A moment passed and Jilly leaned back. "But…" She gulped more air. "But, you won't be able to find me."

"Of course I will. Why would you say that?"

"Because, Daddy said if you sold the house…" Jilly paused to draw in a breath and let out a whimper. "He said we have to move." She sniffed. "…and because of buying his business, he doesn't have much money… and…and…" The faucet of tears went full pressure.

"And what, sweetheart?"

"Henry might have to live somewhere else."

"What? No!"

The truth smacked her in the face like a blast of freezing air on a humid August day. While she realized they lived in this cottage, she'd given only a little thought to what impact moving might have on them. Owen had never once said moving would be difficult for them. Especially with a pet and finances.

"Oh Jilly, please don't cry." But she did, each sob breaking Willow's heart into tiny fragments. "Just let me think."

Jilly dragged the back of her hand across her dripping nose. "And now I'm going to get in trouble."

"Why?"

"Because I wasn't supposed to tell you. Daddy said so."

"He didn't want me to know?"

She shook her head. "He said it wasn't fair to you to know his problems."

Of course. Just like Owen to hide his own problems. All the times he'd reacted strangely had happened while discussing the cottage sale. No doubt worried about moving his daughter.

Willow felt horrible. Did she wear blinders, so worried about herself she'd forget about those in the path of her goal? And Henry. The idea of Henry anyplace but with them crushed Willow's chest. The poor dog, he wouldn't understand why he'd been separated from the people he loved.

No. Willow couldn't live with herself if they had to get rid of the dog. Jilly needed him. And she needed to stay in this cottage. A place where her mother's memories were everywhere.

Willow placed a finger under Jilly's chin and tilted it up. "Don't you worry about anything. I won't tell your dad what you told me."

Her lower lip bowed. "But that's lying."

"Yes, well, I don't want to lie. But I need to think about what I can do. Let's keep this quiet from your dad while I try to come up with a solution. I promise to do everything I can to make this all right." She hoped she could.

Jilly's frown slowly but surely flipped right side up, her smile stealing a little piece of Willow's heart. The promise she'd made to this little girl suddenly meant everything.

* * * *

"One, two, three...." Owen stood across from Willow, moving to the dance and holding his breath that she'd finish these last steps successfully. When she did, pride swelling inside him made him yell, "Perfect! You're smashing it!"

Jilly and Bea sat on the sofa, clapping and yelling, "Brava! Brava!"

Willow dramatically tossed back her golden hair and held her chin high, like a diva taking in the applause of fans. "I'd like to thank the academy of motion pictures and my first, and only dance teacher, Owen Hughes. Who only suffered two broken toes to help me reach my dream of dancing at the Jane Austen Regency Ball."

She curtsied, holding the flowing hem of a mini dress that had belonged to her mother and now served as Willow's shirt. A psychedelic print with large belled sleeves that she wore with gray leggings and white sneakers.

Owen loved the carefree way she wore the unusual outfit, and found her adorable. A fact he couldn't deny if he tried.

Bea rose from the sofa and took Jilly's hand. "Come on. Time for sweets. We need them after that workout."

"I'll move the furniture back in place." Owen went to the sofa, still smiling from the way Willow hammed it up a bit. He sensed she often held back, strangely confident and lacking confidence at the same time.

"I'll help." Willow made her way to the other end, leaning over as she grabbed the end and exposing a little peek at her slightly exposed cleavage. He glanced up and she watched him, making his neck get all hot. How did she have this effect on him?

"Ready?" They lifted together and returned the sofa to its usual location in front of the fireplace.

Henry scratched at the door. Owen glanced at Willow. "Want to join me while I take him for a short walk?"

"Sure."

He yelled, "Back in a sec, Bea. We're walking Henry."

Jilly yelled from the other room. "Can I—"

"Shhh," Bea said. "You stay and help me."

Thank you, Bea. He wanted a few minutes alone with Willow. How did single parents ever find time for romance?

"Come on, Henry." Owen patted his leg and the dog followed them out the door.

The second he stepped outside, the chilly mid-September night air blasted him. "Hold on."

He jogged to his van, took out a zippered sweatshirt, and returned to her side, holding it open. "Put this on."

She slipped her arms into the sleeves that dangled to her thighs. She laughed and pushed them up so they bunched at her forearm.

"Thank you." The full moon made it bright enough to see her smile. "You're every bit the gentleman, Owen Hughes. In case you didn't know it."

"Anything for you, m'lady." He bowed, and remembered Tracey whispering in his ear. *You're too nice, Owen. Too damn nice.* "Is that a good thing?"

She tilted her head. "Heck yeah. Has someone told you it isn't?"

"Once." They started to walk. He was just about to whistle for the dog when Henry shot out of the woods ahead of them. "Women are complicated."

She drew the sides of the sweatshirt together, keeping it closed by folding her arms across her chest. "We can be."

"I think you are, too." He glanced her way, happy to see her smile.

"Oh, I know I am."

"But you are in a way that leaves me wanting to know more."

"To be honest, I find myself curious about you, too."

"Do you now?" He kicked a small rock off the path. "Some people think I'm an open book."

"Then they aren't watching close enough. Can I ask you a question?"

"Shoot."

"If I sell this place, where will you and Jilly live?"

"We'll figure something out. Why?"

She stopped and turned to him. "Because the visit from the estate agent got me thinking about it."

He didn't believe her. This morning at breakfast, Jilly still talked about what she'd overheard and Bea said his daughter had spent the afternoon with Willow. "You sure that's the reason?"

She resumed walking so he followed at her side. Finally she drew in a deep breath. "It's one of the reasons. The other is because of a confidence I won't break."

Yes. Jilly must've broken down, but Willow had stuck by her. "Loyalty is a quality I admire in a woman."

A hint of smile crossed her lips. "And honesty is a quality I admire in a man."

"Ouch. So it's the truth you seek?"

She nodded.

He drew in a breath. "Truth is…I'm a little worried about you selling this place. The cottage is the only house Jilly's ever known. She's been worried about moving ever since she lost her mum."

"It's understandable."

"I had to take her to a therapist for a while."

"Oh." Willow frowned. "I'm sorry. I had no idea."

"How could you? I never told you." He dug deep for strength to share this next half. How would she feel about a man who struggled financially? "Because of that, I was happy to take the job as caretaker. But I had other reasons. At the time, I spent my savings on buying a franchise with Wanderlust Excursion. Living in the cottage solved my money problems while I waited for my business to start turning a profit."

He exhaled. The truth was out. Without waiting for a response, he put his hand on her back and whistled for the dog. "Let's head back."

She allowed him to guide her and they started their return. He held his breath waiting for a response.

She finally said, "It makes sense you'd want to stay here. I appreciate your honesty."

His tense shoulders relaxed. Her answer showed no judgment for the state of his personal affairs. "Seems my reputation depended on it." She laughed. "I'm a ruthless businesswoman who demands the truth. What more can I say?"

He shook his head. "A businesswoman, yes. Ruthless, no. Listen, I meant what I said. This is your property to do with as you want." He swallowed, already feeling like an idiot for his next words. "I have a confession."

"Uh-oh."

He sucked in a breath. "When I took you sightseeing, I sort of hoped you'd fall in love with the Cotswolds, Stonehenge, the whole area. I figured if you did, you might decide to keep the house. It was a ridiculous and selfish move on my part."

"So you were trying to trick me?"

"In an idiotic way." He stopped and took her by the shoulders. "That day, what started as a half-assed plan with ulterior motives ended up being a wonderful day with you. Far better than I'd expected."

She frowned. "Because you didn't want to be with me?"

"God, no! You were the best part of it as we set out. The sights around here have grown tiresome for me."

"I'd never have known you were tired of it here. You talk very passionately, like you feel something for what you are discussing."

"My theater background comes in handy as a tour guide. Who'd want to go on a tour with a guide who doesn't show interest?"

She nodded. "So you're faking it, but you'd rather be traveling the world?"

Would he? "Initially, yes. But by leaving my tour director job around Europe and coming back here permanently, I realized how much I'd been missing of Jilly's life by being away so much. Sadly, it took her mother's passing for me to realize it."

"Why do you dislike it here? It's beautiful. I know I'll miss this place when I leave."

"Personal reasons."

"Like…"

"I told you about my dad. I left decades ago because of him."

The dog flew out of the woods and ran over to Willow. After an obligatory pet, he ran ahead of them. They resumed walking.

She bumped his shoulder with hers. "Kind of ironic, huh?"

"What's that?"

"I'm looking for my father, while you have one and it isn't always perfect."

Her words sank in. Some would call him ungrateful. Maybe he was. "I suppose I could work a little harder at trying to understand him instead of always arguing."

She shrugged. "Perhaps. Or maybe you are justified. It's something to think about."

He'd never discussed this part of his life with anybody, let alone a woman he barely knew. Telling her his innermost thoughts came easily. It had since that minute they sat together on the train.

They resumed walking, each silent. Henry darted into the dense woods along the path. Owen reached over and took Willow's hand. She glanced over and smiled, settling at his side and walking comfortably. As if they'd done this a thousand times.

A rabbit hopped out from the woods and they stopped. A split second later, Henry screamed his battle cry and shot out from the woods and brushed against Willow's legs. Her footing wavered, but Owen reached out and grabbed her by the elbow and steadied her.

"Sorry about him."

"It's okay. After all, it was a rabbit."

They both laughed. He kept his hand on her elbow and drew her close. "Remember our Frank Sinatra dance?"

"I'll never forget."

He slipped a hand around her back, drawing her close and humming the song. As her arm fell to his shoulder, he moved her on the path to the music tempo.

She stared into his eyes, and he got so lost in the way they glistened from the moonlight, he almost took a misstep.

Her voice softened. "I like dancing with you. You make me feel comfortable."

"You do the same for me."

"You mean it?" She smiled.

"Do I joke around?"

Her smile vanished and her hand drifted to the back of his neck, where she softly massaged his nape. "All the time."

He stopped dancing. Lifting his hand, he brushed away a strand of hair near her temple and slowly ran his finger along her cheek, her skin every bit as soft as he'd imagined.

Her gaze locked on his and he wandered, lost in their sparkle, mesmerizing as the stars above. He tilted her chin up, wanting to feel her mouth on his. He pressed his lips to hers, finding them soft, eager.

A rustle in the woods that turned out to be Henry broke the kiss, but Owen didn't step away. Some part of him wanted to hold her like this forever.

Chapter 18

Owen pressed the phone closer to his ear, trying to ignore Margo as she stood in the doorway of his office waving her arms. God, she could be the most impatient woman in the world. "Yes, Mr. Como. I'm certain we can accommodate your group tour needs."

Barely a second passed before she marched over to his desk, grabbed a pad, and wrote something then pushed the note in front of him.

It's important!!

"Could I ask you to hold for a moment?" He pushed the hold button on his desk phone. "What's the matter, Margo?"

"There's an emergency. Your mum is on line two."

His blood ran cold, and he quickly explained to the prospective client he had to go, promising to call back. He pushed the other line. "Mum, what's wrong?"

"Thank God I reached you." The trembling in her voice set Owen's gut on edge. "It's your father. He's at Royal United Hospital."

"The hospital? What happened? Will he be all right?"

"They think it's his heart." Her voice cracked. "I'm waiting for the doctor to learn more."

"I'm leaving the office right now." She gave him the room number. Owen searched his desk drawer for his keys and hung up.

"Will your dad be all right?"

"Don't know anything yet." Owen found the keys, along with his wallet, and grabbed both. "I'll let you know when I do. Can you follow up with each tour that's out and make sure they're on schedule?"

"Will do."

"Thanks." He hurried past Margo and out the office door to his van.

Owen drove, his body numb, his mind turned to practical details. He called Bea to let her know what had happened and make sure she could pick up Jilly from school.

As he sped along the road on autopilot, he grappled with the news. Dad's heart. Owen knew he wouldn't live forever. What if the call had been to say his father had died, that Owen would never have a chance to speak to him again? A swift pain pounded him hard as a sledgehammer to the chest. Guilt. All those stiff conversations. All the tension when they stood in the same room. All the times Owen could've tried harder, but didn't. He pressed the gas pedal and picked up speed.

After parking the van, he rushed into the lobby and took the elevator to his dad's floor. Breathing in the antiseptic-smelling hallway, he said a prayer the old man would be okay. At the room number his mother had given him, Owen paused to inhale deeply before entering.

Dad lay with eyes closed on bleached white hospital sheets, a tube running from his arm to a drip and an electric monitor flashing digital readings.

Across the room, his younger brother stood looking out the window, rubbing the back of his neck. His dirty jeans and wrinkled T-shirt hinted that Graham had come straight from work as well.

Owen went over and gave his brother a hug.

Graham let go, shaking his head, a pained stare on his boyish face. "I'm glad you're here."

"What happened?"

Graham's eyes teared and his Adam's apple rolled along his throat. "Dad passed out at our job site."

"Oh bugger that!" Owen's father grumbled from his bed. "I'm fine. Just needed a little something to eat."

Owen's mother entered carrying a plastic pitcher of water, which she placed on a table near the bed. "Hush, Frank." She tossed an annoyed glare his way, but her tired eyes showed her worry.

Owen hugged his mother, but stopped himself from going to the bed to hug his father. Dad had never been the type for hugs. "Do they know what's wrong?"

"Not yet, but they're worried it might be his heart."

"It isn't a big deal, Ginny," Dad growled, ever the angry bear.

His mother's cheeks blasted bright red and she glared her husband. "Frank Hughes! Don't you say another word."

A rare rise of his mother's voice. One Owen figured—if Dad were smart—he should pay heed to.

She took a deep breath and slowly blew it out. "Now the doctor told you to relax. And it wasn't nothing."

His father pressed his lips tight, then tipped back his head and closed his eyes.

Graham left the window and came over to them. "I'm going to get myself a coffee downstairs. Mum, Owen, can I get you one?"

Both shook their heads and Graham left the room.

Owen's mother collapsed into a chair near the bed. They were getting older. Where they'd need both their sons around to help them. If he hadn't moved home to be with Jilly, he could've been far from here during this crisis. Unable to offer them the immediate support he could today.

He dragged another chair to her side and took her hand. "How did this start?"

"Your father, too damn proud to tell me how he's been feeling, finally confessed to the doctors that he's had shortness of breath, been feeling tired, and lightheaded. Because he passed out, they suspect heart valve problems. They did a chest X-ray as soon as he arrived, but this afternoon they'll do an echocardiography to confirm their findings."

He glanced at his father, lying with his eyes shut again. Every inch of Owen wanted to go sit at his side, share his worry, tell him he'd hate to lose his dad. Hell, if there ever seemed like a time to resist a lifetime of letting his dad dictate the distance of their relationship, it was now.

Yet he didn't. He stayed frozen in his seat, terrified of rejection. Again.

Instead, he turned back to his mother. "And if it's his heart valves, can they fix it?"

She blinked away the wetness in her eyes. "The doctor says if that's it, then yes."

"And if it's not?"

She shrugged. "He didn't say."

Owen stood and went to the window, looking out at the manicured lawns surrounding the hospital. With the snap of a finger, life could change. His father could've died if he'd continued to say nothing. Gone, no longer there to put Owen down. But the idea of Dad no longer being there left a hole inside his chest.

Every fight they'd had through his teenage and college years seemed petty. Stupid things, really, all started because they were alike. Both knew what they loved and had strong opinions about it. Problems came when their likes fell on opposite ends of the spectrum and Dad's resentment over their differences put a wedge between them. Leaving England had allowed

Owen relief from his father's disdain. Relief from the constant reminders that he'd failed the man he'd looked up to as a child.

Today served a dose of reality. The clock of their lives could stop for either one of them any minute. Could they ever get to a better place after a lifetime of separation?

His throat clogged and eyes filled with tears, blurring the view outside. He stayed in that spot to pull himself together.

Once he had, he turned around. "I told the office not to expect me back, so I'll be here all day."

His mother nodded and gave him a sad smile.

Owen slowly walked over and stood by his dad's bedside. Drawing from a force inside of him that always wanted his father's love but never seemed to get it, he rested a hand on his father's shoulder. Still muscular, like Owen remembered from his childhood, but bonier with age.

His father stiffened and his eyes flashed open. "I'll be fine, Owen." He shrugged his shoulder, but Owen kept his hand in place and sat on the edge of the mattress.

He stared at his father. "Now listen to me, you grouchy bastard. Start listening to these doctors and start taking care of yourself."

Dad grumbled and shut his eyes tight, but Owen didn't care. He'd do everything in his power to heal the rift between them, even if it meant swallowing his pride.

* * * *

"Ouch!"

"Sorry, Willow." Edna removed the bobby pin she'd just poked into Willow's scalp. "A hairstylist, I'm not."

"Are you kidding? What you've done is beautiful."

Willow stared at her reflection in the round makeup table mirror. Edna had twisted her hair into a loose bun, leaving soft tendrils to sweep her cheeks. The finishing touch a thin headband of pearl beads, positioned like a crown of jewels.

Edna stood back and studied Willow. "Lovely. Just lovely. Stand up. Let's see it from top to bottom."

Willow rose, gathering the long gown in her hands. She stepped aside from the seat and went to a full-length mirror. As she let go of the light blue brocade fabric, it fell over the petticoat to her feet. While the dress covered more than usual from the waist down, the low scoop neck and back, short puffy sleeves, and snug bodice exposed more of her chest and neck than most of her blouses. Both the skirt bottom and the bodice had a delicate embroidered pattern. She pointed one foot, admiring her silk navy slippers.

This gown empowered her, filling her with a breath of femininity. Locked up inside her but rarely used because she never believed she could pull it off. Right now, she felt dainty, almost light on her feet, despite the heaviness of the dress.

"Do you think I have on enough makeup?" She moved closer to the mirror, studying the mascara, shimmery pink lipstick, and two sweeps of rose-petal-colored rouge.

"It's perfect. Women didn't wear a lot of makeup back then."

Willow stared at her reflection, that of a stranger. The woman before her radiated beauty. Not only outwardly, but giving rise to a new feeling inside of her, as well. The inner voice of judgment, always present with each glimpse in the mirror, had gone silent for once. A new voice emerged, one whispering a phrase she rarely heard. *You look pretty.*

Owen's attention made her feel that way, too. She couldn't wait to see him, although this happy tale would end. One date with a man who lived thousands of miles away from New York wouldn't have any staying power. And yet, nobody could steal from her memory of his tender kiss, a moment that had caused butterflies to stir in her in anticipation of tonight's date.

"Wait'll Owen sees you. He's likely to make sure you never leave town." Edna handed her a pair of long gloves. "You need these, too."

As Willow slipped them over her bare arms, she smiled at Edna. "You look beautiful, too. Has Eddie seen you yet?"

Edna blushed, turning close to the color of her crimson gown. She pushed away the compliment with a wave of her hand. "He's getting ready. After all our years of marriage, I dare say he'll not even notice."

"He'd have to be blind."

"Enough about me. What time is Owen expected?"

"About twenty minutes." She reached down and picked up her phone. "I know this is silly, but can you take a picture of me? Nobody at home will believe I did this."

Edna stuck out her hand. "Are you kidding? You look like you were born wearing those clothes."

"Do you think? I'm strangely comfortable dressed this way."

Edna snapped several photos. Just as Edna handed Willow her phone, Eddie hollered from downstairs. "You ladies almost ready?"

"Yes, dear." Edna pointed to the bed. "Don't forget your reticule."

Willow reached for the beaded drawstring bag Edna had loaned her earlier, used like a purse in the Regency era. "Oh yes. I need a place for my cell phone." Willow laughed. "If that isn't ironic."

Edna smiled politely, like it hadn't been the first time she'd heard that one, and left the room.

Willow picked up the accessory, tossed in her cell phone, and followed Edna downstairs. Eddie sat at the lobby computer desk, typing away while dressed in a short-waisted coat with tails, fitted cream-colored pants, and thin white socks covering his full calves. The marvelous juxtaposition of the modern world and simpler times again made her laugh.

Eddie looked up, his gray brows lifting as they neared. "Well, my oh my. You two look stunning." His gaze rested on his wife. "I'll be the luckiest man there, my dear. Well, me and Owen."

Willow's cell phone rang. She pulled it from her bag. Owen's name appeared on the display. "Hello?"

"Willow, it's Owen."

His serious tone and use of her proper name made her stomach dip. "Everything all right?"

"I had no idea about the time. I'm at the hospital and the doctor came in when I'd started to call you earlier—"

"Hospital?" Her heart stilled. "Are you all right? Is Jilly all right?"

"We are. It's my dad." His voice cracked. "He passed out midmorning. They've been doing tests all day here at Royal United. I wanted to make it tonight, but—"

"Owen, don't be silly. Your father comes first."

"Yes. He does." The sadness in his tone tugged at her heart. "I apologize for calling so late. I just kept debating about what to do, but I can't leave until we speak to the doctor. He hasn't come in yet."

"Don't even worry about me. What's wrong? Why did he pass out?"

"It's his heart. We are told the problem is fixable, so that's the good news. But another physician is stopping by sometime a bit later with more details." He sighed loudly. "God, Willow, I'm so sorry."

"Owen, please don't be sorry. I completely understand. Can I do anything?"

"Yes, please still go. It's an event you really shouldn't miss."

"Of course, I will." Disappointment bubbled inside her chest, but she firmly tamped it down. He must be sick with worry for his father, which made her worry about him. "Call me if you need me."

"I will." His voice softened. "I'll be with you in spirit. If someone asks you to dance, you should. You'll be the best dancer there."

She laughed. "I'm pretty sure you're lying now."

He chuckled, but without his usual pep. "Rosebud, I *will* find a way to make this up to you, I promise."

"There's no need, Owen."

"Hold on." As she waited, low muffled voices sounded in the background before he returned. "The nurse just confirmed the doctor will be here between 8:00 and 9:00, so I'll have more answers then."

"Good. I'll say a prayer for your dad."

They said goodbye and hung up. She explained what happened to Eddie and Edna, who were happy to drive her.

Soon they arrived in Bath. In their search for a parking space, they drove past the ball venue, Guildhall, a Georgian-styled building made of whitish-gray stone and tall palladium windows. Eddie pulled over and let them out to wait while he parked, returning five minutes later from a spot a few blocks away.

He offered them each an arm and they entered the building. Willow stepped into another world, surrounded by folks decked out in Regency attire while music piped in from centuries past filled the air. Even with all the excitement, Owen's dad was never far from her thoughts.

Eddie saw a friend and wandered off, but Edna looped an arm through hers and they kept walking. "Did you know a Georgian or Regency lady couldn't turn down an invitation to dance unless she could claim a previous engagement to dance, or unless she planned to sit out the remaining dances of the evening?"

"No. I didn't. What if she was tired?"

"Then her dancing for the night was done. Of course, we don't do that now."

Edna continued talking about customs of the era while they wandered in a sea of formality. Women in gowns made with silky fabrics, accessorized with pearls, cameos, and jeweled hair clips. Men in tall hats and fitted pants, almost all in short-waisted jackets with long tails.

This spectacular scene revived history, in a way. The history of her mother's people. Willow lifted her chin a bit higher as they neared propped-open double doors leading into the ballroom. Yes, this event was *her* history, too.

Eddie met back up with them as they entered the ballroom. Enormous chandeliers hung from lofty ceilings, casting a subdued light on the mint-colored walls, a sharp contract to dark wood floors. Evergreen molding, carved with an intricate design, outlined the ceiling. Tall windows filled one wall, each one with a smaller circular window above it. She turned in a full circle, taking it all in. Oil paintings galore graced the walls, large canvases of both men and women from the Regency era.

Eddie turned to them. "Shall I get us drinks? White wine okay, ladies?" They both said yes.

He walked off and Edna put a hand on Willow's arm. "So? You're impressed."

"I feel like I've time traveled."

Edna laughed and took her hand. "I see my friends. Let's go over."

Edna guided her to a group of several woman and men, including Kathleen, who'd loaned Willow the dress. She was introduced to the others while a small group of musicians readied their instruments in the far corner.

Her new acquaintances were friendly people, happy Willow could share this night with them. Soon music filled the room. Violin, flute, and piano harmonized to make a beautiful, lively sound, encouraging people onto the dance floor.

Willow watched mostly, simply amazed to be in this setting. She imagined dancing with Owen and sadness took hold, although she heard the disappointment in his voice when he'd called to cancel.

"Willow?" Eddie appeared in front of her. "May I have this dance? Edna says it's one you learned for tonight."

"Oh, yes. I'd love to." Willow took his hand, counting her blessings that she'd stumbled on the kindness of this sweet man and his wife on this trip.

He led her to the dance floor. For once, she put aside her sarcastic, down-putting remarks about herself. Confidence guided her with nary a slipup, and even when she did, Eddie was too much of a gentleman to say a word.

When it finished, she returned to her seat. Owen weighed on her mind. He'd have fit right in here, almost naturally so. She sighed. Family duty called, but she wished for a way to help him.

The music ended. As Edna walked toward her, an idea crossed Willow's mind.

"Whew, I'm exhausted." Edna dropped into the seat beside Willow and kicked off her shoes. "I told Eddie to dance with my friend. I can't keep up with him."

"You two dance so well." Willow's little idea nudged at her, but she debated.

"Well, thank you, but it didn't happen overnight." She fanned herself with her hand. "We took classes."

"They paid off." Willow glanced at her watch. 8:40. Her idea clicked into place.

She turned to Edna. "Where is Royal United Hospital?"

"Right here in Bath."

"Walking distance?"

"A short cab ride, I'd say. Why?"

"I'm worried about Owen. Do you think he'd be happy to see me if I went over to keep him company? It's possible his dad is sleeping by now, but I just want to show Owen some support. He's been such a big help to me, and I want to return the favor."

Edna grinned. "I think Owen would be thrilled to pieces to see you walk through that door. Go. If you need us to pick you up later, call Eddie's cell phone."

Willow retrieved her shawl and reticule. She called for a cab. Five minutes later a driver pulled in front of Guildhall and whisked her off to the hospital.

As she approached the reception desk, she vowed that if anything clued her into this being a bad move, she'd scoot out before Owen saw her.

She found out the room number and headed up to the floor. Heads turned as she walked the hallways, presumably because she dressed as if she'd time traveled here.

Once at the room, she stood outside. A television mounted high on the wall cast a shadowy glow in the dimly lit room. Owen sat in a chair, his gaze trained on the floor, his brow furrowed. Maybe the news hadn't been good. Her motives to visit suddenly seemed selfish. She'd leave, before he saw her.

That second, he glanced out into the hallway and their eyes met.

* * * *

Owen blinked, certain he'd fallen asleep and only dreamed about the gorgeous vision in the hallway. She smiled and waved. He straightened in his seat. "Willow?"

She moved to the door threshold and whispered, "Is it a bad time?"

"No. Not at all." He'd just been thinking of her, wishing he'd been able to go tonight. Spotting her, his wishes had come true. "Hold on."

He stepped behind the curtain to where his mother sat at his father's side watching the TV. "Be right back."

She nodded.

Owen found Willow away from the door, pacing the hallway. He hurried over to her and took her hands. "Why aren't you at the ball?"

"I had fun for a while, but couldn't stop thinking about you."

"Me?"

She frowned. "Yes. This must be stressful. I could go get you some dinner, or help with Jilly."

His heart swelled. When had someone last cared about him? Every single relationship he'd ever had, he'd been the giver. Giving until it hurt, asking for little in return.

He held out her arms. "You, in that dress." Her lovely curves filled out the bodice and the gown color accented the hues of her gorgeous blue eyes. "I thought I was dreaming."

"Dreaming?" She laughed. "Now don't go…" Willow paused, lifted her chin. "You know, I feel pretty great tonight."

"Good because, by God, you shine."

Her cheeks flushed, adding a hint of naiveté to the strong woman who stood before him.

"I can't believe you're here," he said quietly. "There must've been men queued up for a mile to dance with you."

"Owen?" His mother came to the door. "Everything all right?"

He took Willow's hand and guided her over. "Yes, Mum. Remember Willow?"

"Nice to see you again, Mrs. Hughes."

"Ginny, please." She glanced at their joined hands for a brief moment. "You look stunning. You were at the ball tonight?"

"I was."

"I'd planned on taking Willow, until Dad got sick."

A little smile crept up his mother's lips. "Ah, I see. Well, come in and see Frank. He's awake and in better spirits. We just got news the procedure should fix him up like new."

Willow followed his mother into the room, and he joined them.

"Frank, you have a visitor. Owen's friend."

"Willow! What a nice surprise."

It shocked Owen to see his father so happy and animated with her, given his disposition most of the day. But Dad always put on a smile for others. Just like Owen.

Yup, they were two peas plucked from the same pod. If this moment didn't make that crystal clear, then none would.

"You didn't get dressed in costume for me, did you?" His dad grinned.

Willow laughed and put her purse and shawl onto the table near Owen's chair. "Of course I did."

"Uh-oh." Dad glanced at his wife and Owen. "I think we have us another kidder in our midst."

Willow went closer to his bed, her presence bringing new life to the room. "You caught me. I attended the Jane Austen ball, not far from the hospital. I wanted to see how you were feeling."

His father talked about the day, quite openly in fact. Owen stood to the side and watched. How easily his father spoke to Willow, when he often barely spoke to Owen. When the conversation died down, Owen said, "I've been teaching Willow how to dance for the ball. She's a natural."

Willow rolled her eyes. "Your son is prone to exaggeration."

His mother sat on the edge of his dad's bed. "Come on, you two, show us how it's done."

Willow waved a hand. "Oh, I'm not very—"

"Nonsense." Owen took her into his arms, before she stopped him. "Now come on, just like I showed you."

He hummed music and, with only a stumble or two, she kept up beautifully. When they finished, his parents clapped.

"Wonderful." His father yawned, but hid his tiredness with an overdone smile. "You two should go on *The X-Factor.*"

A curly-haired nurse walked in. "So this is the party room?" She smiled. "I'm Lola, the night-shift nurse, here to take vitals for Mr. Hughes."

Owen turned to his mother. "I suppose it's a good time to let Dad get some rest."

"Yes. Go. Enjoy what's left of the night with Willow." She reached up and gave him a hug.

Owen went to his dad's bed and placed a hand on his shoulder. "Dad, I'll be back in the morning."

"Yes, yes. If you want to. Your mother appreciated having you here."

Owen shook his head, buried the urge to flee, and understood change would only happen if he made the effort. He wrapped his father in an awkward hug, feeling his muscles stiffen as he did. "I love you, Dad."

Owen straightened and turned away. He couldn't look at his mother, but Willow's gaze stayed on him all the way over, understanding in her eyes. He took her hand and they walked toward the door.

His father said, "Owen?"

He turned, prepared to swallow back whatever negative remark his father might say. "Yeah?"

Dad stared, blinked a few times. "I love you, too."

Owen smiled, nodded. More than he could've asked for.

Willow squeezed his hand as they walked down the hallway in silence. At the elevator, she turned to him. "You're a good son."

He shrugged and pressed the elevator button, but stood a little taller knowing he'd done the right thing. Outside the hallway window, a full moon shone bright. Had some cosmic force lined up today's events simply so he could see how much his father's love meant?

They stepped on the elevator and as the door bumped shut, he slipped an arm around Willow's waist and drew her close. Lowering his head, he kissed her tenderly, hoping she'd feel the power of his newly opened soul, capable of deeper caring than he'd possessed in the past.

She drew back and placed a soft hand on his face. "I'm glad your dad will be all right."

"Me, too. How do you feel about surprises?"

She tilted her head, her eyes shining, her smile sweet. All aimed at him, causing his heart to flutter in the most unexpected way. "Tonight, Mr. Hughes, I feel game for anything."

Chapter 19

Willow sat in her seat staring out the van's passenger window, curious why Owen had disappeared into her house without a word as to why. Had he left something of his inside while helping her the other day? Or did this have to do with the surprise he'd promised when leaving the hospital? Without electricity, and given the hour, it seemed unlikely.

She shifted onto her hip and adjusted the skirt of her ballroom gown. Why hadn't he wanted her to change clothes? When she'd suggested they swing by the B and B so she could put on pants, he'd only smiled and said she should stay dressed as is.

Radiohead flowed from the van's speakers. What kind of man had tastes ranging from alternative rock to Sinatra to Regency-era ballroom dancing? She hummed along with the song "House of Cards," one she liked. Passion and taking chances. Two things this trip had given her, leading to a more thought-provoking question: how far did she want to go with a man on another continent?

Owen had taken a chance earlier. Witnessing the heart-squeezing moment between him and his dad had warmed her soul. Second chances didn't always present themselves. Tonight offered an opportunity to be with a man who'd helped her see qualities in herself she'd always overlooked. A second chance she'd be a fool not to embrace.

At that moment, a light brightened the living room windows.

The beam of a flashlight came toward the van. When he reached the door, she saw that he'd changed into the clothes he'd worn for the Jane Austen reading at the library.

He opened her door and extended a hand. "M'lady."

"You've changed clothes." She took his hand and carefully stepped to the ground.

"All part of my plan."

"You look so—so handsome."

He lifted her hand to his lips and brushed it with a kiss. "I can't hold a candle to you." He placed her hand on his bent arm, guiding her toward the house.

Her heart swelled. She couldn't remember a single time in her life when anyone had done anything this special for her.

They entered the foyer and a soft glow shimmered on the walls, from a more powerful light in the living room. "Did you light the fireplace?"

"I did." He slipped a hand on her waist and turned her toward the living room. "Go in. Look."

She lifted her skirt hem and went in. The fireplace blazed and gave off the woodsy scent of burning logs. Candles stationed on the fireplace mantel flickered shadows on the walls. Only a short time ago, this place had been dark and dusty. But the warm light, cheese and crackers arranged on the coffee table, and a bottle of wine next to it brought this place alive.

Owen came behind her, placing his hands on her hips and brushing the back of her neck with a kiss. "For you, I'm turning back time."

She turned into his arms, and slipped hers around his neck. "You're amazing. I love this."

"Good." His gaze darkened and swept over her face. "Let's have a drink." He took her by the hand toward the coffee table, where two winelglasses had already been filled. He picked them up and handed her one.

Raising his, he said, "To Jane Austen."

They clicked their glasses. "To Jane."

The cold, crisp wine warmed her belly. Or maybe it was all this attention lavished on her by a man she might not have even noticed in Manhattan. What a shame that would've been.

He lowered his glass to the table. "I forgot something. I brought along a little necessity Ms. Austen didn't have."

He went to the cardboard box sitting on a chair, one he'd taken from his house on their way over here. From it, he removed an iPod speaker stand. After slipping in his phone, he pressed a few buttons and Sinatra serenaded them.

Yes, he truly amazed her. "You've thought of everything."

"I hope so." He raised a brow. "May I have this dance?"

"Certainly."

He took her wineglass and lowered it next to his. Then he gathered her in his arms. "Who'd you dance with tonight at the ball?"

"Just Eddie."

"And...?"

"It went pretty darn well, if I say so myself."

He smiled. "I knew it would."

They danced as one. Owen moved and guided her effortlessly. Subtle touches, all done with an understated boldness. The same way he'd drawn out a newfound belief she now had found in herself, lacking when she arrived.

He spoke softly, his voice near her ear. "Back in the Regency period, dancing was an important part of courtship."

She snuggled against him. "I think it still is."

He chuckled. Stepping back, he put a hand on her waist, guided her in a slow twirl, and reeled her back into his arms. "In *Pride and Prejudice*, Austen wrote, 'To be fond of dancing was a certain step toward falling in love.'" Their eyes met and he shrugged. "It's a...well, you know, a beautiful sentiment."

The sudden shyness from a man who rarely showed it came as a surprise, but she shouldn't read into it too much. "Yes, it is."

"And back then," he said with a confident, husky tone, "dancing offered a chance to publicly touch the opposite sex. Like hands." He took hers off his shoulder and kissed the inside of her palm then replaced it. "Waists." He slipped a gentle hand on hers. "All forbidden under normal circumstances." He moved his hand to her lower back and slowly caressed the area, his gaze filled with need. "Very risqué things for that time."

A heated rush weakened her knees. An ocean would soon separate her from this wonderful man, but she tossed aside concerns and slipped fingers through his thick hair while stretching on her toes and brushing her lips to his.

He lowered his head and his warm breath whispered sweetly against her cheek before his mouth met hers. Tender kisses followed, escalating quickly while the grooves of their bodies joined, as if they were meant to be one. The faded scent of his cologne wrapped her like a cloak. She could taste the wine he'd just sipped, a tang leaving her woozy and responding to the way his hands skimmed her body. Slipping her fingers beneath his jacket, she pressed her hands to his chest and moved along his slim, muscular torso.

Owen leaned back and ran a gentle finger along her throat, slowly following an imaginary line that swept to her shoulder, where he eased the puffy dress sleeve to her midarm. He leaned forward and suddenly stopped. "When we're apart, I can't stop thinking about you."

"Me, too," she whispered as her heart expanded. Even if leaving meant the beautiful thing she'd found with Owen was only temporary, at least they had this moment.

* * * *

Owen opened his eyes. Early morning light peeked through the cracks in the shades. He lifted the blanket and slid off the sofa, careful not to jolt Willow.

She mumbled something incoherent then curled into a ball beneath the blanket and drifted back to sleep. He slipped on his jeans and tiptoed from the living room to the kitchen, where the old floor groaned as he made his way out the back door. A blast of cold morning air reminded him the season knocked on autumn's door. He grabbed a few logs off a pile and hurried back inside.

He pulled his phone from his back pocket and checked the time. Two and a half hours until Jilly had to leave for school. Good. He sent a quick text to Bea to let her know he'd be back in time to get Jilly to school. Once back in the living room, he moved quietly while restarting the fire.

Just as he tossed in a match, Willow said, "Good morning."

He glanced back over his shoulder. Sleepy eyes. Hair mussed. Damn, the sight of her was as comforting as tea and toast. "Hey, gorgeous."

"Now I know you're messing with me. There's no way I'm gorgeous at this hour."

"Just you wait'll I get this fire stoked. I'll show you how gorgeous I think you are."

"Promises, promises."

He chuckled, happiness overflowing inside him. Waiting until the fire took hold, he anticipated climbing next to her soft body and touching those sexy curves. He stiffened just thinking about her. "Rosebud, you are one helluva a troublemaker, you know that?"

"I try."

He finished then turned around, drinking in every inch of her. Head propped on a few pillows. One arm bent behind her head, while the blanket slipped down her chest, leaving those gorgeous full breasts to taunt him.

She raised her brows. "See something you like, kind sir?"

"You know it, baby." He sat on the edge of the sofa and cupped her face in his hands. "Are you good here? Tell me if you want to go back to the B and B."

"No way. I may never leave this spot."

Willow shifted. The blanket fell forward and he smoothed a hand along the curves he loved so much. She kissed him hungrily and reached for the button of his jeans, which he quickly tugged off and returned beneath the covers to make love to her with all the tenderness she'd uncovered in his heart.

Afterward, they curled together on the sofa with the blanket around them, watching the fire while nibbling on the snacks he'd brought last night.

She broke a piece of cheese into two and brought one half to his lips, which he took but nibbled on her fingertips as he did.

She smiled. "Did you get a chance to look at my stops along the Cotswold Way and book me a hotel for each night?"

"I did. Booked the rooms yesterday morning. I wanted to cover the distances between towns you noted. A few of them are long walking days."

"I know. I can handle it. Sure, I don't exercise like I used to, but since I came here, I've been walking more. I feel pretty good."

"You used to exercise a lot?"

"Sure. When I first lost a lot of weight back in college, it helped me get skinny. Exercise matters."

"But didn't anybody ever tell you that you got too thin?"

"Not a single soul." She laughed, but her smile quickly disappeared. "I had to kill myself to get and stay that thin. Now, I kind of just don't care anymore."

"Good. So that means you know you're a beauty, just the way you are."

Her face softened with a weak smile. "Last night when I put on that gown, for the first time in perhaps my whole life, it didn't matter what dress size I wore. What I saw, I loved." She bit her lower lip for a second, then narrowed her eyes at him. "Maybe you've brainwashed me into believing I look good at this size."

"Well, my dear. If I have to brainwash you to see the truth in your appearance, then I will do it time and time again."

He leaned forward and kissed her with all the joy bubbling in his heart, trying to forget that soon she'd be leaving. His daughter wouldn't be the only one who missed Willow.

Chapter 20

Owen stood behind Willow and Jilly as they stared out into the main room of the Roman Baths. The rectangular pool's green water glistened from the strong afternoon sun, the area walled in but opened to the skies.

Tourists packed the walkway surrounding the pool, many of them leaning against the evenly spaced columns while getting their photos taken. From the roofline, statues of Roman emperors looked down on their subjects, the ancient stone blackened by nature's elements.

Yesterday afternoon, Owen had offered to take her sightseeing at the Roman Baths today, the only way he could think to cheer her up. Willow had contacted a company to handle removal and sale of large items in her grandparents' home. They'd even packed his van with all the belongings to be donated. She'd been quiet the whole time. He'd asked why a few times then she finally admitted that getting rid of their things, especially after sleeping at the house with him the night before, was bittersweet.

Willow glanced over her shoulder at him. "Why were these built here, in this location?"

"Bath is located on a natural geothermal spring." She bit her lower lip while listening, her gaze drifting between him and the surroundings. An urge to give her a kiss swept over him, and as he leaned forward Jilly looked up at him.

"Remember what you told me last night, Daddy? That the Roman bath system was one of the most intimate of ancient times."

"Very good, Jilly. It is the most *intricate* of ancient times. Intricate means it's very complicated." He glanced at Willow, who watched him with hooded eyelids and a tiny smirk.

Yup, this place was pretty intimate today—at least for him. And this thing he had going with her, boy oh boy, it was doing some complicated things to his heart.

He gave Willow a quick wink and gently squeezed Jilly's shoulder. "I think we have a future tour guide here."

Her eyes went wide. "You mean when I'm grown up, I can do tours in the van?"

A pride swept through him like no other. Jilly was a sponge. Smart, observant. He imagined handing off the keys to his company to her years from now, seeing his efforts to build a name for himself in the area's tourism become rooted by generations to keep it going...

And that's when a childhood moment hit like a brick dropped on his skull.

As a young boy, he'd often say to his dad how he wanted to be a master thatcher when he grew up. Sure, there were days he wanted to be a policeman, a TV star, or a circus lion tamer, too.

For the first time in his life he understood his father's personal stake in wishing Owen had joined the family business. Willow watched him, a knowing expression on her face. He glanced down at Jilly. "Of course, you may change your mind by the time you're an adult. I always want you to pursue your personal dreams, Jill. Okay?"

"Sure, Daddy."

Willow nodded, all the confirmation needed to know he'd given his daughter the right response.

"Now, a little bit more history. The Romans built baths as far more than a source of hygiene. There were rooms for mental and physical cleansing..."

While he talked about the pool, Willow listened with a gleam of admiration in her eyes that had him offering details he might otherwise have ignored. He wanted her to appreciate the landmarks and structures he'd known his whole life.

More than appreciate, though... He wanted Willow to love what he had to share.

Not because of his prior motives, but because the baths said so much about a civilization of long ago. Because he hoped she'd feel awe learning about them, the way Owen always had. To understand history connects people and places through time with language, culture, traditions and even faith.

He wanted his passion to be hers.

Her gaze traveled the length of the pool. "Fascinating, really. I had no idea how far-reaching the Roman Empire was. It's amazing how layers of history can be found in something as simple as a pool."

Pride filled his chest. Yes, she got it.

Jilly reached out and took Willow's hand. "I'm glad you're here. Do you like the baths?"

"They're amazing. So ancient and yet so modern in a way."

"An impressive observation." She glanced his way and smiled, all the confirmation he needed to keep going. "The restoration you now see was done in the Victorian era." He tapped Jilly's shoulder. "Look across the pool, sweetheart. That woman in the long white dress sitting at the pool side is an actor playing the part of a person who worked in these pools two thousand years ago."

"Wow! That's a long time." Jilly eyes widened and her mouth dropped open.

Willow pressed her shoulder to Owen's but looked at Jilly. "This tour with your dad has been very informative. He's an excellent tour guide. Don't you think?"

Jilly nodded, but kept watching the actor who sat on a bench working with a stone mortar and pestle set.

"In fact," Willow nuzzled closer to him and dropped her voice, "he's the best guide I've had on my trip here."

"Ha-ha. You're a regular John Cleese." Owen slipped his arm around her shoulder. "I'm the only one."

She softly pressed her lips against his cheek. "Still the best."

He inhaled the floral scent in her hair and whispered, "I'll be sure to thank you properly later."

Her lids softened, the same heated gaze she'd passed him frequently since their night together. One that furled around him like a lasso and threatened to bring him to his knees.

"Daddy?" He tore himself away from Willow's gaze to find Jilly staring at them through narrowed eyes.

"What's wrong?"

"Nan says it's not nice to tell a secret in front of someone."

"By God, you're right." He threw up his palms. "Sorry. I told Willow how she looks pretty today."

Something about her glowed. It wasn't just the black-and-white blouse, unbuttoned just enough to drive his desire wild, or the white pants that hugged her familiar curves. Her cheeks glowed and a permanent shine resided in her pretty eyes.

"You're right, Daddy. She does." Jilly wedged closer to Willow, gently pushing Owen aside. "I think it's her new shirt. She got it when we were shopping. When she bought me this one." Jilly motioned to the navy long-sleeved shirt with a sparkle-filled puppy on the front. "Do I look pretty?"

Owen squatted down and wrapped his arms around her. "Baby, you're gorgeous."

Jilly beamed. "Thanks, Daddy. May I go see that lady in the white dress who has worked here for two thousand years?"

"Yes. Go on." Jilly started to leave as he added, "But she's an actor, pretending to be someone who worked here two thousand..." He stopped when Jilly kept going and didn't look back.

He took Willow's hand and they watched Jilly approach the woman and start talking. Owen shook his head. "I can only imagine what she's saying right now."

"Probably that she doesn't look a day over a thousand, nine-hundred ninety-nine."

Together they laughed. He slipped his arm around Willow's waist and her head dropped to his shoulder. His heart bloomed with something so deep it burned his core. This moment, the three of them here, felt more natural than any part of his marriage. If he were granted a wish, it would be Willow would never return to the US and Jilly would stay young and innocent. Always able to find pleasure in the small things and never turn into a teenager who might get angry with him.

But tomorrow morning, Willow would take her walk on the Cotswold Way, the start to the end of her trip to England. And Jilly would grow up, though he'd do everything in his power to make certain she didn't drift away from him. As he'd done with his father.

* * * *

"I can wait until you get underway." Owen stood by the driver's door of his van, coffee cup in hand, reminding Willow of a nervous parent leaving his child at school.

Willow smiled at him and shifted the heavy rucksack on her shoulders. "I'd rather you left."

This morning, she'd woken with a nervous belly, barely able to eat. Owen had picked her up and driven her to the beautiful town of Chipping Campden, a quaint town with honey-colored architecture. He'd parked not far from a stone marker starting the trail known as the Cotswold Way, and had already kissed her goodbye twice.

He tipped his head. "Okay, then." He got inside the van, rolled down the window, and motioned with his finger for her to come over.

She stepped to the window. "Are you trying to get me inside that van again? Like you did the first day we met?"

Owen laughed, exactly the smiling face she wanted to see before she began this journey. He leaned forward and gently kissed her again. "Be safe. Now I'll go."

She reached out and touched his arm, resting on the window edge. "I will be safe. Before you know it, I'll be meeting you right back in Bath, at the other end of this trail."

He winked. "I know you will."

With one last wave, he drove off. She waved, hoping he saw her through rearview mirror. Her reward came when he stuck his hand out the window and waved one last time. She missed him already. How the hell would she ever return to New York when the time came?

She dropped her worries on the curbside and set her mind on the journey ahead.

The plan to photograph and keep a journal along the way would require diligence. As she looked around, she found the perfect object. She crossed the street, stopping adjacent from an old market. Crouching down, she snapped an eye-level shot of the three-foot-high stone marker that read *Cotswold Way - Bath 100 M.*

She drew in a breath and exhaled, easing the flurry of butterflies swarming her belly. Ten and a half miles by sundown. Giving herself mental shove, she took her first steps, relieved and rippling with pride to be finally on her way.

A short walk along the main street led her up a side road near a church. Soon she climbed past the last of the houses and hit farmland. She walked quickly, occasionally glancing back at the beautiful views of Chipping Campden she'd left behind.

Being on her way helped her to relax and she soon hit her walking stride, not too fast, but a nice pace. The sun rose higher in the sky and the morning chill lifted, making her sweat in yesterday's souvenir purchase. A burgundy sweatshirt that read *Tall, Dark, & Darcy* on the chest. A goofy memento of this historic area, but it would forever make her think about Owen. He was her tall, dark, and Darcy.

She hadn't gone but a few miles when she hit a place she'd read about, the Dover Hill escarpment. At the high ground where she stood, land rolled into views of distant horizons, fields dotted with sheep, and neat garden rows. Beauty as far as the eye could see. A joyous force inside of her lifted at the buffet Mother Nature had spread out before her.

She snapped a few pictures and looked at her map. Any downtime would have to be monitored so she didn't get stuck on the trail in the dark. She proceeded on the Mile Drive, a broad, almost straight and level green lane, which took her in the right direction. As she ascended a hill, the Broadway Tower could be seen in the distance.

Her guidebook called the Broadway Tower a folly tower, one built in the eighteenth century primarily for decoration. She studied its three turrets surrounding the central tower and ornate arched windows with balconies on all sides. Then she removed her phone. Flipping through her photos, she found the picture of a painting her granddad had done of the structure and compared it to the actual sight.

After paying a pound, she climbed the structure. An easy climb that took her even higher to observe the spectacular views. This spot was considered one of England's outstanding viewpoints, the second highest point on the Cotswold escarpment providing a sixty-two-mile view.

She finished and went down, and on ground level met two other American tourists on their honeymoon. The woman recognized her and had even once been a member of Pound Busters. After their goodbyes, Willow left and entered the southern edge of the Broadway village. Although early in the day, to be well underway deserved a treat, so she purchased an ice-cream cone.

Some blogs about the trail talked of people occasionally getting lost, or having trouble finding signs guiding them back to the footpath. Yet when she finished her treat, she retraced her steps and located the footpath with ease.

Soon she hit a section of the path where sheep grazed in a neighboring field, the same moment she became aware of a rubbing against the back of her heel. Wearing boots not broken in wasn't her smartest move, but what choice did she have?

She walked through the pain, focusing on the sights around her. Creamy yellow flowers intertwined with tall green grass. A worn wood fence hugging the hillside. A large tree, its trunk leaning toward the bright sun.

She glanced up and blinked into the sun, reminded she had a destination to reach before dusk. Instead of hurrying, she sat on a tree stump and ate the sandwich Edna had packed her this morning, enjoying the endless stretch of land that served as her entertainment. She imagined peasants walking through the fields, or royalty on horseback traveling from Buckingham Palace to these parts.

By late afternoon, she walked the downhill stretch into Stanton, her stop for the night. Despite the rubbing of a blister on her heel, she left the trail and headed to her overnight stop feeling taller, bigger, stronger.

Proving something to others guided everything she'd ever done. Losing weight proved she *did* have self-control over her looks. Starting a business proved to Charlie she *could* make a success of herself. And making Charlie happy made her mother relaxed. Nothing had ever been done with the pure motive of making herself happy. Except this walk.

She entered the village and approached the seventeenth-century-house operating as a B and B where Owen had booked her a room. Part of her wanted to call and tell him about her successful day. Only she couldn't. Alone on the journey meant alone off the trails, too.

Besides, when they met up again in Bath, she'd have even more to tell him. Because in two more days of walking, she'd meet Sean Cooke.

* * * *

"Bye." Willow smiled at Pete, the owner of the B and B where she'd spent the night. "And thank you for a perfect stay."

The beefy man with a bald scalp gave her a warm smile. "You're welcome. Hope we see you again."

Willow exited the centuries-old building, already missing the huge oak beams and floorboards, thick walls, low ceilings, and barely a straight line anywhere. Last night, after a satisfying meal at a local pub and a hot bath, she'd crawled under the covers aching for Owen. Luckily the ten-mile walk had left her exhausted and she fell asleep with her cell phone in her hand before she broke down.

Loneliness had set in during her meal, maybe from the one beer, or because everyone sat with someone else. Only the waitress had talked to her, polite enough, but not Bonnie. Yes, she missed Rory's, although the whole idea of missing a place she'd first entered a few weeks ago seemed silly.

Fact was, she couldn't call Owen after the royal fuss she'd made about doing this alone and cutting off all communications until she finished the journey in Bath. Single-handedly navigating the trail yesterday had filled her with pride. Much as she looked forward to today, though, she understood how sharing these beautiful sights with another person had some merit.

Today she'd risen with the sun and, with more distance to cover, she set a goal to knock off the first four miles in an hour. As she headed for the footpath, one glitch became obvious: her aching calves and shoulders made her move slower than yesterday.

Still, she soldiered on.

Back on the trail, the pretty farmlands lessened the ache of her physical discomforts. She passed the Stanton House, a manor with gardens and a fountain, and Wood Stanway, a tiny settlement.

Soon she hit a mile-long uphill climb. The first steps came easy, but eventually her calves screamed in agony and she panted like a woman in labor. Despite the sweat warming her neck and armpits, she slowly put one foot in front of the other until the crest of the hill finally appeared.

As she hit flat ground, the reward came with another heaven-sent view.

A feast of fields colored in a patchwork of variegated greens, one dotted with black-and-white cows. Trees grew in clusters, leafy tops still green but with bursts of gold and burnt orange. Her throat grew thick and eyes watered. Such a glorious sight. She lowered herself onto the cool grass and gave herself a well-deserved break.

As she sipped her water and studied the scenery, she couldn't think of a single time in her adulthood when she'd given herself a break. Proving herself had become as routine as walking. An unquestioned part of her daily routine. For the first time in her life, she could see how she'd missed out by not slowing down.

She pushed her pitiful history from her head and finished the water. After a few minutes, she stood, brushed off her baggy, drawstring pants, and soldiered on. And on and on. Step. Step. The flatter terrain agreed with her, easier to labor through the ache in her calves and the tug of her weighted rucksack against her shoulders.

At the escarpment, she passed an Iron Age hill front, noted in her handy guidebook. In Hailes, she took a few snapshots of a ruined Cistercian abbey and followed the flatter, grassy footpath to Winchcombe, where she met a German couple who spoke very good English and asked her to join them for lunch.

After the couple left, she wandered the sidewalks of the quaint town and stayed longer than planned to view its historic center and many shops. Hadn't John Lennon said, "Life is what happens when you're busy making other plans"?

For a short while, she allowed herself to forget about schedule demands while exploring a church built during the prosperous Cotswold wool trade era. Well worth the detour with its superb gargoyles, some of which were said to be caricatures of local dignitaries of the era. By the time she returned to the trail, she had no regrets about being off schedule. The only regret came from admitting she should've employed this more carefree philosophy over the span of her life.

As she walked, her mind drifted to the daily operations of her company, left in the trusty hands of her senior management staff. While here, she'd received a few emails on work matters, but only to inform her they'd taken care of something. She'd hired well. Competent and loyal people.

Only after walking for an hour did it dawn on her she hadn't seen a sign for the trail in some time. Plus, the effortless grade of the land seemed to be taking her downhill, not higher as her guidebook had said.

A wave of panic assaulted her, leaving her mouth dry and heart beating fast. In the city, she'd never felt lost. A street sign stood at each corner, making it easy to find your way around. Not so in the woods.

Glancing around, she saw only trees, fields, and a few houses in the distance. A second jittery wave passed through her, leaving her brain frozen. *Now stop. Don't panic. Think. Think!*

Her map. She pulled it out and searched for the last town she'd been in, Winchcombe. Following the map's path with her finger, she came across a turnoff she may have followed by mistake instead of staying on the trail.

Did she keep walking or backtrack? Right now, she had no idea exactly how far off course she'd gone, or if she'd followed the right path.

Standing here alone and exposed, vulnerable to getting further off track if she made the wrong choice, she swallowed back tears. Good God, how silly. She'd handled the rise of a company, ran it like a five-star general oversaw a military operation. So, what was missing now?

Then it hit her... Trust.

Had she ever trusted herself, or was her militant drive based on fear of falling apart?

Maybe the Cotswold Way offered a journey in trust. Perhaps every bad moment that left her feeling "less than" existed to prepare her for today. For this very moment in the wilderness, where she'd stand alone with the challenge of proving she believed in herself.

She turned around and looked up the hill she'd just come down. Digging her walking stick into the ground, she took one heavy step up. Then another. And another. The thick socks she'd put on this morning to cover the sore on her heel rubbed in a whole new area, but she kept going with her chin held high and the confidence of trust in herself as her guide.

At this rate, she wouldn't reach Cleeve Hill until dusk. Too late to view the place Owen had said would give her the most spectacular views of the Cotswolds.

But the views would be there tomorrow. That was, if she found the trail sign she guessed she missed.

Later on, she hoped she could laugh at this mishap and write in her journal about the adventure of getting lost. But in the meantime, she held onto her newfound faith in herself like a long-lost friend.

* * * *

"Come on now." Owen motioned to Jilly's dinner plate, though he'd barely touched his own food. "Eat up if you want to grow big and strong." Jilly crinkled her nose. "But I hate carrots."

"You ate them last week." He took his fork and ate one of his. "Mmmm, good, and quite good for your eyes. Did you ever see a rabbit wearing glasses?" He laughed for his daughter's sake, although it brought little respite to his worries over why Willow hadn't arrived at her hotel.

Jilly frowned and let out a sigh. "Rabbits don't wear glasses."

"Yes, sweetheart. I know. It's a joke. Evidently not a funny one." He stood and took his plate to the sink. "How about I get you an apple? Would you eat that?"

She nodded, even smiled.

He took one from the counter basket, peeled the skin, and sliced it the way his daughter liked before handing her the plate. "Go ahead and watch TV while you eat this, if you want."

"Yay!" She took the plate and pranced off to the sofa while Henry followed, certain to get handouts.

Owen lifted his cell phone from the counter to see if he'd missed a call from the hotel near Cleeve Hill. Willow should've checked in two hours ago, if she'd been sticking to her schedule.

He returned the phone to the counter and wandered to the window over the sink. Blackness greeted him. Images of her in the dark woods set his nerves on edge, although she was probably safe. Just lost.

The vibration of his cell phone on the hard countertop sent him sprinting over and grabbing the phone. "Hello?"

"Owen, it's Stan."

"Stan. Thank God it's you. Did my guest arrive?"

"She did. Just went upstairs to her room."

"Was she…" How could he ask this without sounding like a worrywart? "She's a real stickler for punctuality and I expected her to arrive a while ago. Did she seem okay?"

"Okay? Yes, I guess so. Tired though. Definitely tired. She ordered dinner and asked if we could send it to her room."

"Well, long as she's there. That's what matters." Owen said it, but didn't feel it. What mattered was her being there and happy.

He hung up and told Jilly she had five minutes until bath time. Taking out Willow's itinerary, he reviewed the days ahead. In two days, she'd reach Painswick. The place she believed her father lived. He'd worry about her every second.

In the next hour, he got Jilly ready for bed and tucked her in. As he sat on the sofa staring at the tube, he resisted the urge to call Willow. He'd been itching to talk to her, to hear about her journey.

But he'd better get used to her absence. Soon after her return, she'd leave for home.

So much had changed since she'd arrived. So quickly, too. Her search for her father made him think differently about his dad. Her delight in the Cotswolds revived a love of this region he once had. But mostly, she'd breathed new life into his daughter. For that, and that alone, he'd never forget Willow's visit here.

The last time he'd seen her was the view from his rearview mirror, her standing on the road in Chipping Campden, waving goodbye. He closed his eyes and tipped his head back to the sofa, lost in the way his heart overflowed from just thinking about her.

Of all the gifts she'd given him while here, he treasured most this feeling of comfortable contentment he had around her. It would also be the hardest to deal with once she left.

Chapter 21

Willow tucked the soft sheet beneath her chin and curled onto her side. Sleep. More sleep. She'd never get enough. Behind her eyelids, she sensed the room's brightness and struggled to open her eyes while patting the nightstand and fumbling with her phone.

Shit. 8:05. Why hadn't the alarm gone off at seven? Right, she'd fallen asleep before setting it. She pushed off the covers and sprang out of bed, only to have her sore calf muscles scream.

Once she'd hobbled to the shower, she started the hot water and stepped inside. The moist heat massaged her stiff muscles and cleared the fog in her head.

Today she'd stay on plan and not get stuck on the trail after dark. If she hadn't turned around yesterday, who knew where she'd have ended up? No more daydreaming today. One missed trail marker had been plenty. Walking through the woods in daylight posed no threat, but in the dark, the pretty trees turned into a setting for a Grimm Brothers' tale.

She dried her hair and let it hang to her shoulders but didn't bother with makeup. Tomorrow, when she went to Painswick to look for Sean Cooke, she'd put some on. Today, though, she resorted to her comfortable yoga pants, a long-sleeved, V-neck pullover sweater, and her hiking shoes.

After getting her rucksack situated, she left the room for the hotel lobby.

"Good morning." She smiled at the desk clerk who'd been there last night. "I'm running late and won't have time for breakfast. Is there a deli or store nearby where I could get a few things?"

He gave her directions and she headed out into the sunshine, making a stop to get food for lunch and snacks. All stocked up, she marched straight to the trail, the process almost like a normal part of her life.

Her blister had developed a callus, giving her less pain. She marched toward Cleeve Hill, moving compatibly with the gentle muscle aches. If what Owen said about this hill were true, the potential reward when she hit the crest would be worth every bit of sweat to get there. Right now, the cool morning air on her face, neck, and hands felt good.

She finally arrived at the highest peak on the trail, each breath heavy, her armpits damp. But one look at the view sent her heart fluttering.

At a one thousand eighty-three feet elevation, Cleeve Hill had the fame of being the largest unenclosed "wold" on the trail. Her physical discomfort vanished as she stood in one spot and turned in a slow circle to bask in the unobstructed view. A horizon that stretched for miles and miles and miles, set against cornflower-blue skies and heavenly bundles of clouds seeming close enough to touch.

She opened the guidebook. From this vantage point, it said, she could see from the Malvern Hills to, on a clear day, the Black Mountains of Wales. Panning the landscape, she had no idea if she viewed either of those things. Owen would know. She snapped several photographs. When she reached Bath, he could tell exactly what she'd been looking at.

After rolling her rucksack off her shoulders and letting it fall to the grass, she lowered herself beside it. The vistas spread before her possessed a godly grandeur, removing her far from the modern world.

She retrieved a water bottle from her bag and leaned back on her elbows to enjoy the exquisite fabric of the landscape. Soft fields. Sharp trees. All joined by the ebb and flow of gently rolling hills.

Peace washed over her. This view. This place. Discovered by taking a risk. A surge of power pulsed through her veins. She *was* strong and it felt damn good.

Once before she'd captured this feeling. When she'd finally gained control over her eating. Yes, losing weight gave her power that she'd harnessed to create a company, marry, gain financial independence.

And it all slipped away when Richard's rejection broke the thin thread holding her together for two decades. Circumstance usurped what little faith in herself remained. An ache swallowed the part of her that once had power and control. A cavernous ache that shadowed her even as she'd landed at Heathrow.

Between now and then, though, she *had* changed.

The day she'd met Richard at the lawyer's office to sign the divorce papers forced its way into her mind. She'd just exited the elevator on the fifth floor. On her way past the men's room, the door swung open and Richard stepped out. She'd walked faster. After all, a man who'd announced he no longer loved her so publicly didn't deserve her civility. But he yelled her name and, when she didn't stop, he caught up and took her by the arm.

"Willow. Please, I want to talk to you before we go in there."

She'd jerked her arm away. "Oh, now you want to have a private conversation?"

He'd looked down at the ground and slowly lifted his chin. "I'm sorry, Willow. Sometimes…" He'd drawn in a deep breath. "I tried so many times to hint to how unhappy I was. But all you ever cared about was that firm."

At the time, she'd reminded him of his own dedication to his political career and stormed off seething in hatred for him.

Later, at home, while drowning her sadness in a bottle of wine and a pint of Ben & Jerry's, she'd admitted his words held some truth. Her entire self-worth had been caught up in the firm's success. It served as a safety net, so she'd never get fat again. Her entire being depended on the company's success, its existence proof she was no longer that chubby kid.

Lifting her head, she again scanned the vista, only this time the gentle throb of her sore muscles reminded her of the hard work it took to find this treasure. A journey testing her physical endurance and leaving her too tired to fight a growing realization…

She'd wasted a lot of time trying to prove her worth to the world.

A need to prove herself again and again. All her life, she'd learned one lesson. The fight to perfection seemed the only way to get attention. To get love.

Be smart, Willow.

Lose weight, Willow.

Always win, Willow.

Ideals foisted upon her primarily from her stepfather, a man whose confidence demanded people meet his expectations of them. Not only for Willow. Just about anybody who crossed his path. Even Willow's mother, whose own happiness had been tied into her daughter getting her stepfather's approval. The message Willow received, over and over, had always been the same.…

You aren't good enough "as is."

Willow's throat thickened and tears blurred the view. Love. It's all she ever wanted. To be loved for who she was, without a care for what she looked like.

The hard pressure in her chest cracked, and she buried her face in her hands. Even this journey to England had started with a demand: to get cash and win back her standing at Pound Busters.

But what had all this winning given her? Nothing, really. At the end of the day, she stood alone.

But in England she saw what she'd been missing, found in watching the love between Owen and Jilly. Love that didn't come with requirements. Just pure loyalty for each other.

She sat there for a long time, her body weightless and immobile, almost as if she were one with the landscape.

People came. People went. But she remained. For how long, she didn't know or care.

She finally stood and ambled down the trail. A glance at her watch showed her behind schedule again but who cared?

She'd been lost her whole life.

These days spent on the trail were perhaps the first time she'd actually been on the right path. Tomorrow, when she reached Painswick, she might even get the answer to the biggest question of her life.

* * * *

Willow pulled out her itinerary. Day four. Halfway through her trip. This morning she'd woken early and now walked the main road toward the footpath. A knot in her belly since rising tightened. In a few hours, she'd reach Painswick. Hours from meeting Sean Cooke, and she still hadn't come up with anything to say.

Hi. Remember Chloe? Well, I'm her kid.

Hey, ever wonder if you got a woman pregnant some forty years ago but she didn't tell you?

She groaned and kicked a small rock in the path. To ease her mind, she tried to concentrate on the wooded area surrounding this stretch of the trail. Every so often, the trees parted to a clearing, proving the countryside hadn't gone away.

She neared a place in the guidebook called Coopers Hill, known for its famous annual cheese rolling competition. Cheese rolling, a new sport to her, surprisingly was covered by ESPN, and she found a video on YouTube.

As she watched a large group of eager contenders racing down this incredibly steep hillside to chase a round block of cheese, it only proved that people had more guts than brains. Many of the racers fell about halfway down, bouncing to the finish line. In one case, an ambulance had hauled a participant away.

She took a few snapshots and continued along the path. When the sun disappeared, she glanced up to find the clear sky gone and a blanket of gray clouds took its place.

She carefully treaded downhill into Painswick. As she passed a stone marker for the Cotswold Way, she paused and went over. Forty-seven miles to Chipping Campden. She'd walked almost half the trail.

She breathed in the joy of her success. Not only had she found her way alone, but she'd submerged herself in the countryside of her ancestors and walked in the footsteps of her grandfather. She'd seen more than beautiful views. More important, she'd uncovered valuable insights about herself. Patterns of a lifetime, too close for her to truly see, but now that she did, she vowed to make her life different, better.

She neared the marker and took a photo of it. Standing beside it, she squatted down and made three attempts to get a selfie that included both her and the marker. Luckily, a couple entering the trail took pity on her and offered to snap it for her.

She thanked them and they walked away. Owen would love this. She broke her own rule and texted the photograph to his phone with the words "Halfway there!"

Seconds later, he replied, "So proud of you! I knew you could do it. Good luck in Painswick. Call if you need me."

Of course he'd remembered her schedule and exactly where she'd be headed today. The phone pinged with a second text from Owen. "I've been thinking of you."

For only a brief second did she consider her response. Then she typed, "I've been thinking of you, too. See you in Bath."

She took out her guidebook to read about Painswick. Another stone Cotswold village. Maybe she'd look around before interrupting Sean's work morning and instead stop by closer to lunch.

She headed for town, stopping at New Street. Painswick was a historic wool town. New Street seemed a real tourist destination, and not far from the shop Sean Cooke owned. She adjusted her rucksack on her shoulders and took the walking tour suggested in her guide. First she found the oldest building in England to hold a post office, and Painswick's only example of exposed timber framing.

Next came the Beacon House, with its magnificent Georgian Frontage, followed up by a stop at the Falcon Hotel, owner of the oldest bowling green in England. As she hit Bisley Street, where New Street ended, the map showed she was close to the real reason for her stop in town.

With a hammering heart, she followed her GPS to the auto body shop. For a long minute, she stood across the street and stared at the garage attached to a stone building. Two men worked inside the garage on a BMW.

She drew in a deep breath and headed for the building, where a sign on a glass door read the business name and hours.

The large room contained two metal desks behind a counter. A poster on the wall listed work prices and, near it, a doorway led to a private office. She moved closer and peeked inside the office at photos hung on the wall. A pretty blonde stood with a man who had intense blue eyes and strong chin. A numbing sensation traveled her spine as she recognized the aged face of Sean.

A woman came out from a back room. "Well, hello. Can I help you?" The blonde in the office photograph smiled at Willow. Sean's wife, maybe? "Yes. I'm here to see Mr. Cooke."

"He's not here right now. Just stepped out to the pub for a bite. May I help you?"

"Oh, uh… You know, I can come back. I was just walking the local trail and I think we have a mutual friend from Bitton. I figured I'd pop in a say hello."

"Oh, how nice. Yes, Sean grew up there. Are you're visiting from America?"

"I am."

"Oh, I'm Sean's wife. Sylvia."

Willow couldn't find the words to answer. She hadn't stopped to think about Sean having a wife or a family. *Snap out of it!* "Nice to meet you. How about I come back?"

She studied Willow for a few seconds and said, "Why don't you head into town? You'll probably find him at the Pig and Pen."

"Great. Thanks."

Willow turned and just as she opened the door, the woman asked, "It was nice to meet you. I didn't catch your name."

A smile frozen on her face, she said, "It's Willow. Have a good day."

She hurried out before the woman asked for more. This wasn't the person to whom she should confess the reasons for her visit. On her way down the street her heart pounded so rapidly against her ribs she thought it would pop through.

Should she go into this pub? She continued in the direction, debating with each step.

Hadn't she come too far too turn back now?

Standing in front of the pub's old wooden doorway, she took a deep breath and entered. At a bar to the left, several men sat on tall stools talking with the bartender. She spotted Sean easily. His white button-down shirt had an emblem to his repair shop on the pocket, and his name embroidered beneath it. She selected a table on the opposite side of the room, right near a multipaned window looking out to the street.

After resting her rucksack against the wall, she glanced at a menu already on the table. Every so often she'd glance in Sean's direction, but quickly go back to the menu. He had a kind face. No longer the thin young man in the photos, he'd grown into his body. His shirt, tucked into navy, baggy workpants, showed a fuller torso and broad chest.

The bartender stopped at her table and she ordered a beer and burger. While she waited, she pretended to be looking at her guidebook while covertly watching the men talk. A lively conversation about an upcoming football matched solicited a range of emotions.

Sean showed great loyalty for one particular team. Perhaps the kind of undeserved loyalty he gave to her mother, who didn't have the decency to mention their baby. Anger inched its way into her veins as she faced this awkward moment, one that could have been avoided if her mother had chosen honesty instead of secrecy. The bartender delivered her beer. She took a long swig, but it didn't quell the unresolved irritation.

More people entered and the tables slowly filled. Good camouflage, making it so Willow didn't stand out as much.

As she watched Sean's mannerisms, she grew increasingly aware of a pattern. Some of his facial expressions mimicked hers. A motivational video she'd recorded for Pound Busters had once showed her several facial expressions she used regularly, a humbling observation. Yet as she watched Sean listening to his friends, he displayed the same twitch of his lips combined with a slightly arched brow she saw in herself on that video. When he smiled, his eyes squinted almost a bit too much, just like hers.

Sean laughed loudly at something one of the other men said. Wasn't that her laugh?

Or was she imagining it all?

The men finished and paid the tab. Two of them left, but Sean went the opposite way and disappeared through a door marked *Men's Room*. She gulped the last of her beer and stood.

He came out and hurried toward the exit. She strode toward him, her mouth dry and heart banging in her ears.

As he walked past her, she said, "Mr. Cooke? May I speak with you for a moment?"

He stopped and gave her a friendly smile. "Hello. What can I do for you, young lady?"

Willow froze, suddenly at a loss for words.

Chapter 22

The bartender delivered a frothy pilsner glass to their table and set it in front of Sean, who smiled. "Thanks, Mac." His gaze drifted back to Willow. "You're from the States, you say, with family in Bitton?"

She nodded, still stunned to sit across from the man she'd been wondering about for not only these past weeks, but for her whole life.

"Did you spend much time in Bitton?"

"Yes, I've been staying at the Clemmens Bed and Breakfast."

"Oh? Nice to hear the B and B is still in operation. I haven't been to town in years." He scrutinized her face and his forehead wrinkled, almost like a question had formed in his head. "And what mutual friends do we have there?"

"My grandparents lived there most of their lives."

Just then, Mac the bartender delivered Willow's burger.

"Can I get you anything else?" Mac glanced between them.

"No, thanks," they said at the same time.

When she returned her gaze to Sean, his smile had vanished. "And who are your grandparents?"

Her heart beat so hard it echoed to her ears. "Derrick and Sarah Armstrong."

His brows furrowed and his gaze skipped around her face. His mouth slowly opened. He squinted. "Are you...? Oh my God. You're Chloe's daughter?"

Willow nodded while keeping in mind her mother had hidden the pregnancy from him. "I am."

"Of course. I can see a resemblance."

"Yes. Only slight." Shit. How did she tell this man everything she knew?

He wrapped his hand around the base of his glass. "My goodness. I haven't thought about Chloe in a long time." He snorted a little laugh while staring out the window. "Your mum and I used to have to sneak around to date after our fathers had a huge fight over politics." He shook his head and looked at her. "Two stubborn men. A bit like your mum, too. How is Chloe? Still in America, is she?"

"She was. Unfortunately, I lost my mother in a car accident years ago." The nostalgic gleam in his eyes slipped away. "Oh, God. I'm sorry." His eyes watered. "She was a special one. Knew how to make everyone comfortable around her, always happy. Losing her must've been hard for you and your father."

Willow's mouth went dry. She nodded. Of course. He talked with the ease of a man who'd just met the daughter of a woman he once dated, because that's all she was to him.

"My grandparents' house has been left to me. While cleaning, I found something you might remember." She reached into her rucksack and removed the photo Owen had found in the kitchen.

She handed it to Sean. He studied it, his mouth lifting in a smile, his eyes shining in a way that needed no words. He sighed and handed it back to her. "For years, I couldn't get past your mother's leaving. How did you figure out that was me in the photo?"

"Oh, long story. But she did write about you in a diary I found in her childhood bedroom."

"Did she?" He frowned. "I'm surprised. When she ran off, I figured she didn't love me like she'd said." He laughed, his gaze drifting toward the bar and a distant look of reminiscing in his eyes. "When she didn't show up for our afternoon plans the day after New Year's, I went to the house. My gut told me something was wrong. Mr. Armstrong answered. One look on his face confirmed my worries."

"What did he tell you?"

"He invited me in. Said he'd found Chloe's diary and knew what we'd been up to. He patiently listened to my rant about how much I loved his daughter and no longer wanted to hide my feelings for her. That's when he told me she'd run off to London. I didn't believe him, accused him of trying to keep us apart. Then he..." Sean paused. "Never mind."

"What? Please, Mr. Cooke."

"Young lady, I don't want to tell tales. You should remember all good things about your mother. What happened with us, well, it was so long ago."

"But the whole reason I searched for you is because my mother kept so much from me. I'd hoped you might help fill in the blanks."

He pursed his lips. "Blanks?"

She drew in a breath, exhaled. "I never knew my father. Mom told me he was from the States, but based on some things I learned since arriving here, I suspect my mother got pregnant before she left England."

Sean jerked his head back, his graying brows rising to his thin, sweeping bangs. "And you think—" He glanced around the bar, then leaned in and lowered his voice. "You think I might be your father?"

She stared into his eyes, wishing she saw something besides shock. "Based on the timing, yes. In my mother's diary, her last entry wrote about leaving. It even wrote she wasn't going to tell you about the baby. About me."

He shook his head. "That's impossible. Chloe would've told me. I'm sure she would've—" He drew his lips into a thin line and a shadow of anger flashed in his eyes. "Or maybe not."

"What do you mean?"

He leaned back in his seat and folded his hands, choosing to stare at them for a long moment. Slowly, he lifted his head. "What I didn't want to share with you a moment ago...well, it's possible I'm not your father."

"Why?"

He dropped his chin, gaze focused on the rustic table as he shifted in his seat.

"Mr. Cooke, please."

"Just call me Sean. Anyway, it seems Chloe's dad had caught her in her bedroom with Elliot Williams, an older boy who lived in their neighborhood."

"Caught doing what?"

His cheeks turned pink and his gaze drifted toward the window. "Nothing a man my age should be talking about to a young woman like you."

"So my mother hadn't only been involved with you. She'd been with another man at the same time?"

He nodded and lifted the pilsner glass to his lips, still avoiding her eyes.

Had her mother been having sex with two men? The diary read that she couldn't tell Sean about the baby, but maybe if Willow had read all the entries instead of hopping ahead to those final days she wrote in it, she'd have learned a fuller picture of her mother's life.

He slapped his hands on the table, making her jump. Tension balled in his jaw. "God damn her. For cheating. For lying."

Willow couldn't budge or agree with his anger. Her heart ached, bruised and battered by the unimaginable. Two men. Two possible fathers. Were there more?

The joy she'd expected upon catching up with her father nose-dived down a dark hole. Each and every deception by her mother had grown into an ugly beast.

She sat quietly, her body numb as one thought pounded in her head, over and over and over…The one person who'd claimed to love her was a fake. Thickness blocked her throat. She turned her head and stared out the window, trying to grapple with the reason her mother insisted on having her instead of giving her up for adoption or having an abortion. Instead, she gave birth to a child conceived from deceit and raised with a lifetime of lies. Her existence was a joke.

"I'm sorry, Willow." Sean spoke quietly.

She slowly lifted her head and found him watching her. "Is there a chance you could be my father?"

"It's possible. But…" He shrugged, folded his hands onto the table and dropped his gaze to them, not an ounce of curiosity in his face.

But she wanted answers. "There are tests. We could find out for certain."

Sean glanced up and frowned. "After Chloe left, it took me a while to move on. Now I have a family. What would this do to them?" He pinched his fingers to the bridge of his nose, shaking his head. "Good God, my wife, she'd be so upset."

"I'm sure it would be a shock," she said gently, so he'd hear her sympathy for his dilemma. "But, it's not as if you knew what my mother had done."

"No, my wife, she's a good woman but… This would upset our family, Willow. She can be jealous, and we have grandchildren now. I just don't want to upset the family with this old news."

"Please, just think about it. You might feel different in a few days."

He silently watched her for a moment then shook his head. "I don't think I will."

His words hit like a door slammed in her face, escalating her disbelief over what she'd uncovered at this stop.

She pushed back her chair and it scraped the floor. "Sorry to take up your time. I'd better get going." She dug into her pocket, removing a twenty-pound note and tossing it on the table. "I need to get back on the trail."

"What?"

"Yes, I'm walking the Cotswold Way and need to get somewhere before dark."

Sean stood. "Willow. I'm sorry. I have a good life and don't want to jeopardize it."

She grabbed her rucksack, swallowed hard to stop tears. "No. It's okay. I understand, Sean. Really. Thank you for your time."

Hoisting the rucksack on her shoulders, she rushed out the door.

* * * *

Where the hell is she?

Owen tossed his cell phone on the passenger seat of the van and bit back his frustration. Three hours ago, Willow should've checked into her hotel in Stroud. Since then, every text or call he'd made had gone unanswered.

He pulled up in front of Bea's house and turned toward the back seat, where Jilly sat dressed in her pajamas. "Here we are, pumpkin. Nan's excited to have you for the night."

"Me, too. Henry loves sleeping over here."

The dog stood on the back seat next to Jilly, wagging his tail in agreement.

Owen helped her out and to the front door, where Bea waited. After a good night hug, he hurried back to the van. Next stop, Stroud. The GPS said he'd arrive in forty-eight minutes. He'd worry every single second of it.

Willow had had plenty of time to arrive there, especially given her text showing her arrival in Painswick. Things may have gone well with Sean and she'd possibly joined him for dinner. But why wouldn't she have answered one of his three texts or answered any of his calls?

Images of her on the trail with a twisted ankle, passed out from exhaustion, or meeting some unsavory characters—all right, a little far-fetched—forced him to press harder on the accelerator.

He arrived at the Prince of Wales Inn three minutes earlier than the GPS estimated. He ran inside to the reception desk and learned she still hadn't checked in. The room had been paid for in advance and they assured him it would be available for her when she did.

He left his van in the hotel lot and hurried along the street toward town, a place she'd have passed through once off the footpath. At each local restaurant, he stopped to ask if anyone fitting Willow's description had been there.

By the time he reached the edge of the commercial area, no pub or restaurant claimed to have seen her. He jogged toward the trail. Away from the other businesses and closer to the trail entrance, he ran past a white, thatched-roof building with a sign near the door reading *Red Lion Pub*. He stopped and peeked inside the window, though he held little hope he'd find her.

Inside the smoky bar area, a group of men in a far corner tossed darts. Several more sat crowded at the bar, laughing and having fun. His heart jolted when he spotted Willow on a stool not far from them.

He rushed inside just as Willow tipped a short glass to her lips containing a tawny-colored liquid. Probably whiskey.

As she lowered it, she squeezed her eyes, scrunched her nose, and swallowed. She opened her eyes and turned to the brawly man sitting closest to her. "You're right, Leo. This is strong...very strong. But I kind of liked it." She raised her brows and laughed. "What should I try next?"

"Willow." Owen went to her side, both relieved and annoyed to find her so casually enjoying herself.

She slowly turned to him. Her eyes went wide before she smiled brightly. "Owen!" She opened her arms and leaned forward, her body teetering. He rushed forward and slipped his arms around her waist, letting go when she seemed securely on the stool.

Willow laughed loudly, sending a gust of whiskey-scented breath his way. "You saved me, Owen. I almost fell. You always save me. You're a real hero." She leaned closer, swaying on the stool. "A reaaaal hero."

He put his arms around her waist and kept her steady. "What's going on, Willow?"

She frowned, so over-exaggerated it reminded him of Jilly when she didn't get her way. "What? No more Rosebud?" She grinned while her gaze took on a sultry shimmer and she dropped her voice. "I like when you call me that."

Yup. She was bloody pissed and hanging out with strange men in a bar. "I've been worried about you."

"Me? Why you were..." She threw back her head and laughed. "Why *were you* worried about lil' ol' me?" The words blended into one. She abruptly turned to the men sitting nearby and yelled, "Hear that fellas? He was worried about me."

A couple of them laughed. Something was wrong. Very wrong.

"Listen, Rosebud. How about I get you to the hotel?"

Her eyes hooded, desire he'd seen before, and she cupped his face in her warm hands. "So you want to get me to a hotel?" She pressed her lips to his, softly at first. Drawing herself closer, she covered his mouth with hers, kissing him deeply and giving him a sample of the strong whiskey she'd been drinking.

The men nearby whistled and even clapped.

She pulled back and in a husky voice said, "God, I've missed you."

"I missed you, too." Over her shoulder, he could see the men at the bar watching them with smirks on their faces. He could only imagine what had been going on before he'd arrived. "You were supposed to be at your hotel hours ago." She narrowed her gaze and drew back. "How do you know? Are you following me?"

"No. I…I just know. You sent me a text today remember?" Her face saddened. "Yes. From Painswick." She shut her eyes and a tear rolled along her cheek. She slowly opened them and they glistened from the overhead lights. "Why are you reminding me?"

The bartender came out from the back room and went straight to Owen. "Listen, mate. She got here a few hours ago and seemed pretty upset about something. She's been drinking up a storm. I'm glad you got here. I wasn't sure where to send her and she wouldn't offer anything."

"What's she owe you?"

The bartender told him and Owen paid the tab. He couldn't be sure what happened when she met Sean Cooke in Painswick, but based on her current state, it couldn't be good.

"Listen, gorgeous, how about we split this place?" He slipped an arm around her waist. "Get a bite to eat and then get to bed."

"Get to bed." Her knees buckled as he guided her off the stool, but he held her up. "Now you're talking, handsome."

As he swiped the rucksack leaning against the bar, he avoided the eyes of the other patrons and guided her to the door.

"Bye-bye, fellas," she yelled.

"Bye, Willow," they hollered back, mixed with their laughter.

Owen guided her along the pavement, his arm around her waist as she leaned into his armpit. Every so often, she'd pull away to look in a shop window or wave at passing cars. The attention span of a child. He almost laughed a few times, but worried more about how she'd feel in the morning.

Once at the hotel, they went to the front desk. He found her money and passport packed away in her rucksack, feeling damn lucky that in her condition nobody had taken them. As they walked to the room, she got quieter and once inside, she took her bag from him and headed for the toilet.

When she finally came out, she'd removed her clothes and wore an oversized red T-shirt with her company logo, the edge of her pink panties peeking out from beneath. She'd scrubbed her face clean and brushed out her hair, pushed away from her face in a headband. Never had she looked sexier.

She plopped down beside him on the bed. "Guess what?"

"What?" He took her hand.

"My damn mother had been sleeping with two men. Two!" Her voice rose as she shook her head. "Poor Sean. He loved her. He—didn't even know about me until, until..."

Willow dropped her head to the pillow and started to cry. In a matter of seconds, her body shook as tears turned into sobs.

She lifted her head, took a deep breath. "My grandfather, he found out..." Willow let out a sad, low wail. "His dau-daug-daughter was messin' around with two men."

"So there's someone besides Sean?"

She nodded then grabbed a pillow. Drawing it to her chest, she rolled away from him and curled into a fetal position while continuing to cry. He stretched out next to her, wrapped her in his arms, and held her. As her tears subsided, he scooted her over and lifted the blankets. "Come on, get under these."

She did as he asked and her eyes closed the second her head hit the pillow. He drew the blanket to her shoulders and waited at her bedside until her chest slowly rose and fell, assuring him she'd fallen asleep.

He called Bea to let her know he'd found Willow then got undressed and crawled in beside her. Immediately, she rolled toward him and rested her cheek near his shoulder.

"Night, Owen," she said in a soft, sleepy voice. "Thank you for finding me." She snuggled closer, her warm breath cascading onto his neck. Then her voice drifted off as she said, almost in a whisper, "I love you."

Before he could respond, she began to gently snore.

He wrapped his head around her words and the way it felt so right to cradle her in his hold. Love. *Where did that come from?*

Probably the booze. And the pain.

Still, knowing what she'd just said could have come from an entirely different place, he admitted to himself how he might be developing the same kinds of feelings for her.

Chapter 23

Willow slowly moved her lips, dry as a midday desert. She wet them with her tongue and stopped when a searing pain pierced her skull.

Squeezing her eyes tight, she shifted on the mattress, causing every single muscle in her body to silently scream. Had she been run over by a truck?

Flashbacks of last night slowly emerged. The friendly bar, where everybody seemed to know her name. She'd swear she even met a guy named Norm, or maybe she'd only made a joke about it. Especially after having her second drink and sharing all about herself with them. One glass of whiskey to drown her sorrows led to another and another.

A warm hand slipped onto her hip. Owen. His handsome face when he'd arrived at the bar had brought her such joy, and the tender way he guided her to the hotel was the stuff that created heroes.

She rolled onto her back. The room tilted right and left, back and forth. Worse than any carnival ride she'd ever gone on. She shut her eyes, but the room's movement persisted. Her neck and forehead beaded with sweat.

Bile rose in the back of her throat. She tossed off the covers and flew out of the bed, reaching the bathroom just in time to drop to the toilet bowl. She waited a few minutes and got sick a second time. With a washcloth against her forehead, she sat on the floor and waited until the nausea passed.

Getting to her feet, she started the shower and stepped inside. The hot water beat on her skin, slowly waking her as the steam's healing properties rinsed away her hangover. After the shower, she brushed her teeth, towel-dried her hair, and wrapped a towel around her torso.

Tiptoeing into the room, she glanced at the bed. Owen lay on his back with his eyes shut, one arm extended to her side of the bed, the other bent at the elbow and stretched over his head. A sheet covered him from the navel down, leaving his bare torso exposed. She studied the thin, dark patch of hairs on his abdomen flowing in a line to his navel, the hard plane of his chest. Easily aroused by the sight of him, she squeezed her thighs together. She quietly opened her rucksack and took out clean panties and a T-shirt for the day.

As she slipped on the panties and the shirt, he cleared his throat. "You okay, Rosebud?"

She turned around. His sleepy gaze met hers as he patted the spot beside him.

Taking a seat on the edge of the bed, she reached for his hand. "Not when I first woke, but now I feel better." She glanced at the clock on the nightstand. 6:15. "It's early."

He nodded, watching her with a heat in his eyes that burned straight into her core. She stretched alongside him, comforted when he folded his arms around her and tugged her against his side.

She pressed her palm to the dark shadow of his cheek. "Thank you for worrying enough to find me last night. How'd you know where I was?"

"Finding you was dumb luck." He drew in a breath. "I won't lie. I've asked each of the hotels to call me when you arrive and leave each day. Just to keep tabs on you."

"Wow, you did?" Willow couldn't remember a time when anybody cared enough to do such a thing for her, at least in her adult life.

He nodded. "Are you mad?"

"No. Not at all. I'm not used to anyone worrying about me." She leaned over and brushed her lips to his, a minor gift considering how much she valued his concern. "It's nice to have someone care about my well-being."

"Of course I do." He ran a finger along her cheek. "Last night, you told me a little about what happened when you found Sean."

Yesterday's sadness rolled in like a black cloud, but being in Owen's hold made it easier to handle. "How much did I tell you?"

"You don't remember?"

"Not really."

"You said your mother had been involved with two men. And you mumbled something about your grandfather, but it wasn't clear."

To relive the painful journey hurt, but she relayed details on her mother's two lovers and confirmed Hettie's revelation about the reasons her mother and Sean secretly dated.

"So the two men, seems either one could be my father." A wave of disgust for her mother barreled toward Willow. She released a shaky breath. "My mom was a real gem, huh? Cheating on Sean. Lying to me my whole life."

Owen frowned. "Yeah, I'd be upset, too. But she wanted you enough to leave here to keep you."

"When you say it like that, I feel like a schmuck for feeling crummy."

Owen stroked her hair. "Don't. I'm just saying, she did one thing right."

Willow smiled at him, warmth rising inside of her, followed by regret her time in England would soon end.

"Did you see anything about the other guy in your mother's diary?"

"I only read the first few pages and then I zipped to the end. Once I'd read that she got pregnant but couldn't tell Sean, I figured that said it all. Guess it was shortsighted not to read more."

"You know, there's still a chance Sean is your dad."

Her throat grew thick, Sean's lack of interest in her as his daughter tore at her heart, as painful as her mother's lies. "He doesn't want to know." She shrugged, afraid to say more and start crying, but the pity in Owen's eyes coaxed them out.

Owen gathered her tightly and placed gentle kisses on her head, murmured how everything would be okay.

She sniffled and looked up. "How'd I get lucky enough to meet you on this journey?"

"Funny, I was thinking the same thing." He pulled a tissue from the box on the nightstand and dabbed her eyes. She smiled at him while taking the tissue and wiping her nose.

"Better?" He raised a brow.

"Thanks to you." She pressed her hands to his chest, thinking about some other decisions she'd made while on her walk. "There's something I need to tell you."

He shifted his pillow and rose up on his elbow. "Sounds serious."

"It kind of is. I'm not going to sell the cottage."

His thick brows drew together. "So, you're still selling the house but keeping the cottage."

"Yes."

He nodded, but his jaw tightened. "So then you like the area enough to keep a place here?"

"Sort of." She dropped her gaze to the white sheet covering the space between them while searching for the right words. "I...I..."

"Just say what you need to say, Willow. It's me you're talking to."

"I don't want to sell it because I don't want you to have to move."

He dropped his head back onto the pillow. "I don't feel right about this. You need the money."

"I talked to an attorney and he said I *could* sell only the house and keep the cottage. If I keep it, then I'll have a place here if I want to come visit. And then you guys can stay there."

He smiled softly, ran a finger along her cheek. "That's very nice of you, sweetheart. But I insist on paying you rent—"

She put a finger to his lips. "Stop. If I keep the place, I'll need someone to keep an eye on it while I'm in the States."

He flinched. "Yes, you're leaving soon. When you come back, you'll want the cottage. Won't you?"

She groaned and pressed her hands to his chest. "Stop making this harder than it is, Owen. I'll stay with you and..." Their future together held all the uncertainty of a partially sunny day. What if he began to date someone after she left or she did? Visits here would be different. "Look, I just feel like I need to keep a piece of myself here and the cottage is it. So, I'd be honored if you and your family stayed in it. At least until I'm sure what my future holds."

Staring at the ceiling, he ran a hand through his hair leaving the dark ends sticking up. "And I'm honored you'd ask me, but I don't want to feel like charity case. I'm happy to pay you some—"

"No." She moved closer to his side and cupped her face in her hands. "I don't want rent. It's not charity. It's the arrangement you have now, only now you know me. Please say yes. I trust you."

For a moment, he stared at her, then a smile slowly surfaced. "Okay. I'll do it. Thank you," he said softly. "I won't let you down."

Her heart swelled, filled with gratitude for Owen's generosity and caring. She inched closer, curled her fingers through his thick hair. "I know you won't."

Owen dipped his head and brushed his lips to hers. As he drew back, he stared into her eyes, searching as if he were memorizing them. In a tender voice, he asked, "Last night, before you went to sleep, do you remember anything else?"

Flashbacks sorted through her mind, some clear, others fuzzy. "Like?"

"Nothing."

He kissed her again while smoothing his hand along her waist, to her hip, and to her backside, making both a physical need for him and one close to her heart soar. She slipped her arms around his waist and urged him closer, and that's when it hit her...

Last night, he'd crawled into bed, pressed his warm body to hers, sending her heart spiraling upward with something unexpected. A fulfilling sensation she'd never allowed too close: the idea of love.

Had she said the words swirling inside her head? She thought hard and a single moment came into focus. *I love you.* Yes, she'd said it. Because he made her feel all kinds of special. Notice things in herself she'd never seen before. But love? She couldn't possibly love a man in this short time. Could she?

But what if her vague recollection was wrong and she hadn't spoken those words? She didn't need that embarrassment after losing all hope of finding her father.

She leaned forward and kissed him. "I do remember your kindness by helping me to the hotel. That meant the world."

He smiled and nodded, but she swore behind his eyes she caught a glimpse of disappointment.

* * * *

Willow quickly exited the email from her lawyer. His news helped her answer a question she'd been contemplating since getting ready to leave the hotel this morning. Putting her phone on the table, she stared out the small café's window to the quaint street.

While Owen had showered earlier, she'd given much thought to the remainder of her time on the Cotswold Way. A journey where she'd believed she might find her father and solve a mystery haunting her for a lifetime. But like all the recent events in her life, it hadn't work out as planned.

Which got her thinking about everything driving her weight over the years. Once she'd started that company, a slip in the scale held the terror of a noose around her neck. Not a healthy outlook. She needed to find ways to cope when things didn't go as planned.

"Tea and a toast for my heavy drinker." Owen placed a mug in front of Willow.

She glanced up and smiled at him. "Don't remind me." She leaned over the cup and inhaled the scent. Heavenly tea. "Thank you. This is just what I needed."

He stirred sugar into his mug of coffee. "What time are you getting back on the trail?"

She met his gaze. With Abe's news, she really only had one answer to give Owen. "I'm not doing the rest."

He tipped his head and frowned. "Why not?"

"Well, I've been thinking about it and sometimes it isn't always about finishing the journey, it's what you gain while on it. This walk has made me pause and take a good look at my life. I once measured success by a number on the scale. A pretty sad statement. Maybe true success is about loving yourself no matter the number on the scale or finishing the trail." She shrugged. "Does that make sense?"

"Absolutely." He took her hand. "And Sean?"

"I didn't get what I wanted, but he did share some wonderful memories about my mother. Stories I'd never heard before."

He gave her hand a gentle squeeze. "I'm glad. It sounds like you learned more about yourself walking half of the way than some others do on the full hundred miles."

She laughed. "Maybe. That time alone, removed from the day-to-day, taught me to stop and really look around. That's where the important things are all happening in our lives. It's easy to miss them." She sighed, overwhelmed by the idea she'd been so singled-minded for decades. "All that beauty makes you think about your place in the universe."

He reached across the table and took her hand. "Beautiful observation. I may have to walk it again myself."

"Maybe one day I'll come back and we can walk it together. So many times I wished you were with me."

He smiled. "Aw, now you're making my heart sing, Rosebud."

"Are you being sarcastic?"

"Hell, no. I thought about you each and every day. Not just about your safety, but I wished I could've been at your side, shared what I know about the countryside." He brought her hand to his mouth and brushed a kiss across her knuckles. "I'm going to make you keep that promise."

He let go of her hand and they quietly ate.

As she picked at her crust, she searched for the right words to tell him what she'd just read, then opted to just get the truth out on the table. "I got an email from my lawyer this morning."

He looked up, still spreading his jam. "Oh?"

"I've been avoiding the Pound Busters board because they want to fire me. But it seems they're tired of waiting for me to respond and have decided to take a vote in four days…with or without me there."

He lowered his knife, shaking his head. "It's crazy they'd sack you from the company you started. Hardly seems just."

"When I went public I knew the risks, but I'm inclined to agree. Abe, my lawyer, thinks I should come back home. He's convinced enough of them will vote to keep me if I show up. The current board president is losing some favor with them."

"Sounds very political."

She nodded. "Yes, the boardroom can be."

He stared at his plate. When he finally looked up, his Adam's apple rolled along his throat. "So, I guess you're keen to get leaving soon?"

"I'm going to try to get on the flight leaving tomorrow morning." She reached out for his hand, mostly to steady a tidal wave of sorrow knocking her for a loop. "Today I need to talk to the realtor again, but with the work almost done, I'm hoping to get the place listed."

He gave her a closed-lip smile. "I can help you with that." His smile faded. "I really can't thank you enough. Don't ever feel like you can't sell the cottage, though. Jilly, she just needs time to adjust. It was only a short year ago her mother passed and…" He drew in a breath. "Well, I expect in time, she'll be able to cope with a move."

"Owen. It's fine. Right now, I'd feel better if you two stayed. For Jilly and Henry."

She dropped her chin, staring into her tea, much easier than absorbing the pain radiating from Owen's eyes. Jilly. Henry. Owen. They felt like family.

"Hey."

Owen's deep voice made her look up. His sadness had gone and, in its place, he grinned.

"What?"

"Come on. Let's make the most of today. And tomorrow, I'll drive you to Heathrow." His eyes softened. "You're a special woman, Willow Armstrong, and I'm lucky to have met you."

She got up and walked over to him. Placing her hands on his shoulders, she enjoyed a moment lost in his rich, brown eyes. "Owen. It's me who's the lucky one."

She leaned over and pressed her lips to his, thinking about the words she couldn't bring herself to say. Yet every fiber in her being wanted Owen to understand that leaving him behind would be one of the most difficult things she'd ever done.

His hands slipped around her waist and he pulled her onto his lap.

"Hey!" She laughed. "What are you doing?"

"This." He pushed his fingers through her hair and kissed her in a way that told her he understood *exactly* how she felt about him.

Chapter 24

The cab driver mumbled something in Greek and tooted his horn. "Come on!"

Willow dragged her gaze from commuters hustling into Grand Central Terminal for their ride home to the driver, a sweet old man who'd been very talkative since he'd picked her up at her co-op for the board meeting. "I haven't missed the mayhem of rush hour."

"You best to stay in England, yes?" His dark gaze watched her in the rearview mirror.

"It would've been nice. Certainly not much traffic where I visited."

They turned onto 42nd Street and approached Bryant Park, where shoppers mingled in the makeshift shops lining the popular tourist destination. White lights in park's trees twinkled as dusk darkened the cityscape. A perfect New York photo moment, one that would've suited the calendar Willow had found in her mother's room.

When she'd returned to Bitton from her walk on the Cotswold Way, she'd retrieved her mother's diary from a box about to be mailed to the US. The next day, on the long trans-Atlantic flight home, she'd devoured every last word. She'd cried a few times. The words carried her mother's voice, as if she'd returned from the past and were speaking directly to her.

She learned her mother had loved both Sean and Elliot. The college boy had swept her mother under his charming spell, but not enough to alter what she had felt for Sean. That single notion brought Willow comfort.

Earlier entries about Willow's grandfather showed her mom had a close bond with him. Perhaps when he'd caught her with Elliot and learned of her pregnancy, shame made her run and never return. It was a logic Willow would never know, but it would explain the regret often visible in her mother's eyes when she'd share a rare tale about her parents.

Willow watched the activity in Bryant Park. Jilly would love this place, especially the ice skating rink. Longing squeezed Willow's heart in a spot reserved for Owen and Jilly. And even Henry.

Just over forty-eight hours ago, she'd been at Heathrow, holding Jilly tightly and offering promises to return soon, trying to stifle her own tears while the poor child's spilled. And kissing Owen goodbye, wrapped in the warmth of his arms while savoring one last kiss.

Thickness clogged her throat now, as it had done then. The second she'd returned to her apartment, she'd Skyped them. Proof she'd stick to her promise to do so. Since then, she and Owen had texted multiple times a day.

Tension knotted her shoulders. She'd be more relaxed going to tonight's board meeting if he sat at her side.

She studied the people hurrying along the sidewalks. Tall, short, heavy, thin, average. Everyone one of them a unique package on the outside, but not necessarily a wrapping that reflected who they were on the inside. Somewhere along the way, Willow had lost sight of this simple fact when it came to the image she saw in the mirror each day.

She smoothed the front of the pencil skirt she'd selected for the board meeting, worn with a jacket that buttoned at the waist. An outfit she'd put on many times since gaining this recent weight, but this afternoon when she'd looked in the mirror, she saw a different woman. She'd ran a hand over the full curves of her torso that had previously caused her to grimace. This time, touching the road map of her body made her think back to Owen's response to it. She must've been crazy to think anything but good things about herself.

This *was* her. Take it or leave it.

Her phone buzzed and she pulled it from her briefcase, smiling when she saw the text from Owen.

About to go to bed, but hope I caught you
before you face the board. Remember this:
"It isn't what we say or think that
defines us, but what we do."
No. It's not an Owen original. It's a quote written
by Jane Austen, in Sense and Sensibility. Remember
those words, stand proud, and don't take any guff

from those cheeky bastards tonight, Rosebud. I'm
at your side in spirit. Good luck, Gorgeous.

Gorgeous. Since she met him, he'd tossed out little phrases or studied her through eyes that tore her from an image of herself she'd clung to over a lifetime.

She typed back.

On my way there right now. Thank you. For
your message and for always making me feel
so good. I will let you know how it goes. Xx

The cab neared the Pound Busters building, sending a flurry of nerves pinging inside her stomach. She took a deep breath and exhaled, though the nerves remained. Hell, facing a firing squad might be less stressful.

She paid the driver and headed through the glass doors into the lobby. Tonight, she had two speeches planned. One would pacify the board, the other they'd deem more controversial. Right now, she wasn't sure which she'd use.

* * * *

"I second the motion." Tom Botsford, a long-time member of the board, passed Nikki Winslow a wolflike smile as he supported the motion she'd just made.

Willow's gaze drifted to Nikki, who nodded but didn't flinch at the suggestiveness in the eighty-four-year-old's eyes. Her skill at dealing with board members' idiosyncrasies helped solidify her power.

"Thank you, Tom." Nikki turned to the meeting secretary. "Please record the motion to approve a loan to cover our losses from the recent abuse by our financial advisor." She flashed a smug glare in Willow's direction.

Willow kept her gaze on Nikki and straightened in her chair. She'd arrived at the meeting early enough to secure a seat opposite Nikki's, at the head of the long, rectangular table. This way, Willow at least held a power corner. She reached up to her throat and took the rose charm between her thumb and forefinger. As she ran her thumb on the grooves, it not only reminded her of the journey that started the day she had slipped this on, but the powerful insights gained each step of the way.

Abe tapped her forearm and pushed a notepad toward, pointing to the margin with his pen. He'd scribbled *Stay strong, kiddo,* along with a happy face.

She lifted her gaze his way and smiled. Over the tops of dark-rimmed reading glasses, he did the same, making the corners of his eyes crinkle. The day she'd returned from England, they'd met for lunch and she'd laid out plans for a new way to run Pound Busters, using the awareness found on her journey. A plan she hoped she could present to defend her role as CEO. Abe had liked her fresh look at the company image, but warned her some of the members here tonight might not.

The question, how much was she willing to risk to keep her job?

"Last item of the night is…" Nikki's voice rose and she paused to read from the agenda before her.

Willow forced her attention to the head of the table.

"…the replacement of our current Chief Executive Officer, Willow Armstrong." Nikki glanced up, looking everywhere but at Willow. "Before we vote, I've told Willow she can have an opportunity to speak. A last chance to explain her current physical condition and decisions she has made that have taken us to this regretful decision."

Willow stared back and refused to look away.

Nikki's gaze drifted briefly to Willow and she just as quickly pulled it away. "I do remind you all that, in her role as figurehead for this organization, Willow hasn't presented an image some of us believe best represents our views. And in case any of you have forgotten, her pizza-eating episode made national TV." She looked to the end of table, her superior expression wielding the power of a weapon. "That said, Willow, the floor is yours."

The mention of the horrible video stung like a blow to the chest, but Willow drew in a deep breath, remembered her mission, and got to her feet to address the group.

She glanced around the sea of faces intently waiting for her to speak. Both friends and foe, each with very different wishes for her.

Her gut quivered. The new approach to running this business that sounded so good in her head had lost some steam. Risk never stopped her in the past, but if this speech went sour, she might lose the company. And if they liked it and employed it, what if her new idea proved wrong? Her reputation in the business world was at stake.

She took a deep breath, and opted for her safer speech. "Pound Busters was my creation. It's a method for weight loss I believe in. Our philosophy has impacted so many people across our country, leaving our members happier and healthier. Despite the problems I've had with my image for a while now, I still believe in our message and..."

The words were a lie.

She studied the faces around the table, some nodding and understanding. Others' staring down at their hands or the table. Nikki watched with the smugness of Stalin about to have his guards toss a traitor in the Gulag.

Rage churned through Willow. This board's interest lay in a philosophy she could no longer stomach. In a way of viewing people's struggles with weight that she hadn't understood until forced to face this fate. As her anger propelled her to speak honestly, she debated the outcome.

It isn't what we say or think that defines us, but what we do.

Owen's text. Did she want to leave here tonight wishing she'd done the right thing or not doing it?

Perhaps someone needed to speak out on behalf of those who struggled with weight loss every single day. Who proudly slipped on pants in a new size that might *not* be the one society deemed perfect, but were perfect for them. A realistic outlook, not a "do or die fat" mentality geared to overly thin images of women seen on TV and in magazines. But an approach for real women, who possess a plethora of qualities that make them special. Who aren't inferior because they aren't pretty enough or skinny enough or not suitable enough to run a company.

"You know what?"

Several of the members who hadn't been watching looked her way, and those who had raised their brows.

"I'm going to forget about the excuses I'd been prepared to offer to this group. Here's why." She took a step back from the table and paced, aware of how they watched and knowing she had their full attention. "Weight loss is tough and the reason is simple. It's because we are human. Humans feel things. Happy things. Sad things. And those emotions—even the good ones—can sometimes trigger us to turn to food. Up until now, I hadn't seen a fundamental flaw with the philosophy here at Pound Busters."

"Oh, come now, Willow." Nikki's sunken cheeks turned crimson and her jaw went tight. "A flaw in a philosophy you once touted as indispensable?"

Willow had a hundred angry retorts, but all sidetracked her from her true goal. "Yes, a flaw, Nikki." She stopped pacing and canvased the group. "Can anybody guess what it is?"

The others glanced uncomfortably at each other and Willow waited it out.

"Well, let me tell you. We drive our members hard and accept no excuses. I suppose for some members, that is what they want. But nothing we do truly allows for forgiveness. Because sometimes we humans are fragile beings and we mess up."

A few board members slowly nodded, giving her the power to continue. "We eat something we shouldn't. We eat because our friends are. We ignore exercise in place of a movie. Or we eat because we feel sad, like when we get bad news. But who are we to perpetuate a myth that the alternative to being thin is unacceptable?" She stood a little taller, pulling her shoulders back and raising her chin. Waving a hand along her frame, she said, "When we act like looking like *this* isn't acceptable?"

Murmurs filled the air.

She resumed her pacing, aware of the intent eyes following her. "Yes. I've put on weight. So what? It doesn't change who I am or my abilities. Confidence from the inside out is what people need. And it all boils down to one thing..."

She stopped, the room's silence quiet enough to hear a pin drop.

"Acceptance."

More nods.

"Yes. Everything I've been through has showed me acceptance of who I am—flaws and all—has been missing my entire life. It's been missing from our company philosophy. Did you ever question why people leave our centers?"

"Honestly, Willow." Nikki smirked. "Are you trying to tell me that you're fine with your current weight and that's how you are going to suggest our firm move forward?"

"Good question. Am I fine with this weight?" She thought about the past weeks and the evolution inside her when she finished walking the Cotswold Way. "Yes, I am fine with it. Someday I may want to lose a few pounds, but never be as obsessive as I used to be. Because at this weight, I'm normal. Normal! Do you people understand what that means? Do you understand why our current philosophy makes us un-relatable to so many people who might want to lose but don't carry such an extreme view about it?"

"Don't be ridiculous." Nikki slapped her palm on the table. "What you're suggesting is a huge departure from our current philosophy. Our members are happy with the more militant approach."

"I disagree." Willow stared at Nikki, confident in her new belief and sad she'd let such an extreme view dominate her ambitions for decades. "We need to open the door and let customers know we have a better understanding of what happens when our weight loss doesn't go as planned."

Nikki snorted. "Fine. Need I remind you the board has other issues with your performance? The money stolen by the financial advisor is still an issue."

"I stood by someone I believed loyal to me. To my firm. While the company suffered, he stole my personal funds, too. Hindsight is twenty-twenty. All I can do is move forward. It's all the firm can do."

Nikki shifted and her gaze hopped to each board member, perhaps searching for support. The majority sat with rock-hard expressions. "Is that all you have to say to the members here?"

Willow scanned the group, certain a few were with her, but not sure how a vote would go. Yet it almost didn't matter. For the first time in her life, she felt amazing. Satisfied with her weight with self-doubt about her appearance not even slowly creeping into her mind.

"One more thing. No matter what the outcome, I thank the board for their time and am still committed to Pound Busters, as I have always been."

She took her seat, mentally exhausted but lifted by her own words, committed to a new cause no matter what happened here.

Based on frowns around the table, not all of them seemed convinced about her new outlook.

"Thank you, Willow." Nikki's gaze panned the table. "Back to the matter at hand, the replacement of our current Chief Executive Officer.

As if on cue, Alistair Lockwood glanced briefly at Willow, then to Nikki. "I move this board release Willow Armstrong as Chief Executive Officer of Pound Busters. Do I have a second?"

Traitor. Willow had figured he'd vote against her anyway.

Nikki smirked and straightened her shoulders, sitting a bit taller in her seat. "So moved. Do I have a second?"

The man sitting next to Alistair grumbled, "Seconded."

Nikki nodded. "Those in favor of her removal say aye."

Willow's heart pattered fast as a hummingbird's wings. The battle had ended. No matter what the outcome, she'd won a war fought with herself for her entire life.

Chapter 25

Two months later...

Willow studied the faces of her senior executives. As they listened to the two marketing gurus from Gilmore & Gilmore Creative Services, their expressions seemed engaged, positive, like they were as excited as her over this new direction for the firm.

Beverly O'Hare, senior VP at Gilmore & Gilmore, smiled and gave a thumbs-up to Willow. Since the Pound Busters' board voted 5-4 to keep Willow, she and Beverly had worked day and night to arrive at this moment. Willow nodded and turned to the screen to see the image she'd approved three days before.

Beverly waved toward a screen at the front of the room. "And now, we'd like to unveil your firm's new slogan..."

The ad they planned on launching in the late spring showed an aerial shot with a group of people huddled together, smiling up at a camera. Men and women of varying sizes, shapes, and ages. Beneath them read the words, "Pound Busters, Find Your Inner Strength."

The applause started slowly. Soon the entire room of her employees clapped louder and louder as they rose to their feet. Willow fought tears. Not only had her new vision been so succinctly captured by this award-winning ad firm, but based on the applause, her upper management loved it, too.

Willow walked over and shook hands with Beverly, then with her senior ad staff. "It's perfect. The exact message I wanted to get across." She turned to the room. "We'll take a lunch break and meet back here afterward to talk about the impact of this across the board. Folks, we're going to be very busy. Before we break, let me also add one thing. You all impressed me while I visited England. Each and every one of you played a role in keeping this company afloat. Saying thank you hardly seems like enough, but, from the bottom of my heart, I'm so grateful. Teamwork is what has made our firm great. With our new outlook, we'll continue to be a competitor. Not only in the arena of weight loss, but in understanding good health and why it's critical to keep a positive outlook about yourself. See you back here at 1:30."

She hurried down the hallway, hopped on the elevator, and removed her phone from her blazer pocket. Owen had sent a text during the presentation.

Have you heard the news?

News? Maybe Jilly lost a tooth? Owen got a new client? She typed back,

No. Don't keep me in suspense...

Bitton. Far away but never far from her thoughts.

Two floors up, she exited the elevator into the reception area to her office suite.

"Yes, those three pictures should go centered above the sofa against the wall." Becky pointed to an area above the sleek, modern office furniture to the two workmen standing nearby, waiting with hammers and a ladder.

"I'm back, Becky."

Becky turned away from the men, her dark eyes going wide. "Oh, I didn't hear you come in. What do you think?"

Willow glanced at the suite walls. Gone were the old poster-sized photographs showing thin, muscular people who represented the old Pound Busters. New photographs showed people active. Smiling. Eating. Each with a positive energy. Satisfaction that always came with a job well done swelled inside Willow's chest.

"Looks perfect. Thanks for getting that done so fast."

She continued to her office and Becky hollered, "Someone named Hope Jenson called and said to call her back on Skype."

An offer on the house, maybe? "Thanks."

She hurried across her office threshold, her heart beating wildly. Going straight to her desk, she clicked on the computer and returned the call.

After a few rings, Hope's smiling face appeared. "Hello, Willow. I told you I'd call if I had good news."

"You did. So…?"

"We've had an offer on the house, and they're willing to pay your asking price."

"That's wonderful. Who is it?"

"It's a developer. They want to turn the estate into a multifamily dwelling. God bless Owen. He happened to know one of the guys and recommended the house to him. Really talked the place up and I think got you top dollar."

Owen. She had so many things to thank him for. "That's fantastic, Hope. What are the next steps?"

Hope said Willow would have to return to England to meet with lawyers, sign papers, and clear out the few remaining items left on the premises. Willow kept quiet about the fast and furious pace, especially when she learned the developer wanted to start work as soon as possible.

She said goodbye and hung up, a bit uneasy. This had been everything she'd wanted. So why did a weird feeling nag her? Where was the joy she'd expected upon getting a call like this?

She still had the cottage, a small slice of her past, that just happened to house the two people she cared about more than anyone else on the planet. Well, two people and one dog.

Excited about having to return to England, she texted Owen.

> *Just found out about the house! Thank you!! Guess what this means?*

She hit Send and waited, knowing she needed to get lunch, but too anxious to budge from her seat. Every night, she fell asleep thinking about seeing him again. Christmas was a little over a month away, and she'd thought about surprising him with a visit, but now she had a reason to return sooner.

Her phone pinged and she picked it up, happy to see Owen had replied.

> *It means I'll get to hold you in my arms soon, I hope…*

She smiled, her entire soul filling with joy she held only for him. Even if neither one of them had the courage to admit it aloud to each other, imagine what could happen if they did?

She typed a response, knowing the next thing she'd do was book a flight.

Yes. And I can't wait.

Chapter 26

Willow sank into the sofa at the Bristol nursing home, one hand on the oil painting resting against the sofa, the other firmly holding Owen's. He leaned close. "Remember when we danced last time we were here?" She turned to him, smiled. "I do. A magical moment, but you're not getting me to do it again."

He grinned. "Why? Chicken?"

"Yes. I forgot all the steps."

"Nah. You'll remember. It's like riding a bike. You never forget."

Hettie's voice carried from across the lobby. "What a grand surprise to see you two!"

They both looked her way, waving, but Willow quickly turned to Owen gave him a quick kiss on the cheek. "Ha! Saved by the bell."

He chuckled as they both stood. "I'll get you later."

"We'll see about that." She arched a brow and walked off, letting out a little shriek when he caught right up and gave her a pat on the bottom.

Laughing, she went toward Hettie's wheelchair. "I'm back in England for a short while and wanted to make sure I visited you again. There's something of my grandfather's I want you to have."

She lifted the painting.

"Oh, my." Hettie's eyes instantly turned glassy. "I'd know one of Derrick's paintings anywhere. And you're giving it to me?"

"Yes. For your help in my search to get answers about my family."

"Oh, you didn't have to—"

"But I wanted to."

Hettie took her hand, urging Willow to come closer. She gave the painting to Owen, while she gave Hettie a hug.

Hettie turned to the orderly. "Sammy, do you mind taking that to my room?"

He took the painting from Owen, who walked to the back of Hettie's chair to move her toward the sofa, so the three could sit and talk.

Willow told her about the journey on the Cotswold Way and finding Sean. When she shared the news about her mother's possible involvement with two men, Hettie winced and shook her head. "Ah, no wonder Sarah was so quiet and upset."

"Yes. But on a happier note, when I got here five days ago, the first thing Owen and I did was meet with a second cousin in Canterbury. If you hadn't identified my mother's cousin, I'd never have known to look them up."

Hettie patted her hand. "So happy for you, dear. So happy."

While the two women talked and she shared about her company in the States, every so often she'd glance at Owen. He silently watched her, his eyes bright and not quite smiling, but he looked happy. Especially whenever she talked to him this week about the changes at the firm.

Half an hour later, they hugged Hettie goodbye and left. As they reached the van, he opened her door.

"Thank you, kind sir. The men in Manhattan could learn from you."

He smiled, and as she moved to get inside, he grabbed her hand. "Have I told you how proud I am of you?" He drew her tightly to him and secured her arms around his waist.

Of course. The look he'd given her. It was pride. "Thank you. I'm not sure anybody has ever been proud of me."

"No? Well, you'd better get used to it, Rosebud."

Then he kissed her, one of many she'd received since landing at Heathrow. Making her think about how much she'd miss the cozy little life she'd settled into these past five days. A couple of days left then she'd sign the papers and return home.

As she slipped into the car, he said, "We've got one more stop. A surprise."

"More surprises from you, huh?" Willow studied him as he stared straight ahead at the road with a slight grin. "Do I get a hint?"

"Nope." He glanced her way and winked.

They drove, and no matter how many different ways she asked, he refused to tell her.

Soon they passed a sign reading "Welcome to Painswick."

She turned to him. "What are you doing?"

"Sean's expecting you."

"What? Why?"

Owen shrugged. "I stopped in to see him one day." He glanced over at her, hesitation in his gaze. "He's expecting us but, so it's not a total shock for you, I'll tell you why we're going. He says he'll do the paternity test." Willow's eyes watered. She'd tried to justify not knowing, telling herself it no longer mattered, but it really did. "You went to see him?" He shrugged. "I know you were fine if he didn't take it..." He exhaled loudly. "Look, I can see you when I look at him. My gut tells me he's the one. And..." He rubbed the back of his neck. "I don't know. Now that I'm working hard to make things better with my dad, I just know having a relationship with your dad *does* matter."

Owen. A true prince of men. She took his hand and squeezed it tight. "Thanks. I owe you so much."

"No, dear Willow." He softly smiled. "I truly owe you."

Leaving here this time would be even harder. Because this place, with this man, felt more like where she belonged than anywhere else in the world.

* * * *

Warm air brushed Owen's ear. Willow in his bed sure made him happy. He smiled into his pillow and turned his head to the side. As he slowly opened his eyes, he said, "Good morning, sweet—" Henry stood at the sofa's edge staring at Owen, wagging his tail while one of Owen's socks dangled from his mouth.

Owen rolled onto his side. "Blimey. You're not Willow and I'm not in her bed."

Henry jumped onto the sofa, squeezing his long body alongside Owen's.

Owen threw an arm around him and quietly laughed so he didn't wake the others. "Good thing you aren't a mind reader, Henry."

Not exactly where Owen wanted to be right now but for Jilly's sake, he'd given Willow his bedroom while he slept on the sofa during her stay... At least from about three a.m. on. Each night, once certain Jilly had fallen asleep, he'd crawl into his own bed with Willow, always sneaking out hours before sunrise in case Jilly woke before them.

A noise came from his room and before he could grab the dog's collar, Henry leapt off the sofa and raced down the hallway. Owen planted his feet on the floor, stretched his arms over his head, then got up and slipped sweatpants on over his boxer shorts.

When he reached his room, he found Henry on the bed snuggled next to Willow, who smiled at him, her hair mussed and eyes sleepy. The sock still dangled from Henry's mouth.

"Sorry. He woke me, too."

"It's fine. How could I ever get mad at that face?" She took an end of the sock and tugged to Henry's delight.

Owen sat on the edge of the mattress and Willow let go of the sock and rubbed his back with her warm hand, her eyes hooded. "I wish you'd woke me."

He chuckled. "Me too. Henry came over and whispered sweet nothings in my ear. I woke thinking it was you."

"Hmmm." She grinned. "I'm not going to even ask how you confused me with the dog."

He took Henry's sock, tossed it on the floor, and crawled into the bed beside Willow. Henry jumped right back up, but Owen had already claimed the coveted spot near Willow so Henry plopped down at the foot of the bed.

Brushing a few stray hairs from her eyes, he smiled. "Imagine my disappointment when I found out who it was."

She laughed, her happiness igniting a spark inside his chest. God, he had missed her these past months. Since her first trip here, he'd watched her slowly transform. A rosebud opening its petals and revealing a glorious flower. She'd returned with her confidence fully blossomed, radiating an outer beauty that someone could only possess if they believed in it at their core.

"Henry!" Jilly stood at the door, pulling Owen from the thoughts. "When did he leave my room?"

"A few minutes ago." Willow patted on the bed. "Come on in. We're having a party."

"I love parties." She rushed over and pounced onto the mattress, then scrambled next to the dog. "Daddy, can you make pancakes for our party?"

"What?" Owen pulled a face that caused his daughter to laugh. "I'm tired. Maybe you should help me."

"I want to stay with Willow." Jilly crawled into the space between them. "It's fun in this bed. We should all sleep here."

Owen laughed and glanced at Willow, who smiled and raised a brow his way. "I'm afraid there isn't enough room. I mean, Henry is a long dog and likes to stretch out."

"Oh, I had this dream…" Jilly talked about her dream, not responding to Owen's concerns about the potential sleeping arrangements. Willow hung on every word, occasionally asking questions.

Owen's heart swelled, so heavily that for a moment, he thought he'd stopped breathing. These two people were everything to him. He didn't care that he'd only known Willow a short while. Fact was, he'd never cared about any woman in the same way.

She'd leave again soon. They'd resume a long-distance relationship of sorts. And if he didn't speak up, she'd leave not knowing the one thing he knew true, without any doubt.

He loved Willow Armstrong.

* * * *

Willow headed through the trees to the house, leaving behind Owen while he got Jilly ready for their long drive to visit Warwick Castle.

Heaviness followed her over, not from the chocolate chip pancake breakfast. More the idea that tomorrow she'd sign the house over to developers who would change everything about it.

She unlocked the door and walked inside. A far cry from her first time entering. Cleaner, brighter. No stench. Cleaning this house had been a journey of its own.

She walked through every room, making sure they'd removed everything that had remained yesterday. Her gaze traveled to details like the intricate woodwork and the high ceilings. No doubt considered quite lovely back when her grandparents had lived here.

On her way up the staircase, she passed outlines of places where photographs had once sat for decades. Many had been packed in her luggage when she visited her cousin, and the faces now had names. On a future visit, she'd told Willow she'd invite some other family members.

She stopped in her mother's room. The place where all the secrets kept hidden from Willow had unfolded. The odds Sean was her father were fifty-fifty. Even if he wasn't, after talking to him yesterday, she'd learned how much he once loved her mother. His stories about their times together were invaluable, helping to ease anger accumulated as Willow learned the truth.

Her phone buzzed. A text from Becky, asking if a vendor they did business with still fit into their new marketing plan. She typed out a response and hit Return.

As she slid the phone back into the back pocket of her jeans, Willow stared out the window at the barren trees, no longer masking the cottage. Sadness at having to leave burrowed inside her chest, the weight of it heavier than last time she'd have to go. She wished she could stay.

She imagined the house, pulled apart and turned into separate dwelling units. Updated, but would it change the character she loved so much about this house? Worse, it would put an end to the place that represented her family's history.

When her mother had received the will, she could've sold this place and not said a word to anybody. Yet she hadn't.

Money that had driven Willow when she first arrived mattered less now. Some of her funds had been retrieved with the arrest of Tom Comstock, who would pay a stiff penalty for what he'd done to her and a few other clients. And Pound Busters stock prices had jumped after an article about their new marketing strategy.

Her phone buzzed again, Becky thanking her and telling her she'd sent off an email to Willow about a personal matter.

She started to respond but reality slowly settled in. All week, she'd been here, but conducting business. One day, they'd even Skyped her into a meeting. Trans-Atlantic flights were easy to get if she needed to be in New York.

So, what if she kept the house and renovated it over time? She could live here. Work here. Heathrow Airport was easy to get to with the great public transportation in this country. Gosh, she could even start a Pound Busters in England.

This country held everything she'd every longed for. Family, friends, love, and the heritage she always craved. She belonged here.

Excitement coursed through her veins as little details fell into place. She screeched on the brakes of her excitement. Would Owen be glad?

All week he'd been looking at her in a way that sent an arrow straight to her heart. She couldn't deny they had strong feelings for each other, but did he want her to live in England permanently?

From the window, she watched Owen exit the cottage with Jilly. She ran to the swing set while Owen headed through the path.

The sight of him made her stomach flutter, her pulse pick up. Yes, everything here felt right. Including him.

How would he react to the plans she had in her head? Everything could change with a simple call to Hope. When he entered the yard, she opened the window and leaned out. "I'm up here."

He glanced up and his face bloomed into a classic Owen smile. "Should I come save you, Rapunzel?"

She laughed, slowly stopping as his expression became serious. "What's wrong?"

He stepped closer to house and stopped directly beneath the window. "Nothing is wrong. I've just wanted to say something to you all week."

"What?"

He drew in a deep breath, rubbed the back of his neck with his hand for a second then met her gaze. "I'm falling hopelessly in love with you, Willow Armstrong. I want you as part of my life. I'll cross oceans if need be to make this thing between us work out." He exhaled and smiled. "There. Well, that was easier than I'd thought." He frowned. "I couldn't let you leave again without you knowing."

She wanted to pinch herself, make sure this wasn't a dream. "I love you, too, Owen. I did when I left here last time. Listen, I've got some big news."

His brows lifted. "Since I saw you ten minutes ago?"

She nodded. "I'm not selling the house."

"What...since when?"

"It's a last-minute decision. I figured out how I can work from here, and when I can't, I'll return to New York for a few days. And this house, I want to fix it up and live here. I can't give up this place. It's all I have left of a family I wish I'd known."

"That's the best news I've had in a long time." He grinned, raised his brows. "I was thinking, this would be a great conversation to have standing a little closer. Don't you think?"

She laughed. "You're right. On my way down."

She rushed down the stairs and out the front door. Owen approached the porch. When he saw her, he opened his arms, guiding her straight to the path of her new beginning. A path that might have some bumps, and a lot of uncertainty, but she'd never know if it was right unless she took a chance.

The End

The Sweet Life

Keep reading for a glimpse of another installment of Sharon Struth's Sweet Life series!

In Italy, the best attractions are always off the beaten path . . .

Mamie Weber doesn't know why she survived that terrible car accident five years ago. Physically, she has only a slight reminder—but emotionally, the pain is still fresh. Deep down she knows her husband would have wanted her to embrace life again. Now she has an opportunity to do just that, spending two weeks in Tuscany reviewing a tour company for her employer's popular travel guide series. The warmth of the sun, the centuries-old art, a villa on the Umbrian border—it could be just the adventure she needs.

But with adventure comes the unexpected . . . like discovering that her entire tour group is made up of aging ex-hippies reminiscing about their Woodstock days. Or finding herself drawn to the guide, Julian, who is secretly haunted by a tragedy of his own, and seems to disapprove any time she tries something remotely risky—like an impromptu scooter ride with a local man.

As they explore the hilltop towns of Tuscany, Mamie knows that when this blissful excursion is over, she'll have to return to reality. But when you let yourself wander, life can take some interesting detours . . .

Chapter 1

Mamie Weber's hands trembled as she shoved aside piles of neatly stacked clothes inside her luggage. Beneath her underwear, she found the well-worn Yankees cap, tossed it on to cover her unwashed hair, and tugged her ponytail through the back opening. She left her luggage on the bed and hurried to the hotel room door, officially fifteen minutes late. She inhaled a deep breath to steady her nerves and hoped the bus hadn't left without her.

One step into the hallway, she stopped. A room key. She propped the door open with her hip and slipped off her backpack. Halfway through her search of the pockets, she remembered seeing it on the nightstand after waking from the nap that now made her late.

She hurried inside, swiped the plastic key card off the nightstand and ran back to the door. As her hand fell on the knob, the shrill ring of the phone made her pause.

For half a second, urgency made her ignore the call and she turned the knob. Her boss had said she might call, but so soon? What if it was an emergency at home, like her parents?

She let the knob go and hurried to phone. "Hello?"

After seconds of silence, a man with a deep voice and American accent said, "Uh, hello. Wanderlust Excursions here. I'm looking for Felix Carrol, room 324?"

"Felix is..." Crap. Hadn't anybody called the tour company to tell them she'd be taking Felix's place?

"This is Julian Gregory. Tour director for a group who is expecting him." He paused, as if he expected her to say something. She debated between lying about the change in plans until she got downstairs or telling him the truth now. "Is this Mr. Carrol's room?" He sounded annoyed now. "We have a bus full of people waiting to leave and he's the only one missing. So—"

"He'll be right down." She hung up and hurried out to the hallway. Explanations like this were better face-to-face and she was determined to get on that bus.

At the elevator, she caught a glimpse of herself in a mirror on the nearby wall. Wrinkled peasant blouse and the same yoga pants she'd worn on the plane. Not exactly the Italian high fashion she'd seen in photos. An outfit that screamed to the world she didn't care enough to even tidy up her appearance. Exactly how she'd felt since that damn car accident.

She slapped the elevator button again, afraid she'd slip into the despair that almost stopped her from accepting this assignment in the first place. As she glanced around the elevator alcove, she saw a sign for the staircase and headed for it.

Each quick step aggravated her sore hip, but she worked hard to concentrate on the bigger problem of getting on this bus, not the accident.

Like how should she deal with the tour director. He expected Felix. Even though she'd packed all his documents, including a faxed note transferring the ticketing paperwork ownership to her, Mamie assumed Felix had called to confirm the change.

Felix Carrol, a.k.a. The Covert Critic, was Mamie's favorite author to edit for in her job at Atlas Publishing. He traveled the globe incognito while reviewing tours for his bestselling series with the same pseudonym. One month he'd be on a safari in Kenya, the next swimming with the sharks in Bora Bora, another mingling with the rich in St. Tropez. And now Mamie had agreed to stand in for him when he canceled last minute.

She entered the marble-floored lobby, glancing around for someone from the tour. Outside the glass doors was a gold mini-bus parked with the words *Wanderlust Excursions* emblazoned on the side. As she pushed through the doors, the hot July air blasted like a slap across the face. She stood on the sidewalk staring at the full bus, prepared to make a case worthy of Clarence Darrow if the paperwork she carried wasn't good enough.

This trip was for work, but it also would test the waters of the life she'd been wasting. Inhaling a breath, Mamie slipped the long strap of her purse across her chest and rushed to the open bus door.

In the driver's seat sat a square-faced man with a full Romanesque nose and short, dark hair. He greeted her with a wide smile. "Ciao, bella."

She climbed the steps and smiled back. "Hello. I mean, Ciao. Sorry I'm late."

Before the nice man in the driver's seat could respond, a man standing about halfway down the aisle said, "I'm sorry, miss. You've got the wrong bus."

Whoever he was, his cargo shorts and faded Led Zeppelin T-shirt didn't carry any authority. But he held a clipboard, and his tone suggested he meant business. His Gaelic-looking face carried a slight boyish quality, hardened into a manly appearance due to his trimly cut mustache and beard. Wavy hair the color of cognac peeked out from beneath a gold cap with orange and blue lettering reading *Wanderlust Excursions.*

"I'm sure the hotel front desk can help you find the right tour." He gave her a now-hurry-along smile and turned back to the man he'd been talking to.

"Did I just talk to you on the phone?"

He lifted his chin and raised a brow. "We're waiting for Felix." His gaze traveled her from top to bottom then he looked her in the eyes. "I'm pretty sure you're not Felix?"

"No, but..." Mamie became aware of the silence and scanned the passengers.

Everyone in the full bus stared back. Quiet. Curious. She squirmed and her gaze drifted back to the man who seemed to be in charge.

"No. I'm not Felix, but if this is Wanderlust Excursions, it's where I'm supposed to be."

He squinted. "Wait. Are you the woman who answered Felix's phone?"

"Yes. I'm taking his place on the tour."

He snorted. A short, patronizing laugh. "I don't think so."

"Why not?"

"Because you're clearly not Felix."

"But he transferred his vouchers to me."

"Nobody told me. Our company rules state that purchased seats are not transferrable without prior home office approval." He frowned and studied her again. "Besides, this is a specialized tour and you're not a member of this group. Felix is."

"How do you know I'm not?"

His lip curled into a little smirk. "Did you attend Woodstock?"

"The concert?"

"Is there another one?"

"Well, no, but..." Mamie scanned the other passengers more carefully. Other than the guide—everyone else was probably over fifty-five. Maybe even over sixty. "What group are they part of?"

"They are"—the guide, whose company sponsored tag read *Julian,* glanced at his clipboard—"the Woodstock Wanderers."

"Felix may not have been part of it either." Mamie never heard him mention them before.

"Are you kidding? Felix was one of our founder members." A man with thinning white hair, dark-rimmed glasses, and a full white beard sitting in the front seat winked at Mamie. "Bernie" in capital letters sat square in the center of a nametag with a tie-dyed background. Beneath his name it said, "Favorite Woodstock Song: 'Let's Go Get Stoned,' Joe Cocker."

Mamie would've never put Bernie together with that song, but... The bus's silence and everyone watching her jarred her back to the problem at hand. "Felix never mentioned your group to me."

Guess she *knew* Felix but didn't *know* him. The truth about how she and Felix knew each other, though, wasn't something she could share.

So she did the only thing she could do. Staring Julian square in the eye, she said, "Uncle Felix wanted me to take this trip. I'm his niece. He insisted I go in his place."

"His niece, huh?" The tour director rubbed the back of his neck and considered her again. He shook his head. "I'm sorry he's decided not to come, but on the transfer, I can't budge. Rules are rules."

A thin gentleman sitting a couple rows behind Bernie, with salt-and-pepper patches of hair above his ears, piped in. "Julian. Dude. Can't you just go with the flow? She looks harmless. Let her come."

Mamie squinted. His tag read *Bob*, but before she could read more, the others joined in with choruses of "yeahs," and she looked away.

"You know what they say, Julian." A woman with curly brown hair, peace sign earrings, and a pretty smile said, "Don't sweat the small stuff."

Mamie noted her nametag read *Martha* and her favorite Woodstock song was "Suite Judy Blue Eyes" by Crosby, Still, and Nash.

Julian pursed his lips. "All due respect Martha, me losing my job isn't exactly small stuff."

Martha grinned slyly and winked. "We promise to keep it a secret from the boss." She glanced around. "Right everybody?"

Another chorus of loud "yeahs" filled the bus.

One slim man with thinning hair who sat in the last row fist bumped the air. "We aren't afraid of the man."

The passengers murmured and nodded, complete agreement on that one. Mamie loved this solidarity. Though she'd never considered herself a hippie—more like a loner—she had an incredible urge to be part of this group.

Julian watched them, frowning. He refocused his attention on Mamie. "Sorry. I'm going to have to ask you to step out so we can start. We're already running late."

Normally, Mamie respected timeliness, schedules, and rules. But she had a job to do. A mission to accomplish.

"Please. My uncle, he *really* wanted me to go and—"

Julian took several swift steps to the front of the bus and stopped close to her. He dropped his voice. "Listen, this isn't personal. The last thing I need is to lose this job. Do me a solid and go see if you can get any of your money back."

She quietly replied, "You don't understand. I *need* to go on this tour."

He narrowed his hard green eyes, but before he could say a thing, a chant filled the air.

"Let her stay. Let her stay. Let her stay."

A blond-haired woman with a cherub face who sat at Bernie's side spoke up over the chant. "Doesn't she remind you of Tracy, Bern?" Her nametag read *Sandra* and her favorite Woodstock song was "Amazing Grace" by Arlo Guthrie. She patted Julian's arm in a very maternal way. "Tracy's our daughter. We'd love having some young energy around. Tracy's just too busy working to spend any time with us."

Julian's lower lip dropped. He drew in a deep breath, looked at Mamie, and motioned to the door. "Let's talk outside."

She turned and headed off the bus. Little did he know, she wasn't about to back down. Nothing would stop her from getting on this bus or making the most of this adventure. Two very good reasons existed for fighting the good fight.

The memory of her husband and daughter.

* * * *

Julian grabbed his satchel off his seat and stopped near Beppe. "Keep the bus running."

"Don't be hasty," the driver said, his smile almost a leer. "There's no ring on her finger, *sì amico?*"

The passengers up front laughed, adding to Julian's annoyance. For a man with a wife and two kids, Beppe never missed a chance to ogle a nice-looking woman. "Head in the game, Beppe. We're working."

He lifted his dark brows, clearly surprised. Julian's childhood friend, who'd found him this job, knew him better than most. Normally a cute, single female would've captured Julian's attention. Not today.

He hurried down the steps. Holding it together since this morning hadn't been easy. An old friend from the show had called him at breakfast with a warning. Seemed Gary Simon was considering asking him back to the show. The shrewd producer was getting pounded by audiences who wanted more of *Exploring the World with Eddie*, not the replacement host they'd found.

But Eddie was dead—at least in Julian's mind.

Julian's television alter ego, Eddie Morrison, was the thrill-seeking adventurer and former star of *Exploring the World with Eddie*. Nobody knew Julian Gregory, but a wide audience around the globe knew his fake persona.

Eddie feared nothing, lived dangerously, and mocked the word *risk*. Julian hated Eddie. Perhaps even more than he hated himself these days.

He stepped onto the sidewalk, stopping at a bench. The woman waited near the hotel doors and searched through her purse, a very determined gleam in her eyes. Over the years, he'd handled bigger problems than a stubborn female. A black caiman alligator in the rainforest. A run-in with Hezbollah militants in Lebanon. One persistent passenger would be easy.

He placed his satchel onto the bench and looked inside for his employee handbook. Other directors for Wanderlust Excursions, including his roommate, had told him the tour company owner had no sympathy for employees who didn't follow her rules. Julian kept this with him at all times. He located the book and opened to the page listing five simple rules Claudia expected her staff to follow.

No deviating from the predefined tour schedule or route.

Only previously authorized passengers can board our buses. Transfers of tickets on site are not allowed.

All stories guides share with our travelers must be true. We encourage passing along appropriate stories of your own travels.

No kickbacks from local merchants, who will often bribe you in order to lure your guests into their stores.

No fraternizing with the passengers off tour.

Before Julian had watched Carlos Lopez die in a wing suit jumping accident, he'd have scoffed at those rules. Anybody's rules.

Now, he desperately needed to live within the constraints of them.

Fear and guilt trapped him daily for the last twelve months. He could've stopped the jump that day. But he hadn't. What had Carlos called the winds? Questionable? Self-hatred pounded at Julian's head. What an idiot. A self-absorbed idiot.

Bravado that once led him to take on the show's challenges disappeared after that moment, the reason he was fired. This tour company provided the perfect hideaway to his shameful existence. Its strict policies helped him regain control of the life he'd forfeited when he'd encouraged Carlos to jump. Footsteps nearby drew him back to the problem at hand. The woman clutched an envelope and lifted her chin as she neared, her legs long and frame lithe. She had a slight limp, a fact he hadn't picked up on until now. Yet it didn't undercut the bull-like determination in her gaze.

"Now listen," he said before she could speak. Best to keep an unpredictable bull grounded. "I'm not an unreasonable guy."

Her large brown eyes softened. "Did I say you were? It's just that the others don't seem to care if I'm on this bus or not. Bernie and Sandra, they'd even feel like they have their daughter along. It obviously means a lot to them. Wouldn't my presence make them happier travelers?"

"I told you. Rules are big in this outfit. Look." He offered her the handbook, opened to the rule page. While she scanned them, he said, "If it was my company, I might let you stay. But as you can see, miss—"

"Mamie." She looked up from the book. "Mamie Weber."

Julian found himself drawn to the innocence in her eyes, hiding behind her tough facade. "My problem is that you've come out of nowhere and want a seat on my bus. I don't have one piece of paper telling me I shouldn't still be waiting for this Felix Carrol."

She opened the envelope in her hands, pulled out some papers, and thrust them in Julian's hands. "I have the entire trip itinerary, with Felix's name on it. And a faxed note from Felix saying he's transferring the trip to me. The hotel gave me the room."

He flipped past the itinerary to the faxed note. "Anybody could've written that letter. If the passenger who booked the trip didn't take the time to call it in, well..." He worked hard to think of an excuse as a bead of sweat dribbled past his ear. Julian batted away the moisture, not sure when it got so hot outside.

"Excuse me?"

He glanced up to find her staring at him.

"Do I look dishonest?"

Of course she didn't. He reread the note from the original passenger. The package contained the full itinerary. Everything seemed legit. He removed his phone to call Claudia.

"Who are you calling?"

"The boss."

She frowned. "But if she says no, then I can't go."

"She probably will."

As he dialed the phone, he could see her lips pressed tight and she started to pace. Finally, Nicola, Claudia's assistant, answered. Julian explained his problem.

After a minute of searching the office, Nicola returned to the phone. "*Nein*. Nobody contacted us regarding a transfer on that passenger."

Damn. "Nothing, huh?" He glanced up at Mamie and caught her eyes watering. "Okay. Thanks."

A sadness Julian hadn't expected took him by surprise, overpowering him with the idea this trip of hers was about something more. "Why are you really so eager to go on this trip?"

"I told you. My uncle wanted me to..." She stopped. "Why are you shaking your head?"

"The truth. It'll go a long way with me."

She wouldn't meet his gaze for a long moment, but then she glanced up. Dark circles that he hadn't noticed before hung beneath her eyes. "This trip is a chance of a lifetime. I may never get here again." She drew in a breath and, he swore, she trembled. "It took everything for me to board the plane and fly here." She rested her soft hand on his forearm, the effect cracking a piece of him that always stayed tough. Or maybe that strong facade had been broken this year and made vulnerable to more damage.

"Please don't ask me to explain why, but doing this means *everything* to me." She dropped her hand from his arm, adding, "Everything."

The rules flashed like a warning, but his softened resistance buckled at the knees. He could only think of one reason this trip meant so much to her.

There was a chance she was sick, especially considering the limp. What if she was so sick this was her last chance to travel the Tuscan countryside?

She lifted a hand to wipe away a tear, drawing him to her high cheekbones and ivory skin, with a few faded freckles near her nose. Simple and pretty. But tired. He wanted to ask if it was her health, but to do so seemed invasive.

He glanced in the bus's direction. Inside, the passengers watched from the windows with expectant expressions. He didn't want to face their disappointment.

Julian rubbed the back of his neck and dragged his gaze away only to have it collide with Mamie's doleful eyes. Damn it! Every ounce of common sense said to end this now. Only he couldn't. Each time he glanced her way, a pain in the far recesses of her eyes mirrored his own sadness...or was he imagining it?

"Do you have a passport?" he asked.

She tipped her head. "How do you think I got into the country?

"Can I see it?"

She dug into the bag and pulled out a navy-blue US passport and handed it over.

It had been issued eight years ago. In the photo, her face looked fuller and eyes brighter. From her birthdate, he worked the figures. Thirty-nine. Further snooping showed she was born in New York. He flipped through the pages used for immigration stamps. "You haven't used this once."

She shrugged. "Like I said, taking this trip—it's a big deal for me."

Guilt sucker punched him. Damn rules! No wonder he'd ignored them most of his life. A quick risk calculation on a visit from Claudia was low. During his employment here, the home office only got good feedback on Julian's tours—so he'd been told.

If he did this one little thing, how would she know?

He looked again at the bus. Several occupants gave him eager nods. When he looked to Mamie, she watched him.

He kicked a stray stone gently off the curb. "If I say yes, will you promise to be low key?"

"Low key. Of course."

"I'd like to keep this letter from your uncle. For my records, in case my boss finds out your uncle transferred his paperwork to you."

"So, I can go?"

"Yup."

Twirling to face the bus, she flashed a thumb in the air. A loud cheer erupted from inside. She slowly turned back to him and smiled sweetly, the relief in her eyes a reward he wasn't sure he deserved. "Thank you. You won't regret this."

He motioned to the bus before he changed his mind. "Get on. We're behind schedule."

As she took a seat toward the front, the other riders whooped loudly. With any luck, he'd skate by without Claudia finding out.

How much could go wrong with a bus full of people over sixty-five and a thirty-nine-year-old who'd never left the US?

Meet the Author

Sharon Struth believes you're never too old to pursue a dream. The Hourglass, her debut novel, was a finalist in the National Readers' Choice Awards for Best First Book. She is the author of the popular Blue Moon Lake series, which includes Share the Moon.

When she's not working, she and her husband happily sip their way through the scenic towns of the Connecticut Wine Trail, travel the world, and enjoy spending time with their precious pets and two grown daughters. She writes from the friendliest place she's ever lived, Bethel, Connecticut. For more information, including where to find her published essays, please visit www.sharonstruth.com or visit her blog, Musings from the Middle Ages & More at https://sharonstruth.wordpress.com/.

Printed in the United States
by Baker & Taylor Publisher Services